The PRIZE WINNERS of PIEDMONT PLACE

Meet the Talaskas

Dad: He loves to rhyme, all the time.

Mom: A star athlete . . . sort of. Not really . . .

Cal: The mastermind who will make their dreams come true

Imo: A know-it-all inventor whose name means "In My Opinion"

Bug: He may be the baby, but he's smarter than he looks!

Butler: Gets blamed for *everything* because . . . "The butler did it!"

The PRIZE WINNERS of PIEDMONT PLACE

Book 1

by **Bill Doyle**

illustrated by **Colin Jack**

SCHOLASTIC INC.

ISBN 978-1-338-18537-9

12 11 10 9 8 7 6 5 4 3 2 1   17 18 19 20 21 22

Printed in the U.S.A.   40

First Scholastic printing, January 2017

For the Macatawa crew
and racing backward up the hill
−B.D.

To my lovely wife, Michelle
−C.J.

What's on YOUR wish list?

A go-kart,

a waterslide,

 or maybe a robot best friend?

King Wonder wants to grant <u>your</u> wish!

ENTER THE GREAT GRAB CONTEST!

You and your family could win a run through
the new WISH SHOPPE superstore in your town.
Grab and keep EVERYTHING you want!

The contest starts Tuesday at exactly 7 PM
on Palmer's Farm in Hawkins, Michigan.

WILL YOU BE THERE?

KING WONDER'S WISH SHOPPE
WISH WELL!

When the pancake hit the fan, Cal Talaska wondered if he'd gone too far.

The pancake was still raw, like watery pizza dough.
So when the eleven-year-old tossed it up at the ceiling
fan, it exploded. *Splith! Splith! Splith!*

As gooey globs of batter rained down in the kitchen,
Cal ducked. But the family dog bounced straight in the
air like a mini pony on a trampoline. Butler's long tongue
snagged falling pancake drops while his tail whirled like
a propeller. Cal's little brother, Bug, tried to reach the
batter first as it splattered on the kitchen table and the
counters. But the four-year-old was half the size of Butler, and the dog kept beating him to the prize. Finally,

they crashed into each other, knocked over a chair, and tumbled to the floor.

A smudge of pancake had dripped onto Butler's back. The dog spun around and around on his side, trying to lick it off his fur. Trapped against Butler's belly, Bug spun with him and giggled hysterically. They were a swirling, slobbering ball of nuttiness. It was exactly the kind of noisy chaos Cal wanted.

Just as he knew she would, their mom pushed open the kitchen's swinging door. "What the cheese is going on?" Mrs. Talaska demanded.

"The Butler did it!" Cal cried.

"Not funny, Cal." Mrs. T. switched off the fan, but not before a glob of pancake flew onto her forehead.

Cal didn't want her to be mad. He pushed back his black hair and put on his most adorable face. "Surprise! I'm cooking pancakes for dinner! In the microwave!"

Mrs. T.'s green eyes softened. "Honey, I was thinking of making baked chicken and a salad." She bent over to untangle Bug and Butler. Bug reached up and dipped his finger in the blob on her forehead.

"Gron't!" Mrs. T. said, saying "Gross!" and "Don't!" at the same time.

Too late. Bug popped his finger in his mouth. His

eyes lit up as he got a taste of the pancake goo. It was like giving a drop of water to a man dying of thirst. He had to have more—and if he didn't get more, a tantrum would be on its way.

Bug was going through a phase. He didn't really talk except to bark with Butler. Mrs. T. said he would grow out of it in a few weeks or so. His tantrums, though, had become epic. When cranky, Bug might dig a hole in the backyard with Butler for hours. Or he might twirl in the kitchen for half an hour until he threw up.

Holy Aristotle, Cal thought. He and his mom shared a look across the room.

"Get your dad and sister in here," Mrs. T. said. "STAT!"

"Dad!" Cal yelled at the top of his lungs. "Imo!"

"Criminy, Cal, that's not what I meant—"

Mr. Talaska burst into the kitchen. He was even taller than Cal's mom, and his broad shoulders barely fit through the door. His glasses were slanted across his face. He turned them diagonally when he wrote music. He said it helped him see the notes better.

"We've got a BTA on our hands," Mrs. T. told him.

At the code for *Bug Tantrum Alert,* Mr. T.'s eyes darted to the door, as if he might run for it.

"No, you don't," Cal's mom commanded. "We need pancakes—"

"—and we need them now!" It was Imo. Cal's nine-year-old sister ran into the kitchen and opened a drawer next to the sink. "Ground Control to family: Why are you just standing there?" Imo said, tucking a whisk and measuring spoons into the pockets of her overalls. "Don't you see what's about to happen?"

Cal did, and he was suddenly nervous. His plan had been to gather his family and eat early. That way, he could get them out the door to a top-secret spot by seven PM. But he was playing a dangerous game. If he didn't get Bug a pancake, they wouldn't be going anywhere but Meltdown Town.

The tiny batch Cal had made in the microwave was useless. They had to start from scratch.

"Talaskas together!" Cal said. "Let's make pancakes!"

Mr. T. manned the griddle as if it were one of his favorite musical instruments. Imo took charge of the kitchen tools. And Mrs. T. looked through her box of recipes until she found just the right one. Cal moved like lightning around the kitchen. He cracked the eggs, gave advice on the right time to flip, and kept everyone on track.

Six minutes later—a Talaska record—the first

pancake hit Bug's plate. Everyone took a seat with a plate of pancakes. The family waited: Bug didn't move. In fact, he looked more ready to blow than ever.

"What's with the look?" Mr. T. asked. "It's perfectly cooked!" He rhymed when he was excited or nervous.

"Oh!" Cal realized what was up. He rushed to the dishwasher and grabbed Butler's dog bowl. He slid a cool pancake into it and put the bowl at Bug's feet. Once Butler had a flapjack, too, Bug grinned . . . and stuffed an entire pancake into his mouth.

"Disgusting," Imo said.

"Better not laugh, Bug," Cal said. Which he knew was the worst thing to say to someone you didn't want to laugh.

Bug's pancake-filled cheeks quivered, ready to explode.

"Stop!" Imo yelled at both Cal and Bug.

"I'm serious, Bug," Cal said. "Don't laugh."

Bug's lips stretched into a smile, and a tiny pancake glob slid out, like air seeping from a balloon that was about to pop.

"Quick!" Cal said. "Distract him. Somebody say something sad!"

"Like what?" his mom asked.

"Homework!" Cal yelled.

Imo looked offended. "That's not sad."

"I don't know what to say, then," Cal said. Actually, though, he did know. This was going just the way he had hoped. "Let's talk about something *not* funny. Say something you want. Mom, you start."

Mrs. T. seemed anxious, watching Bug's mouth like it was a ticking bomb.

"Mom?"

With a distracted shrug, she finally answered, "I want to get in shape."

"How? Specifics, please!" Cal said. More pancake drool slid down Bug's chin. "Like, for instance, *I* want the Wonder World Video Game System—"

"That costs almost eight thousand dollars!" Imo protested.

"Dream big!" Cal said. "Now you guys go, fast!" He pointed to his mom.

"I want a home gym," she said.

"Great," Cal said, and pointed at his dad.

"I want a new piano," Mr. T. said. "No, wait, I want an orchestra!"

"I want a laboratory to make spacecraft," Imo said without hesitating.

★ 7 ★

Bug mumbled something like *mmmph*, which shot a small spray of pancake juice out of his mouth. Butler barked in agreement. And then the pancake slid down Bug's throat, reminding Cal of a boa constrictor swallowing dinner.

Bug thanked the family with a happy thumbs-up. Everyone breathed easier as Mrs. T. put another pancake on his plate. This time, she cut it up for him.

"Could there be anything better than breakfast for dinner?" Mr. T. mused, sopping up the syrup on his plate with his last forkful.

There might be, Cal thought, glancing at the kitchen clock. But they'd have to hurry if they were going to find out. He needed to get his family to the secret spot in under half an hour.

"Whipped cream might've made it even better," Cal said, knowing this would get his mom thinking about walking.

"True," Mrs. T. said. "But all that extra sweetness would've meant an even longer walk after dinner, and I have so much work to do tonight."

Mrs. T. was always busy. Her job was bringing sports stars to their small town in Michigan. The athletes gave speeches at the auditorium about reaching goals and staying healthy. Cal's mom sometimes laughed that she should practice what they preached. She was always trying new fitness routines. The latest one involved a lot of walking.

That walking could work into Cal's plan. He just needed to plant an idea. "The park, the park, the park," Cal mumbled softly.

"What, Cal?" Mr. T. asked. "Did you say 'the park'?"

"The park?" Cal repeated at full volume, as if his dad had just come up with the best idea. "The park it is! We can all walk with Mom once we're there. Here we go!" He grabbed the family's plates in a big stack and put them in the sink.

Before anyone could protest, Cal rang the small bell they kept on the kitchen counter. The Talaskas rang it when someone had a good idea or wanted to call a family meeting. Once Cal had their attention, he herded everyone toward the back door. His mom went in the other direction, toward the griddle. "I need to clean this—"

Cal gently steered her away. "I'll clean up everything when we get home."

Mrs. T. stopped. "Hold on, mister. What's going on here?"

By offering to do something for nothing, Cal had

gone too far. He needed to tone it down. "I mean . . . ," he said, "I'll clean up for a small fee."

That seemed to satisfy his mom, and they hustled out the door. On the driveway, Bug and Butler were already in the back of the Flying Monkey. That was what the family called their beat-up car. Imo poked at the compact's front-right tire, which had sprung a leak a few days earlier. "The patch I put on is holding up pretty good," she said. "In my opinion, I'm one awesome mechanic. Probably the best in the world, don't you think, Cal?"

Cal bit his tongue. He didn't have time to argue. "That's right!"

Imo frowned. "Why are you agreeing with me?" she asked. "What are you up to, Cal?"

Cal didn't answer. He squeezed into the front with his mom and dad, and Imo got in the back.

"Buckle up, kids," Mrs. T. said as she turned the ignition. Then, as the car wheezed out of the driveway, she added, "Tight."

The Flying Monkey trundled down Piedmont Place. "We Are Family" played on the car's stereo . . . as always. The CD was stuck in the Flying Monkey's old-fashioned CD player and ran on a loop whenever they turned on the car. Imo had offered, and sometimes begged, to get it out, but Mr. and Mrs. T. always shook their heads. "It's our song now," Mrs. T. would explain.

They were driving past Palmer's Farm when they spotted a group of cars and people at the side of the road. Mr. Palmer had rented out space along the road for a giant billboard for the new Wish Shoppe superstore. And the crowd was clustered between the sign and the cornfield.

"What's going on at Palmer's?" Mr. T. asked.

"It looks like a rally or something," Imo said. "The

Donegan Diner's food truck is there. And so is the mayor's motorcycle."

Cal looked at his watch: 6:57. Just in time. "We should check it out," he suggested. "We can walk to the park from here."

They pulled in next to the other cars and piled out of the Flying Monkey. Over the heads of the crowd, they could see a bald man with a megaphone jump up onto a small stage.

"Hello, folks!" the bald man said with a big grin. "I'm Paddy Vance, Vice President of Fun at Wish Shoppe. Welcome to the first stage of our Great Grab Contest!"

The crowd clapped and cheered.

"King Wonder is opening a Wish Shoppe in your town that will have over five acres of amazing products," Mr. Vance announced. "One lucky family will get twenty minutes to run through those acres and grab whatever they want! But let's not get ahead of ourselves. First, families need to pass through today's elimination round!"

"Wow," Cal said to his parents. "Sounds cool, doesn't it? Want to take a closer look?" Without waiting, he squeezed by people toward the front of the group.

"Hold on a second, Cal," Mr. T. said, trying to pull

him back. "I think that's my boss, Mr. Wylot, and his family over there. I don't want to see him right now."

Cal kept leading the Talaskas through the crowd. People shook their hands and patted Butler on the head. A neighbor, Constance MacGuire, reached out to squeeze Mrs. T.'s shoulder. "Good luck!" she said warmly.

"Uh, okay, thanks," Mrs. T. replied, confused. "We're just going for a walk in the park."

"There's a space right here." Cal moved them into an empty slot in a line of other families.

Once they were in place, the Talaskas had a clear view of Mr. Vance.

"Hello to those of you who are just joining us!" Mr. Vance said through the megaphone. "As a child, King Wonder, the founder of Wish Shoppe, was inspired by his pet butterfly. The flapping wings made him want to soar. Today, your challenge is to capture your own butterfly!"

Mr. Vance pointed dramatically to thirteen wooden poles that were lined up along Palmer's cornfield. They were twenty feet high and looked like telephone poles. Each one had a stuffed purple butterfly the size of a toaster stuck on the top and a treasure chest at the bottom.

"Which three families will get the butterfly off their pole first and become finalists in the contest? Let's find out!" Mr. Vance took a breath. "Ready?"

The audience hooted and applauded, some yelling out different family names.

"Why are people cheering?" Imo asked nervously. She looked down at the white line on the grass at her feet. "And what's this?"

"That's a starting line," Cal said. No point in trying to trick anyone anymore.

"Set?" Mr. Vance cried.

"Uh, Cal," Imo said. "Why are we standing at a starting line?"

Cal shrugged. "Because we're about to run a race."

This caught Mrs. T.'s attention. "Wait, what the goat cheese is going on?" she said in a panic.

As if to answer her, Mr. Vance shouted, "Go!"

KA-BLAM! A starter cannon fired. And, just like that, the Talaskas had entered their first contest.

The other families around the Talaskas raced off. Cal sprinted a few steps toward the pole meant for them, but he realized his family wasn't moving. He turned back. "Let's go! Let's go!"

His parents looked more stunned than mad. But not Imo. She was just mad. "I'm not going anywhere with you," she said, driving the heels of her sneakers into the ground. "You tricked us."

"For your own good!" Cal shot back. He glanced over his shoulder. The other families had already reached the poles with the butterflies. "If we win today, we'll be in the running for the Wish Shoppe Great Grab! We'll get whatever we want in the store for free!"

Imo dug her heels deeper and wouldn't budge. "You just want the world's biggest video game."

That's not all, Cal thought. But he said, "Absolutely! And you want stuff, too." Cal turned to the rest of his family. "You said it yourselves. A home gym, an orchestra, a spacecraft laboratory, and . . ." Cal pointed at Bug and Butler. "You two want *mmmph* or whatever." Butler wagged his tail and barked, "Rabbo!"

Mrs. T. lightly tapped Cal's forehead. "We're not puppets," she said. "And you're not a puppet master."

"We'll talk about it at home, pal," Mr. T. said. He didn't like causing a scene. "My boss just heard everything you said, Cal."

Now it was Cal's turn to panic. They couldn't go home and lose this chance! "If I'd asked you, what would you have said?"

"NO!" his family shouted back.

"See? I was right to do what I did!" Cal insisted. "We just have to be one of the first three families to get a butterfly down from a pole. But we need to move now!"

Most of the families had climbed up on the chests at the bottom of their poles. Some tried to shake the butterflies loose, and others tried knocking the poles over with kicks and shoves. Cal spotted his best friend, James, and James's dad climbing their pole. After just a few feet, though, James's hands started slipping and sliding and he dropped onto his dad. They both tumbled onto the grass, laughing.

"Hey!" James yelled, rubbing his hands on the ground. "The poles are covered in slime!"

Other families were finding that out for themselves. People were sliding down the poles all along the field. Getting desperate, a few tried jumping up to grab the butterfly. But it was twenty feet off the ground, so they weren't even close. The football coach from the high school leapt in the air, landed off balance, and slid onto his rear.

"You'll need wings to make that jump, Coach Eaton!" Mrs. Moylan, owner of the Hawkins gas station, shouted from the audience.

The coach chuckled, and the crowd laughed with him. But not Cal. He had his eye on the treasure chests next to the poles. He had a feeling there was something inside those chests that could help with the challenge. But it might already be too late.

"Look at that!" Mr. Vance, the VP of Fun, yelled into

his megaphone. He was watching the Wylots, and soon everyone else was, too. "Have you ever seen anything like it?"

Mr. Wylot was Mr. T.'s boss at the factory, and Leslie Wylot was in Cal's class. But it was the older daughter, dressed in hunting clothes, who had snagged all the attention. Emma Wylot was like a ninja. Somehow, the thirteen-year-old had shinnied up the greased pole, even though it was as slippery as ice. Emma plucked the butterfly off the top. She held it out and, with her legs extended in a straight line, slid down the pole one-handed, like she was a human flag.

Once on the ground, Emma handed the butterfly to her dad. And the family lifted Mr. Wylot into the air, as if he had done all the hard work. He waved at the crowd like a king home from battle.

"We have our first winners! The Wylots!" Mr. Vance shouted. A few people clapped. "And the second family doesn't look far behind!"

It was true. The Rivales, who lived next door to the Talaskas on Piedmont Place, were just inches away from nabbing a butterfly. Mr. and Mrs. Rivale and their identical triplets—three teenage boys—had built a human pyramid that would have wowed the ancient Egyptians. The parents stood next to each other, forming a base. The first triplet stood on their shoulders, with the next triplet on his shoulders and the third on top. Like a circus act, they formed a tower rising twenty feet in the air. A few families stopped what they were doing to stare as the top triplet grabbed the butterfly and slid down his other family members to the ground.

"We have our second family!" Mr. Vance cried. "Who will be the third and last one?"

"We will!" Cal yelled. "Come on, Talaskas!"

Still, his family wouldn't move. Cal couldn't take it anymore. He ran by himself to the chest at the bottom of their pole. He tried to open it, but the clasp was held shut by a combination lock.

By now, many other families had started thinking like Cal. No one else could climb the pole like Emma

Wylot, and no family was able to copy the Rivales' pyramid. People wanted to get inside the chests, and they were trying different four-number combinations. A few were kicking the chests, trying to break them open.

"This is silly, and I have way too much work to do!" Mrs. T. called to Cal. "We're just not a contest kind of family. We'll wait for you in the Flying Monkey."

"Hold on, please!" Cal said. He was reading words carved into the top of the chest. "There's a clue here. It says, 'To open and use the chest, you need to know two things: the birth date of the royalty of marvels . . . and that the time of the message is past!'"

A few contestants around Cal mumbled that they had no idea what that could mean and went back to shaking the poles. But Mrs. T. had stopped in her tracks on the way to the car. "Oh, that first part is easy," she said automatically. "The answer is twelve zero two."

The families close by heard her, and immediately spun the dials. Cal did the same. "She's right!" James shouted, pulling his lock free. "Thanks, Mrs. T.!"

Cal shot her a look. Some people collected snow globes or stamps. His mom hunted strange facts about the ancient Olympics, the speed of a ferret's sneeze, what aardvarks ate—whatever! But this probably wasn't the best time for her to show off her trivia skills.

Mrs. T. shrugged. "*The royalty of marvels* is another way of saying *King Wonder,* and his birthday is December second, or twelve zero two. Doesn't everyone know that?"

If anyone had missed her spilling the answer before, they heard her now. One by one, the rest of the families spun the locks and popped open the chests. Kids and parents laughed, pulling back in surprise as three helium balloons with pictures on them drifted up out of each box. Strings kept them from floating away.

"We like our shoppers to be resourceful and find the best value in our Circles of Dreams!" Mr. Vance yelled. "To help you prove you can be smart shoppers, we put a few other things inside each chest."

Mr. Vance was right. Cal spotted a three-foot-long piece of thin steel and two pieces of wood at the bottom of the chest. What were they supposed to do with these?

Cal held them up for his family to see. They had been walking away. But now they were back at the starting line, like moths drawn to a flame.

His dad had turned his glasses on a slant and was

smiling. "The three balloons tell you what to do with that stuff," he called to Cal. "The balloons are a rebus— it's not too tough!"

Cal looked more closely at the balloons. One had the letter *I*, the second had an eye, and the third had a sheep with a pink bow on its tail. It *was* a rebus!

Cal read the symbols out loud. "I eye sheep." No, he knew in an instant that wasn't right. An eye could mean *see* in a rebus. He tried again. "I see sheep."

"Look at the bow on the sheep's tail," Mr. T. said. "It's a female!"

Right. A female sheep was a ewe. Cal replaced the word *sheep* with *ewe*.

"I see ewe . . . ," Cal said. Then he got it. "I see YOU!"

he yelled, and slapped his hand over his mouth. He was just as bad as the rest of his family at giving away clues.

But it didn't matter if people overheard him. How would a rebus message that said "I see you" help anyone get butterflies off poles? Cal reread the words on the chest, focusing on the second part of the clue: "The time of the message is past!"

The message was "I see you." How would you say that in the past?

"It should be 'I *saw* you,'" he whispered to himself.

"*Saw?*" someone said right next to him. Cal jumped. It was Imo. He knew she couldn't resist cracking the code. She was pulling one earlobe, the way she did when her brain was really humming.

"I've got the answer," she said. "It's a—"

For some reason, her mouth snapped shut. Cal turned to find that Mr. Vance's cameraman was pointing his lens directly at her. Imo went pale, and she put her head down so the spaceship-shaped clip in her hair sparkled in the setting sun, like she was trying to hide.

"What's wrong with you?" Cal asked. "What's the solution?"

Imo didn't answer. Instead, she took the three items from Cal's hands and snapped the pieces of wood on either end of the strip of steel. With her eyes, she made back-and-forth gestures along the pole. Almost as if she were using her gaze to cut the pole. Or *saw* it!

Cal finally understood. "I *saw* you."

Aha! He grabbed one end of the saw that Imo had made, and she held the other. They put the steel blade next to the pole and started pushing and pulling. It took them a second to get the right rhythm as they cut into the pole. Other families had caught on by now and snapped their own saws together. But Imo and Cal had a head start.

They quickly sliced into the wood, and, like a tree, the pole started to fall over.

"Timber!" Mr. Vance cried.

As it tipped over, the top of the Talaskas' pole headed straight for the Wylots. They already had a butterfly, but Cal could see them getting ready to grab this one, too. Leslie Wylot shoved her sister out of the way, trying to get to it first. Her arms reached out to catch it.

Luckily, Cal was a pretty good athlete. He jumped between the falling pole and Leslie. He snagged the stuffed butterfly off the top just before she could touch it, and the pole slammed into the ground. *WHAM!*

"Yes!" Cal said, holding up the silly-looking butterfly

like it was the world's greatest trophy. He turned around so the crowd could see him. A stuffed toy had never felt this good in his fingers.

"And we have our third finalist family!" Mr. Vance shouted. The audience went berserk, yelling and clapping. As Cal jumped up and down, he saw that even his parents were cheering. Bug was spinning in circles with Butler.

Mr. Vance gathered the Talaskas, Wylots, and Rivales together. "Congratulations to the finalists!" he said.

"We're the winners!" Leslie Wylot shouted.

"Not quite," Mr. Vance said with a chuckle. "To make it to the Great Grab Contest, the three families have to survive two more elimination rounds. First, you must create a thirty-second video to show you are perfect Wish Shoppe shoppers! Not only will the winning family keep whatever they grab in King's new store, which will open in a few weeks, but also their video will appear on billboards all over the country!"

Imo got a panicked look on her face. "That's never going to happen," she said under her breath.

Hearing her, Mr. Vance rushed over to Imo. "What's your name, little girl, and where are you from?" he demanded as his cameraman zoomed in.

Little girl? Imo hated being talked down to, and this

should have been enough to send her into a rant. But she just kept her head down. Since when was she so shy?

Finally, Cal stepped in front of her and looked straight into the camera. "We're the Talaskas from Piedmont Place," he said proudly. "And it turns out that we *are* a contest kind of family!"

The next morning at school, Cal met up with James in gym class. They were early and shot a few baskets while they waited for the teacher.

"Stellar performance yesterday, Captain," James said after going in for a layup. He had a habit of wiping his nose with his hand, so Cal gave him an air fist bump.

"Thanks, my man," Cal said. He was still buzzing from the race. "Sorry your family didn't nab a butterfly."

"No big deal," James said. "My dad and I had a blast doing it. Did you convince your parents and Imo to keep going with the contest?"

He glanced across the gym at Imo. Cal and his sister were both in fifth grade because Imo had skipped a grade two years ago. She was at the other basket, shooting with her friend Simone.

"I haven't convinced them yet," Cal said. "But I'm working on it."

Actually, Cal's parents and Imo had come right out and said they had zero interest in the contest. Mrs. T. was way too busy for something so "silly." Mr. T. didn't want to compete against his boss. And they sure as heck didn't want to make a video about their family for the next elimination round.

But Cal was more determined than ever. Just the thought of grabbing whatever he wanted from the Wish Shoppe's aisles of 3-D printers, giant TVs, go-karts, automatic bowling balls—you name it!—was enough to bring a grin to Cal's face. Plus, the whole country would see his family in the Wish Shoppe ads and know how perfect the Talaskas were.

Cal's grin disappeared when Leslie Wylot bounced into the gym, her three perfect braids snapping an angry rhythm. Cal's class had stopped having show-and-tell years ago, but Leslie held her own version pretty much every day. This morning was no different. She carried the Wish Shoppe stuffed butterfly for all to see, as if it were a major movie award. She strutted across the gym and took a seat next to Alison Mangan on the bleachers.

Without missing a beat, Leslie started talking. "I can't wait to get whatever I want in the Great Grab Contest, Alison. I know I get what I wish for every day. But this is different. Because everyone will be watching. I'm so glad we're best friends, Alison. We can tell each other everything!"

The whole gym could hear every loud word she said. People on other planets could hear her. Alison said something, but it was like talking into a hurricane. Cal liked Alison. She laughed at all his jokes, even the dumb ones, and she used to stand up to Leslie. Now Alison did everything Leslie said—and Cal didn't get why.

Leslie just kept rolling along. "It's totally cute and so sad the way those Talaskas think they have a chance to win the contest." She pointed at Imo and then Cal. "Look at them! Aren't they hilarious!"

Cal stopped dribbling. "I'm right in front of you, Leslie."

"Oh, Cal," Leslie said. "Can't you take a joke?"

Before Cal could answer, Ms. Graves rushed into the gym. "Sorry, folks, your gym teacher, Mr. Price, is out sick today. You've just got me."

Cal couldn't have been happier. Ms. Graves was usually their English teacher. Cal was a fan of Ms. Graves. At the beginning of the year, he had almost convinced her he was allergic to homework. *Almost.*

"Why don't we play a game of—" Ms. Graves started to say when the intercom buzzed. The voice of the school secretary came over the speaker. "Ms. Graves? We need your help in the office. Principal Cahill is locked in the supply closet again." A split second later, the intercom buzzed once more. "Better bring Imo Talaska with you."

"I'll be just a minute, Ms. Graves," Imo said, and ran to the locker room to change.

"We have to rescue the principal from his prison of paper clips," Ms. Graves told the class. "I'll return in a few minutes. Until then, behave, and play . . . a gym game . . . or something."

Imo was back in a flash, rushing through the gym to follow Ms. Graves out the door. Imo had put on the overalls she kept at school for helping out with quick fixes. The pockets were filled with tools like screwdrivers, a spud wrench, and even a plugging chisel.

Leslie gave her a once-over. "Nice outfit, Jessie!"

Either Imo didn't hear her or she pretended not to. She just kept moving.

"Knock it off, Leslie," Cal said.

"What? It is *nice*!" But the way Leslie had said *nice* definitely wasn't nice. "I just think it's a shame that my family is going to win the Great Grab Contest and Jessie won't have the chance to grab more things. You know, like those *nice* hair clips from *Star Wars* she always wears."

Cal trotted across the room after his sister. He caught up to her in the hall. "Imo!"

Imo turned around impatiently, tapping her foot. They were standing next to the sports trophy case—a spot where their mom always stopped when she came to school.

"What is it, Cal?" Imo demanded. Ms. Graves had already turned the corner to the principal's office. A banging sound was coming from the supply closet.

"Why don't you stand up to her?" Cal asked.

"Who? Leslie?" Imo said. "Who cares what she says? And Jessie *is* my real name."

It was true. Imo's real name was Jessie. But her nickname, Imo, was so much better. Her first word as a baby hadn't been *Mommy* or something like *apple*—she'd said "in my opinion." After her toy elephant had splashed into a bowl of milk, she'd fished it out, licked it, and said, "In my opinion . . . blech!"

As she got older, she kept it up. During dinner when Mrs. T. had forgotten to thaw the fish sticks, she said, "Fish sticks make good Popsicles, in my opinion." Another time, she said, "In my opinion, ghost stories are better without ghosts." Just a month ago: "To keep the water in the kitchen sink at forty psi, in my opinion, we'll need to exercise that valve with sliding-head pliers."

In my opinion this. *In my opinion* that.

The Talaskas started calling her IMO for short, and it stuck.

"Just let Leslie play her games," Imo said. "Stuff she says doesn't matter."

"But it does," Cal insisted. "It matters how people treat us. That's why this Great Grab Contest—"

"Ugh with the contest!" Imo said. "I told you I don't want to be in front of cameras anymore." Down the hall, the banging was getting louder. "Look, I've got to go." She took off.

When Cal went back into the gym, Leslie had pulled out the red rubber balls. "We're playing dodgeball," she announced to the twenty-two kids.

A few of them gasped, and one boy shouted, "Dodgeball was outlawed after you lost your temper last time!"

"Besides, it's totally dangerous!" Sheila Hanahan screeched. She was the smallest girl in the class.

Leslie rolled her eyes. "Oh please. Dangerous? That idea is just a conspiracy by badminton companies. And I know about big companies. After all, my dad runs the biggest one in the state. . . . What? It's not bragging if you can Google it."

Cal didn't want anyone getting smacked by a rubber

ball. He trotted over to the canister of lightweight foam balls. Imo had made them for kids who couldn't catch. She had sprayed them with a static glue so they stuck to hands instead of bouncing away.

"We'll use the balls Imo made," Cal said.

Leslie sighed impatiently. "Fine, fine, whatever."

They started to break up into teams. Leslie was one captain and Cal the other. Kids drifted toward Cal.

"I have a fun way of making teams," Leslie announced. "Whoever wants my family to win the Wish Shoppe Great Grab Contest, come on over to my side."

The other kids looked at each other, confused, and still headed for Cal.

"Let me put it another way," Leslie said. "Whoever's parents work for my father in some shape or form, I'm sure you'll make the right decision."

Leslie often made hints that her dad could fire anyone. Most of the kids shrugged, grabbed a ball from the canister, and walked over to Leslie's side. Only James stayed put next to Cal. The two were going to get slaughtered. Buried under an avalanche of yellow balls.

"Poor Cal," Leslie said with a fake smile. "It's not personal. People just have to know their place in life, that's all. There are the winners and there are the losers." She cocked her arm with the ball and waited for everyone else to do the same. "Are you ready, Cal?" Leslie asked.

"Hold on," Cal said. He needed to stall for time. "My shoe's untied."

"Make it fast," Leslie said.

While he crouched with his head down, pretending to tie his shoe, Cal spoke quickly to the class. "Look, I know you all think you've made a decision. But I want you to look at that ball in your hands. If you had to really choose in a split second, where would you throw it?" He took a breath. "Listen to your heart, not your fear."

When Cal stood back up, all the balls were still aimed directly at him. And Leslie was grinning at him. "Sounds good, Cal," she said. "When will you learn? My family and I always get what we want. Here we go!"

At that moment, the gym door slammed open and the noise startled everyone. Ms. Graves and Imo were back. The sound of the door was like a starter cannon, and the kids threw the balls without thinking. *Phlit! Phlit!* Balls whizzed through the air, finding their target.

"Holy Aristotle," Cal said under his breath. The kids had listened to their hearts—and Cal—after all.

Leslie was covered in the static balls from her sparkly sneakers to her braids. She looked like the cartoon character called Princess Fuzzy in cotton ball ads on TV. Except Leslie was bright yellow.

Cal knew the power of nicknames. He had seen Leslie use them to put other kids down or just for fun. He knew that if he opened his mouth and said, "Hey, Princess Fuzzy!" the nickname would stick to her for months, or even years.

But he didn't say it. Instead, he tossed his ball aside and walked over to pull the foam balls off Leslie. Ms. Graves and Imo hurried over, too. But Leslie wanted none of it. Red-faced, she pushed them away and rushed toward the locker room in a huff.

"My family always gets what

we want!" she yelled over her shoulder, her words muffled by the yellow ball stuck on her collar. "Alison, come with me. Now!"

Alison shrugged and followed her. Watching them go, Ms. Graves looked confused. "All right, everyone," she said to the rest of the class. "Give me fifty . . ." Ms. Graves paused. "What's a gym thing? Right. Fifty jumping jacks, please."

As they bounced up and down, James shook his head. "You shouldn't have done that, Cal."

Cal knew James was right. He shouldn't have let Leslie get to him. Cal blamed the excitement of the Great Grab Contest for pushing him a little too far. He shrugged, trying to act like it was no big deal. "She can't get her dad to fire everyone in Hawkins."

"Maybe not everyone," James agreed. "But how about just one person?"

"Hi, Cal?" said Sarah, the babysitter, when Cal walked around to his backyard after school. "Someone left a message for your parents? On the answering machine? Mr. Wylot, I think?"

Uh-oh, Cal thought. Had Leslie already told her dad about gym class? Was Mr. T.'s job at the Wylots' factory in trouble?

Sarah was upside down, her legs hooked around the highest bar on the swing set. The college student's curly hair was so long, it dragged back and forth in the grass. Bug and Butler were sitting nearby on the ground, staring at her, both their heads tilted slightly to the left.

On days when Mrs. T. was busy taking sports stars around Hawkins to give their speeches, she hired Sarah to watch Bug. Everything Sarah said sounded like a question. Maybe that was why she could get Bug to chill out, although no one else could. He and Butler could stare at her for days. And when they weren't staring, they were trying to impress her with their "world-famous" B&B Scooter Madness Stunt.

The fake stunt always went the same way. Bug started by scratching Butler behind the ears and grabbing on to a rope tied to his collar. Butler would race ahead, pulling Bug on his scooter toward a seat cushion on the patio. At the last second, just as they were about to crash, they'd make a wide turn and avoid the cushion.

Bug's hands would shoot up in the air like he was a champion who had just accomplished a dangerous feat. He'd say some kind of gibberish while Butler let out his trademark bark—"Rabbo!"—with his tail twirling.

Cal shook his head to clear it. He had much more important things to worry about. "Is my dad home yet?" he asked. "Has he heard the message?"

"He's home?" Sarah said. "But he went straight to the kitchen? He asked if I could stay for a few more minutes while he works on his music?"

Good. Until Cal could figure out what to do, he had to find a way to keep his dad from playing that message.

He didn't know if Mr. Wylot would really fire his dad because Leslie demanded it. But even if Mr. Wylot was just upset, the message could ruin Cal's hopes of entering the Great Grab Contest. It would be one more reason his parents might give for not making the video.

Cal could hear Imo working on the other side of the overgrown bush on the patio. And suddenly he knew how to distract his parents so they wouldn't hear the message, at least for a while.

"Thanks, Sarah!" Cal said. "Hang in there!"

Imo had changed into her overalls again. She was eating an apple while working on one of her nutty projects. Imo had built a platform twice as tall as Cal. It had a ramp down the front, and on top sat a long board with six wheels. Whatever the wheeled thing was, it could be just what Cal needed to cause a ruckus.

"Wow, Imo," Cal said. "You've gone to a whole new

level with this . . . go-kart . . . sled . . . best Imo creation ever."

Imo rolled her eyes and took another bite from her apple. "It's a lawn luge. Before I make spaceships, I might as well start on the ground." She finished turning a bolt on the ramp with her wrench. "And, no, you can't ride it."

Sometimes Cal had to fine-tune his sweet talk. "We don't do enough as brother and sister," he said, putting a hand over his heart. "We can ride it together, Imo."

"Ugh, weird, Cal," Imo said. She tapped one of the back wheels with her wrench. "Besides, this wheel isn't working quite right . . . and I don't know why."

Then, as Imo tugged her earlobe, Cal could see his sister's brain start to sizzle. When she set her sights on a problem, she *had* to solve it.

"Hold on!" he said before he completely lost her.

Too late. "Here, take this," she said, and handed Cal

the half-eaten apple. Mumbling formulas about energy and wheels, she wandered off toward her fort in the corner of the backyard. Designed to look like a sheriff's office from the Old West, the one-room fort had been Cal's eleventh-birthday present a few months ago. Imo had taken it over and turned it into her workshop, where she dreamed up inventions.

When Imo was inside the fort, Cal asked softly, "So I can ride the luge after all, Imo? If your answer is yes, don't say anything."

He gave it a second. Nothing. Putting the apple in his jacket pocket, he scrambled up the ramp. From up there on the wobbly platform, Cal could see past their backyard fence into the Rivales' yard.

Cal lay on his back on the lawn luge and put his hands to the sides to push off. *Crack!* One of the back wheels snapped free and tumbled off the platform.

"Uh, Imo, quick question!" Cal yelled. He was teetering on the edge of the ramp. "Would your luge work without one of the wheels?"

"Sure," Imo called from her workshop. "But only if you want to spin out of control and crash into the patio!"

"Wait, what?"

Before he could stop it, the luge shot down the ramp, dragging to one side, where the wheel should have been. He nearly plunged over the edge, and then slammed onto the patio.

Umph! The luge spun completely around. Now it was flying across the concrete toward the house.

Cal zipped on the luge through the open back door and shot into the kitchen. His dad was at the table with his back to Cal, his fingers pounding on the wood surface.

"Dad!" Cal shouted.

But it was no good. Mr. T. wore sound-blocking headphones that helped him concentrate. They also made him look like a giant-eared alien as he loudly sang, *"Rutherford B. Hayes, why oh why do you hate mayonnaise?"*

Mr. T. loved to make up songs. He said it was relaxing, especially after a long day at his accounting job. The family didn't have a piano, so Mr. T. pretended the kitchen table was a keyboard.

"Dad, a little help here!" Cal called out.

Mr. T. just kept crooning about sandwich spread as Cal knocked against a chair and zoomed out of the kitchen. With a jolt, the front wheels hit the living room carpet. The luge stopped dead on the shag . . . but Cal kept moving.

Ziipp!

He shot off the luge and into the room like pizza sliding off a tray. He crashed into the files Mrs. T. kept stacked along the wall. Notebook pages and sticky notes flew up and whirled around him like confetti as he tumbled into the corner.

Finally, Cal came to a halt on his side, and he stayed there for a second. Was he in one piece? Yes, thanks to the cushion of his mom's paperwork.

After a few seconds, Cal saw that his plan had gone horribly wrong—or horribly right. Talk about a distraction! The living room was a disaster. He stumbled to his feet and—

Wham!

Cal was tackled from the side by something huge and furry. Papers went flying again as he went down. And then a wet nose was snuffling at his pockets.

What the heck was Butler doing?

Oh, right, Cal remembered. The half-eaten apple! This was Imo's fault!

He tried to stand up. Butler knocked him over again,

this time getting the apple out of his jacket. Reaching for balance, Cal tipped over a side table. The answering machine on the table clattered to the floor with a *BEEP!*

His parents, Imo, Bug, and Sarah rushed into the living room. Mrs. T.'s eyes went wide as she took in all the destruction. "What the Gouda is going on?" she asked.

"The Butler did it!" Cal said. This time, it was true. Well, kind of.

"Thanks for test-driving the luge for me, Cal," Imo said, and then she burst out laughing. She held up a screw. She must have removed it from the lawn luge's wheel while Cal had been talking to her.

Imo had set him up. Cal should've known!

Butler chomped happily on the apple and rolled over . . . right onto the answering machine. It beeped again and announced, "Playing first new message."

No!

Instead of distracting all of them so they wouldn't play the message, Cal had actually gathered an audience.

"Hello, Talaskas," a voice said over the machine. It wasn't Mr. Wylot. It was *Mrs.* Wylot.

Cal didn't know what to do. He was tempted to dance

or just start yelling to keep them from listening. But his parents would hear the message sooner or later.

"I apologize for not sending out our usual high-quality invitations!" Mrs. Wylot was saying in her frantic voice. Every time Cal heard her speak, she sounded as if she were on board a sinking ship. "We'd love to have you over to our estate for a pool party and a big surprise, three Sundays from now at four PM, if you're free—"

"Of course they're free," they could hear Mr. Wylot say in the background. "What else do they have to do? Just hang up."

Click. The line went dead.

Cal didn't feel the relief he'd thought he would. This seemed just like something Leslie would plan as revenge for gym class. In fact, all the Talaskas were staring at the machine in confusion. For the moment, the chaos Cal had caused was forgotten.

"A party?" Mr. T. asked. "The Wylots want to invite *us* to a party?"

"What do they mean by *surprise*?" Imo asked. She glanced around as if the surprise might jump up out of nowhere.

"Oh, I don't know," Mrs. T. said. "Maybe they just want to be nice? Don't you think, Sarah?"

"Yes?" Sarah replied. As always, she answered with a question. And Cal thought that made a lot of sense, especially because he had his own big question:

What were the Wylots up to?

"**W**hat's the big surprise?" James asked. It was the same thing Cal had been asking himself since hearing the message yesterday.

Cal and James were leaning against the Talaskas' backyard fence, watching the Rivales next door like they were a reality TV show.

The Rivales didn't mind the attention. Not only were they finalists in the Great Grab Contest, they were professional coupon clippers, tae kwon do masters, and champion synchronized swimmers. They were used to people watching them.

Right now, they were heading into the huge tent they had set up in the backyard. The parents and the triplets moved in exactly the same way. They reminded Cal of the workings of a clock. Maybe a cuckoo clock.

James raised a hand. "Hello, Rivales!"

The Rivales didn't stop, but each of their five heads turned as if they were prairie dogs. With their slicked-back hair and black clothes, it was hard to tell which family member was which. Without smiling, the Rivales silently waved back in perfect unison.

Cal laughed as if they had just performed an amazing trick. "Holy Aristotle! That's amazing!" he cheered. But instead of taking a bow or laughing along, the Rivales nodded and disappeared into the tent.

Cal and James shared a quick look that said, *Can you believe it?*

And then Cal got back to James's question. "I don't know what the Wylots' big surprise is."

Cal was worried about what Leslie might have planned. But the party was weeks away, and he had more pressing problems.

"If I'm going to win the Great Grab Contest, I have to get my family to make a video," Cal said. "Just think how it will be when I win and grab the Wonder World Video Game System!"

James's face got serious. *"Add more wonder to your world and play* inside *the game!"* he said, sounding just like a TV announcer. James could copy anyone's voice. Once he'd pretended to be the school secretary on the phone and asked Principal Cahill to go buy a tin of anchovies.

Wonder World had been invented by King Wonder himself, and it was sold only at Wish Shoppes. It cost as much as a car, but for good reason. It was the only game that turned a player's real life into a game. Players plugged in the game, and no matter where they were, the game adapted. In other words, players could control the world around them. It was the perfect game for Cal!

"We could be playing Wonder World in my basement right now!" Cal glanced back at his house. The drooping gutters. The peeling paint. The trees that seemed so exhausted they could barely keep themselves from collapsing onto the roof. He loved his giant, rambling house and how it looked like a ship that had run aground—but he wasn't sure everyone else did.

"The video just has to show that my family is the perfect family to shop at Wish Shoppe," Cal said, "and I'll win."

James always looked away when Cal said the words *perfect family*. Cal knew what he was thinking. The Talaskas weren't as rich as the Wylots. And they didn't move as smoothly as the Rivales. But who cared? Cal knew if people could just see how great his family was, the Talaskas would easily win.

"I can help you with the video entry," James said.

"Thanks, my man," Cal said, clapping his shoulder. "But I actually think it's better if I try it alone. I know my family. They won't be able to resist my special plan."

"Are you going with Strategic Pestering?" James asked.

"No," Cal said. "I need something a little fancier."

A whole day of "Take me to the fair, please," repeated

over and over, had worked when he was seven years old. But he was much more skilled now. "I'm going with Turbo Adorable," Cal said.

A car pulled into the Talaskas' driveway. It was James's older sister, and she beeped the horn.

"Got to go," James said. "Good luck, Captain."

Cal waved to James's sister as his friend got in the car. She waved back cautiously. Cal knew she was thinking about the time he convinced her to make—and eat—a pint of tuna-fish ice cream.

Everything was ready for Cal to put his plan into action. He started by propping his old, beat-up camera, which took video, on the patio table. Then he shouted through the screen door into the house, "Mom! Do you have a second?"

His mom came out of the living room, her pencil still in her hand. "What is it, honey?"

"If you put all the products at a Wish Shoppe in a line, how many times would it go around the planet?" he asked.

"Hmm," Mrs. T. said, tapping the pencil against her leg. "I'd have to figure that out. Why are you asking?"

"No reason," Cal said sweetly. "I just know you're the best at trivia, and I'm trying to think like you."

"Um, okay," Mrs. T. said.

She stayed for a second, and Cal was glad. He wanted her to see how he was imitating her. Also, he wanted his whole family to think he was struggling to make the video without them. He hoped they would feel bad and decide to take part after all.

Pushing his hair back the way his mom did, he faced the camera and said, "I want a home gym."

"Cal . . . ," his mom said from inside. Was she already about to crack?

But then Mrs. T.'s desk phone rang, and she had to go answer it. Cal moved on to the next person on his list.

"Imo!" he shouted in the direction of her workshop.

"What?" she called without opening the door.

"Is this something you'd wear?" he asked.

She peeked her head out and saw him holding up a yellow T-shirt with a flower on it.

"Oh brother," she said, and closed the door again.

Cal hoped she was still watching through a crack. He put on the T-shirt and looked at the camera. Getting as close to Imo's voice as he could, he said, "I'd like a space-craft laboratory."

He knew he looked adorable.

A minute later, Cal called, "Dad!" and slid on a giant

pair of fake glasses. After singing a short song about tinfoil in his dad's voice, he yelled for Bug. Cal lifted his hands in the air like a champion, marched around, and barked, "Rabbo!"

When Cal started to put on one of Butler's old dog collars, his parents and Imo finally came out onto the patio.

"Okay, this is just—" Imo said.

"The cutest thing ever?" Cal finished for her.

She shook her head. "No, really, really creepy. Stop dressing up and acting like us."

"But—"

"If you do," Mr. T. said, "we'll make the video with you, okay? But only the video. And then that's the end of all this contest business."

"Your dad and I both work very hard during the day," Mrs. T. said. "So we don't have time for nonsense."

"Thanks!" Cal said. "And, Dad, I'm sure Mr. Wylot would want you to do it." At the name Mr. Wylot, his dad's face clouded over. Cal needed to change the subject quickly. "The deadline to submit the video is seven o'clock tomorrow."

Imo said, "That's just twenty-five hours away."

Bug barked to Butler. The meaning was clear. It was impossible.

"No, Bug," Cal said. "That's plenty of time. Imo, you build the sets. Mom, we need more facts about the store. Dad can write the jingle—you know, catchy music that will get stuck in people's heads."

Mrs. T. frowned. "Let's leave Dad out of this. Mr. Wylot is being a major—" She interrupted herself and started again. "Work is very challenging for your dad right now."

"No, Mom, we can't leave anyone out," Cal said. "We have to be the *perfect* family. Dad is always picking words out of the dictionary—like, I don't know . . ."

Imo chimed in, *"Polyphagous?"*

"Exactly," Cal said. "So writing a jingle about Wish Shoppe should be a breeze!"

Mr. T. nodded. "I'll come up with something on my lunch break. What about you, Cal? What are you going to do?"

"I'll write the script and direct, of course."

Bug barked again. He wanted a job, too.

Cal shook his head. "Bug, you'll just be Bug."

By the next afternoon, the Talaskas' backyard was transformed. Imo had used old cardboard from refrigerator boxes to build a set where they could shoot the video. She had turned the cardboard into walls and started to paint them white with blue trim, just like the walls in Wish Shoppe.

It looked amazing. Then Bug dipped Butler's tail in blue paint and chased the dog around the backyard. Butler's tail smeared blue paint all over the patio and one of the cardboard walls, so Imo ended up painting the whole set blue.

When Mr. T. got home from work, his gaze landed on the muddy ditch Cal had dug. It was his version of the River of Low Prices, which ran between the Wish Shoppe and the parking lot.

Cal wondered if an insect was crawling on his dad's face. Mr. T.'s cheek was twitching, and a vein in his neck had popped out. He turned around and went inside. Cal could hear him counting to ten. When Mr. T. came back out with Mrs. T., he didn't look quite as red.

"All right, I'm ready, Mr. Director," he said, turning his glasses on a slant. "How can we make this thing soar?"

Mrs. T. smiled, and Cal handed his dad a script. Mr. T. flipped through it, and his eyes widened with each page. "Uh . . . okay. Whatever you say."

Ten minutes later, the family had taken their positions.

Cal put the camera back on the patio table. He pressed RECORD and rushed to his place.

"Action!" Cal called out.

Imo had glued a handle on the lawn luge so it looked like a huge shopping cart. Mr. T. pushed it in front of the camera.

"Hello . . . Talaska . . . family!" Mr. T. said in a wooden voice, reading from the script.

"Why, hello there, uh, stranger!" Mrs. T. said back, reading her line. "How are you?"

"I am . . . super great," Mr. T. said. "You know why? Because I am shopping at Wish Shoppe, where I can get whatever I want!" He pretended to pull a mask off his face. "And guess what! It's me, your Talaska dad!"

"Oh! What a, uh, surprise!" Mrs. T. said in fake

shock. "We were having so much fun shopping here at Wish Shoppe that we didn't even know it was you!"

Cal jumped out in front of the camera. "We're the Talaskas!"

Imo threw a bucket of water toward the set just as Butler bumped into her. The water missed its target and splashed onto Cal's pants.

Gasping, Cal stopped acting. "Why did you do that?" he demanded.

"It's rain!" Imo said.

Cal's script said there should be a rain shower, a snowstorm, and a mild hurricane. He wanted to show that the Talaskas were the perfect Wish Shoppe family under any conditions.

"You ready for the snow?" Imo asked.

"No!" Cal shouted.

"What about the butterflies?"

Cal shook his head. "Let's just say our lines and talk about what we want at Wish Shoppe. You go first, Imo."

Imo faced the camera, and she suddenly looked as terrified as if a stampede of buffalo were about to flatten her. Cal didn't get it. How could she argue to the death with him about the perfect temperature of milk but then get frozen by a tiny camera?

Cal stood behind Imo and said in her voice, "My name is Imo. I want a spacecraft laboratory. My mom wants a gym. My dad will grab an orchestra. My handsome, so-much-smarter-than-me older brother will take a video game system. My little brother and our dog want something amazing, too, but only they know what it is!"

That was their cue to start singing the jingle that Mr. T. had written. The family stood together by the muddy moat and sang:

"Oh, Wish Shoppe, you cause our hearts to hop!
Please never stop making those high prices drop!
Oh, Wish Shoppe, you give the best impression!
We have just one or two quick questions:
In your name, what's with the extra P?
Isn't it time to maybe set it free?
Into the River of Low Prices let it flow—"

"Hee," Mrs. T. said in a burst of laughter while the others kept singing:

"It's something we need to know—"

"Hee hee," Imo said.

The hee-hees were like a virus, leaping from one

person to the next. Cal could feel his shoulders shake. *NO! Control. This is too important.*

Still looking into the camera, he tried to keep a straight face. He could feel his mom and Imo struggling, too. Finally, it popped out of Cal's mouth. "Hee hee."

His dad joined in. "Hee. Hee. Hee. Hee." And then his mom. Soon the only ones singing were Butler, who was howling, and Bug, who chirped nonsense sounds. The others were gasping for breath as their laughter picked up steam.

"What's . . . with the . . . extra *P!*" Mrs. T. managed to say, tears streaming down her face as she clutched her sides.

"Let it *flow!*" Mr. T. added, and doubled over. "Set it *free!*"

"What rhymes with *free*, Dad?" Imo asked, collapsing on the ground. "It starts with a *P!*"

Cal stumbled around, unable to stop laughing, and then fell over next to Imo. Soon the Talaskas were rolling on the grass like hysterical hyenas. With his own high-pitched giggles, Bug dove onto the heap. And then Butler jumped on top of all of them. The dog flipped over and started squirming on his back, rubbing against the family and somehow making everything seem funnier.

Cal was laughing so hard, he was worried he would actually set free his own extra P.

"Cal!" Mrs. T. wheezed. "Your pants!"

Oh no, Cal thought, realizing what he must look like. His pants were soaked from the fake rain!

"The Butler did it!" he managed to gasp. His words brought even more waves of laughter, and everyone clutched their stomachs. Finally, after thirty more seconds of complete nuttiness, Cal staggered to his feet and looked at his watch. Oh man. They only had an hour to finish the video and upload it to the Wish Shoppe site.

"All right! All right!" he said, wiping the tears from his face and spitting out a clump of Butler's fur. "From the top!"

They ran through Cal's script quickly. This time, they managed to do it without anyone bursting into hysterics.

"That's a wrap, people," Cal said. "Imo, can you fix it up and add the music and sound effects?"

"Sure," Imo said, taking the camera to make the changes on it.

Half an hour later, when she announced she was done, Cal glanced at his watch.

"Good timing," he said. "Ten minutes to go until the video is due."

Imo perched in front of the computer and opened the Wish Shoppe website. "Uh-oh," she said.

"What is it?" Cal asked. "What's wrong?"

"With our dial-up connection," Imo said, "it will take over fifteen minutes to upload the video."

"We're not going to make it," Mrs. T. said. "There's not enough time."

Cal put his head in his hands. "No, no, no," he groaned.

Tugging her ear, Imo announced, "Then it's a good

thing I can optimize the connection and have it uploaded in nine minutes."

"Do it!" Cal shouted, and Imo got to work. She plugged the camera into the computer, and her fingers flew across the keyboard.

"Go, go, go!" the whole family was chanting. They watched the bar that showed how much of the upload was left. It was going to be close. Then—*bing!*

"We did it!" Cal said.

Just barely. Seconds later, the contest screen was replaced by these words:

Hello, dreamers! The time for Great Grab Contest entries has passed. Good luck to our three finalists. The two winning families of the next round will be revealed in three weeks on the Wish Shoppe billboard in Hawkins, Michigan! Till then, wish well!

—King Wonder

"What do we do now?" Cal asked.

Mrs. T. answered with the hardest words for Cal to hear.

"We wait."

To Cal, waiting was like bathing in his brother's used bathwater. It was torture.

Every day, Cal rode his bike by the Wish Shoppe billboard on Palmer's Farm. He would stare at the sign for almost an hour, hoping King Wonder would announce the two finalist families early.

Instead, the electronic sign showed the same commercial over and over: King Wonder running around a Wish Shoppe with his Butterfly of Savings. The butterfly was a direct descendant of the one that King had had as a kid, and it lived for a month in each new store he built. In the ad, King flapped his arms like a butterfly. He glided around the Wish Shoppe's confusing

Nine Circles of Dreams, or departments, like it was the easiest thing in the world.

Cal thought he'd go crazy from the waiting. The days seemed to stretch on forever. The rest of the family didn't have the same problem.

Bug and Butler practiced their fake B&B Scooter Madness Stunt in the backyard. Bug scratched behind Butler's ears and grabbed on to a rope on his collar. Butler took off, pulling Bug on his scooter toward the patio seat cushion. At the last second, they made a wide turn to miss it. They did this again and again.

Mrs. T. was keeping busy with her work. She brought a famous pole-vaulter to town. He spoke at Wylot Auditorium about leaping over obstacles in life. Cal went to listen to the speech. It had mushy parts and funny lines, but nothing about waiting. So it wasn't overly helpful.

Then it was the day when the last two finalist families would be announced. Well, kind of. It was 12:01 AM, and Cal was lying in bed wide awake. His mind was racing. Whose videos would be picked—the Rivales', the Wylots', or the Talaskas'?

Bug's bed was across the room, and Cal could hear him mumbling something in his sleep. Snuggled up next to Bug, a sleeping Butler grunted, "Rabbo," as if he agreed with whatever Bug was saying.

Cal tried everything to get back to sleep. At 4:30 AM, he finally gave up.

★ ★ ★

He was in the kitchen waiting for his family when they got up hours later. Bug came bounding down in his stunt-car driver outfit, complete with bright-purple helmet and neon-green goggles.

Why was Bug wearing his favorite clothes? Cal wondered. Then it hit him.

Oh man. The Wylots' party. The contest had pushed it out of his head. For some reason, he'd never noticed that the Great Grab announcement was on the same day as the party.

Mr. T. was right behind Bug. "Sorry, little man," Mr. T. said to him. "Today's a big party. You've got to change into other clothes."

Under the helmet, Bug's face started to scrunch.

"BTA!" Imo said, coming down the stairs. She was wearing her overalls, her tool belt, and at least eight hair clips shaped like spaceships from *Star Wars.*

Mr. T. looked at Bug to see if a tantrum might be on

its way. He didn't seem to like what he saw. "Okay, okay," Mr. T. said. "I guess we'll all wear whatever we want."

Bug liked that idea. His face unscrunched and he barked.

"We can't go to the party," Cal said. "We have to be at the billboard for the big announcement."

His mom had just come into the kitchen, still in her robe. "We'll go to the party first," Mrs. T. said. "And then we'll drive by the billboard to check out who won."

"Sounds like a plan," Mr. T. said, and yawned.

Cal could tell that no one in his family thought they had a shot in today's elimination round. But he also knew better than to argue with his parents this early in the morning. It would only backfire.

Instead, he turned his sights on Imo and her overalls. "You know Leslie is just going to make fun of you, right?" he said.

"Why?" Imo said, touching her spaceship hair clips. "Because the *Millennium Falcon* doesn't match my eyes?"

But he could tell she knew what he meant. Cal decided to let it drop.

★ ★ ★

When the Talaskas arrived at the Wylots' mansion, they went straight to the backyard, which was the size of a football field. The entire town had been invited. Hundreds of people were chatting in small groups around the party, but everyone looked a little nervous. Cal knew they were all thinking the same thing: What was the big surprise?

A line of waiters in tuxedos held trays of glasses filled with ice-cold water. Toward the back fence were six barbecue pits with sizzling chicken, steaks, and potatoes. The smells were amazing. Drool dripped from Cal's lips before he could catch it.

But the barbecue pits were blocked off from the crowd by thick velvet ropes. Guests who got too close were hit by little spitballs that shot from the trees behind the pits. *Splat!* Ms. Graves was struck between the eyes. *Splot!* The mailman got hit right on the nose.

After that, everyone kept their distance. Cal wandered off, looking for unguarded snacks and to see if James was there yet. As he walked, he saw a life-sized, gold-covered statue of Mr. Wylot. And beyond it was a pool that held more water than Lake Michigan.

The five Rivales were the only ones swimming in the pool. Well, kind of swimming. Mr. and Mrs. Rivale and the triplets were performing a pretty wacky routine, moving through the water like synchronized otters.

"What are they *doing* in there?" Leslie Wylot said. Cal turned. Leslie and Alison Mangan were walking past him toward the pool. Cal was glad Leslie was too busy focusing on other people to bother Imo.

He shrugged. "It is a pool party, right? The Rivales are just going for a swim."

"Well, I guess there *is* plenty of room in the pool," Leslie said, stroking her braids. "After all, it's the largest one in the county. That's not bragging, you know, because you can Google it."

Cal rolled his eyes. Alison smiled and rolled her eyes, too. Leslie saw it.

"Fetch me a glass of water, would you, best friend?" Leslie said to Alison. Alison's smile disappeared.

"Sure, Leslie, no problem," Alison said in an embarrassed whisper.

"She does whatever I say," Leslie said proudly after Alison left. "My family's company is growing all over the world. Her dad might—or might not—get a promotion from my father. Keeps her on her toes."

"So not cool," Cal said.

"Ground Control to Leslie," Imo said. She had come up behind them. "We regret to inform you that you seem to have lost contact with reality."

"Oh, you Talaskas," Leslie said, as if disappointed. "You still can't take a joke. But I think that's about to change."

Before Cal could respond, a loud screech filled the air, and everyone turned. Mr. Wylot stood on the back deck, tapping a microphone. Cal and Imo joined their family as the rest of the party drifted toward Mr. Wylot. Leslie walked like a princess up the steps and posed proudly next to her dad. Her mom and her older sister, Emma, were already there.

"Welcome to my estate!" Mr. Wylot boomed into the microphone. Several people covered their ears, but Mr. Wylot didn't seem to notice.

"You might be wondering why we haven't served any food yet," he said, wiping crumbs off his chin. "I like the people around me to be hungry. Especially the people who work for me. And, let's face it . . . that's just about everyone here."

"Ha! Ha!" Alison's dad laughed, but no one else did.

Mr. Wylot gave him an annoyed look, then continued. "I want to introduce you to our daughters, Leslie and Emma. Watch out for Emma's little booby traps around the estate—she's quite a military genius, that one. My wife, Olga, and I are so proud of the good work our girls do in the community."

Leslie and Emma took a bow. Emma was holding an

extra-long blow tube. Cal realized she had been firing the spitballs.

"In fact, it was my darling Leslie who helped me come up with today's big surprise," Mr. Wylot said.

Uh-oh, Cal thought. Leslie was grinning straight at Cal, and she mouthed the words *Ready for another joke?*

"And here to introduce the surprise is . . ." Mr. Wylot paused and then shouted, "Mr. Paddy Vance, Vice President of Fun at Wish Shoppe!"

Mr. Vance bounced up onto the deck. Mr. Wylot stepped aside so he could use the microphone.

"Hello, ladies and gents!" Mr. Vance cried, waving both hands at the crowd. "First I want to thank Mr. Wylot for having us here and for convincing Wish Shoppe founder King Wonder to have this elimination round in such a comfortable setting!"

Cal couldn't believe it. They were going to eliminate one of the families now?

"What about the billboard?" he shouted. Mr. T. touched his shoulder. "Sorry," Cal said more quietly. "What about the billboard, sir? I thought you were going to reveal the winners on Palmer's Farm."

Mr. Vance gave him a wink. "Mr. Palmer decided

he didn't want the crowds to come back. And then Mr. Wylot made a generous donation to the, uh . . . Wish Shoppe . . . charity. . . ."

"In other words," the fire chief, Mr. Carmody, grumbled, "Mr. Wylot paid money and got his way."

Pretending not to hear, Mr. Vance kept grinning. "Here's what's going to happen today. Three finalist families made videos about being the world's best Wish Shoppe shoppers: the Wylots, the Rivales, and the Tal-Tal . . . ?"

"Talaskas!" Cal said.

"And the Talaskas," Mr. Vance said. "We're going to show the videos they sent in . . . right now!"

A large screen rose out of the deck behind him. "That's the largest home video screen in North America," Leslie said loudly to Mr. Vance. "Again, not bragging. Google it."

Mr. Vance nodded eagerly as if he would do just that. Then he announced, "The two families that get the loudest applause on the Audience Love Meter will move on to the final round of the Great Grab Contest. So get ready to clap your hearts out!"

A second, much smaller screen slid up next to the

first. This one had the words AUDIENCE LOVE METER over a dial that looked like a car's speedometer.

"King Wonder, owner of Wish Shoppe, is proud to announce the three finalist families in the Great Grab Contest!" Mr. Vance said. "The first video is from the Wylot family!"

A deep voice blasted out of the speakers on the deck. "In a world filled with simple, average people, only one family can dominate and lead. Only one name can rise above all others. And that name is . . . WYLOT!"

The screen filled with an image of the Wylots sprinting like action heroes down a store aisle. Emma pushed a shopping cart with Leslie crouched inside. All four wore full-length fur coats and had bandanas over their faces like bank robbers from the Old West.

Leslie pointed, and lightning bolts shot out of her finger, knocking a giant cotton candy machine off a shelf and into their cart. Mr. Wylot raised both hands and lifted a washing machine into the cart—as if with his mind. Emma performed wild karate moves and chopped a mini refrigerator in half. Mrs. Wylot spun around and became a tornado that sucked in items from the shelves. Lamps, dog beds, stoves, an iguana—all magically flew through the air and into their cart.

Cal's stomach sank. His family couldn't compete with this. It was like watching a Hollywood blockbuster.

The video finished with a huge explosion. *BLAM!* The crowd gasped, and Cal thought he felt his hair blow back.

Mr. Vance grabbed the microphone. "So, folks, what'd you think of the Wylots' video?" he cried. "Remember, your applause will determine the winner!"

A few people in the audience clapped, and the Audience Love Meter ticked up to 16 percent.

"They can scare us into coming to the party," an old man muttered, "but they can't make us clap."

As if to prove him wrong, Mr. Wylot made a twirling signal with his hand. The waiters dropped their trays onto the grass, and they burst into cheers noisy enough to make cheerleaders cover their ears.

The arrow on the meter ticked up to 65 percent. Mr. Mangan clapped and hooted even more loudly, and the Audience Love Meter rose to 72 percent.

"Not a bad score!" Mr. Vance said. "Next up, we have the video from the Rivale family!"

Cal looked for the Rivales. They were right next to him, dripping wet in their swimsuits and standing perfectly still.

"Good luck," Cal said, and they nodded at him in unison.

The Rivales' video popped up on the screen. It showed a single can of corn in a spotlight in a dark tent.

So that's what the Rivales have been up to inside their backyard tent! Cal thought.

With their slicked-back dark hair and black unitards, the Rivales surrounded the can of corn and just stared at it. Slowly . . . very slowly . . . they each moved one hand in little circles around the can at exactly the same time.

Then the screen went black except for the single word *FIN*.

The video ended.

People were stunned. Mr. Vance snapped himself out of some kind of trance and finally said, "Let's hear applause for the Rivales!"

There was nothing. Not even from the Rivales. Finally, Cal gave a little clap. That started a small ripple, and the arrow on the Audience Love Meter turned to 46 percent.

"Thank you for coming, Rivales!" Mr. Vance cried dramatically. The Rivales didn't move a muscle. They were like synchronized rocks.

"Did someone switch them off?" a little girl whispered to her dad.

Mr. Vance announced, "And the third and final video is from . . . the Talaskas!"

"Here it comes," Imo said. She sounded panicky about being up on the big screen. She added, "I'm sorry, Cal. Especially because watching Leslie boss Alison around has changed my mind about things."

Sorry? Why are you sorry? Cal almost asked. But he didn't want to miss a thing.

The world around Cal seemed to slow down, and his heart pounded. Mrs. T. must have known he was about to burst. She put a hand on his shoulder. "Easy."

Cal couldn't wait for everyone to see the video of his perfect family shopping like experts. Instead, something completely different appeared on the screen.

His ears reacted first.

"What's . . . with the . . . extra *P*!" Cal heard his mom say in the video. Then Mr. T. said, "Let it flow! Set it *free!*" When he heard Imo say, "What rhymes with *free,* Dad? It starts with a *P*!" Cal started feeling queasy.

Still, it took a second for him to figure out what he was looking at. He and his family were in a heap on the muddy ground in their backyard, a giant pile of arms, legs, a tail, and six laughing heads.

Then Cal heard himself say, "The Butler did it!" He saw the expression on his own face in the video—and his wet pants.

"What am I doing?" Cal asked out loud.

Mr. Carmody overheard him. "Hmm," he considered. "I'd say you're trying not to pee your pants. And I'm not sure you're succeeding."

For twenty seconds, the video showed the Talaskas laughing their heads off. Then, without warning, the screen went blank.

Once again, the audience was stunned. This time, not even Mr. Vance could recover. The Talaskas were frozen. Cal felt his face burning with embarrassment. The Audience Love Meter sat at 0 percent.

Leslie gave Cal a nasty smile and chuckled. The microphone picked up her laughter, and it went out to the crowd.

The sound was like a stick of dynamite blowing up a dam.

As if they had been waiting for the okay, people opened their mouths, and a flood of laughter and clapping filled the air.

Then the Audience Love Meter arrow shot up to 45 percent.

People were smacking each other's backs and reliving the video.

"What's with the extra *P*?" howled John Salmona, who lived down the street from the Talaskas. "Set it *free!*"

Next to John, Ms. Graves dabbed her wet eyes. "Holy moly," she said in a most unteacherly way. "The Butler did it! That's just awesome!"

"What's happening, Dad?" Cal asked. "Did they like it?"

"I'm not sure what's with all the racket," Mr. T. said. "But laughing is like a cold—you can catch it."

And it was true. The noise of laughter only grew. The dial on the Audience Love Meter raced to 70 percent. Cal could see Leslie looking around furiously. Even Mr. Wylot was starting to get worried. When the arrow approached the Wylots' score of 72, he grabbed the microphone.

"All right, all right, I think that's enough," Mr. Wylot said, putting up a hand. "Let's all calm down."

The crowd's laughter died down to chuckles, and Mr. Vance took the microphone back. "Well, that was something," he said. "Looks like we have our two finalist families! The Wylots and the Talaskas!"

Cal launched into the air and pumped his fist. "That's me!" he yelled at the top of his lungs.

"That's *us*!" Imo yelled even louder. She sounded as excited as he was to have won. Mr. and Mrs. T. didn't seem nearly as happy. Cal knew they had thought the video round would be the end of the contest for them.

"We'll see both families at the brand-new Wish Shoppe in two weeks, at nine AM sharp," Mr. Vance said over the hubbub. "If either the Wylots or the Talaskas fail to show up for the Great Grab, the Rivales will take their slot. So be on time! Remember, there will only be one winning family that day. One family will be allowed to keep everything they grab and will appear in our national ad. Stay tuned for more!"

Mr. Wylot did not look pleased. But he had a fake smile on his face and clapped. "Everyone is free to *grab* a plate and eat now! Enjoy!"

The velvet ropes were moved and the crowd stampeded to the barbecues, with the Rivales and Mr. Vance rushing to the head of the line.

"Not you, Mr. Vance," Mr. Wylot said. "I want to have a word with you."

He pulled Mr. Vance through the patio door into the house.

As his heartbeat slowed down, Cal's brain had a chance to catch up with what had just happened. He knew Wish Shoppe planned to put the winning videos online and on its billboards. The whole state . . . maybe the whole world . . . would see them.

"Why did you send that part of the video, Imo?" Cal asked. "I thought you were going to edit it."

"Sorry, there wasn't time." Imo shrugged. "In my opinion, though, it showed our family at our best. And it worked."

Cal wasn't so sure. He looked around, expecting to

find Leslie Wylot sneering at him. But the Wylots had already gone inside, as if bored with the company.

Cal wanted his family to win the contest so they could get whatever they'd like. But he also wanted the world to know that the Talaskas were the perfect family. Rolling around in the mud might not be the best way to show that.

Still, Imo had a point. The video had worked, and the Talaskas were finalists. They were going to the third round of the Wish Shoppe Great Grab Contest!

With the naming of the two finalist families, the small town of Hawkins exploded with Great Grab fever.

A few junior high kids who lived down the street rolled on the ground every time Cal went by on his bike. The kids acted like they were laughing so hard, they were about to pee their pants. As Cal pedaled away, they would call after him, "The Butler did it!" Cal had to admit it was kind of funny.

Still, something bothered him. He wasn't sure if their video had succeeded because people thought it was great—or because it was just a big joke.

Neighbors dropped off Wish Shoppe catalogs to give the Talaskas ideas for what to grab when they ran through the store. Jenny Vincent, a six-year-old from Brightmore Road, thought Cal should grab a life-sized ceramic ostrich. Other people circled sports equipment, jewelry, and car mats.

Dan MacGuire, an eighth grader from across the street, stopped Cal on the sidewalk. He'd drawn a star next to a roller coaster in a travel magazine.

Cal said, "Uh . . . I don't think that ride would fit in a shopping cart, Dan. Unless the cart was the size of Detroit."

"Yeah, but imagine the fun I can have—" Dan said, and then stopped. "Did I say *I*?" he asked, flustered. "I mean *you*! *You* as in *me*!" Finally, he gave up and said, "The Butler did it!"

Not everyone was as open about giving them ideas. When they stopped at Moylan's Gas Station, Mrs. Moylan left a note under one of the Flying Monkey's windshield wipers. The Talaskas found it when they got home. It read, "Get yourselves a new car! And thank you for standing up to them." By *them*, Cal knew Mrs. Moylan meant the Wylots.

Other people were nervous about openly rooting against the Wylots, too. The twin Weber girls snuck up to Mr. and Mrs. T. outside the library. Looking around as if the Wylots might see them, the twins gave them a list of lawn mowers.

While some of the ideas were pretty amazing, Cal still had his sights set on the Wonder World Video Game System. He'd be able to control the world around him! And owning a game that usually only hotels could afford would be a great way to prove how special the Talaskas were.

At school, Ms. Graves wrote LESLIE, IMO, and CAL on the board under the word CONGRATULATIONS!

"As your oh-so-hip English teacher, I'm not a fan of the old-world spelling of *Wish Shoppe*," Ms. Graves said. "But I'm very proud of the contest finalists in our class!" The rest of the students clapped, and the three took bows.

Imo and Cal managed to keep their distance from Leslie, and they just ignored any nasty comments she sent their way. Which wasn't always easy. Leslie had taped two sheets of paper on the wall outside the cafeteria. One was labeled TALASKA FANS at the top, and the other read WYLOT FANS. Leslie had been using scare tactics to get kids to sign the Wylot page.

So Cal was surprised when they came out of English class to find the Talaska Fans page completely filled in. Names scrawled in bright-purple ink covered the paper.

"Who signed this?" Leslie demanded angrily.

Cal stepped closer to see, and he laughed. "Some very important people."

"Like who?" Leslie snapped. "Wait until I mention them to my father."

"You should do that," Cal said. "I think George Washington, Teddy Roosevelt, and Abraham Lincoln will be very sorry."

"What does *that* mean?" Leslie peered at the Talaska page and snorted when she saw the names. They belonged to all the U.S. presidents and Canadian prime ministers. Leslie tore the sheets off the wall and stomped into the cafeteria, shouting for Alison to follow her.

"Who would dare do this, my fellow Americans?" James asked, perfectly copying the voice of the current president.

"Maybe the Butler did it?" Alison answered with a wink. She stuck her hands in her pockets and rushed after Leslie, but not before Cal saw the purple ink stains on her fingers.

That night, Cal called Grandma Gigi for the third time to tell her the amazing news about being contest finalists. She lived thirty minutes away. He got her answering machine again.

"I'm out and about, but leave me a shout," Gigi's greeting said. "And I'll call you back, without a doubt." Not the best poetry, Cal thought, but it was a clue as to why his dad rhymed when he got excited or nervous.

Even so, the good news kept coming. Ms. Donegan, who owned the Donegan Diner, had started dating James's dad. James helped out there for a couple of hours a week. He called to tell Cal that Ms. Donegan had created two new sandwiches in honor of the Wylots and the Talaskas.

Perfect timing. Cal's family needed all the encouragement they could get to keep going with the contest. Especially his parents.

Mrs. T.'s business was suddenly in trouble. The Olympic swimmer, the diver, and the linebacker who were supposed to speak at Wylot Auditorium next month all canceled on her. The athletes gave fake-sounding excuses, like still being dizzy from changing to daylight saving time or having a sick goldfish. Mrs. T. had already sold tickets to the events, and she would lose a ton of money when she had to send refunds.

Cal had an itchy feeling that Mr. Wylot was behind the athletes' not showing up. "It's called *Wylot* Auditorium, after all," he told his mom.

"No one is that awful," Mrs. T. said. Then, after thinking about it, she added, "But it is true that Mr. Wylot has been tough on your dad since that video elimination."

Saying *tough* in this situation was like saying the sun was *slightly warm*. Mr. Wylot was making Cal's dad's job at the factory almost impossible. Without warning, Mr. Wylot had taken away Mr. T.'s office. Now Cal's dad was stuck sitting in the hallway at a desk smaller than Cal's at school.

What did all this add up to?

Mr. and Mrs. T. were even less excited about the Great Grab Contest than before. "It's been kind of fun, Cal," Mrs. T. had said. "But we need to keep our eyes on real life and real jobs for a while."

That did not sound like a good plan to Cal.

A sandwich named after them could be just what they needed to get back on track! Cal convinced his family to head down to the diner for lunch, and the Talaskas hopped in the Flying Monkey. They drove to Main Street and parked close to the diner.

A chalkboard menu in front of the diner announced:

Come on in and try a . . .

Wylots' Maximum Force
or
Talaskas' The Butler Did It!

They're both a wish come true. . . .
Grab a great one TODAY!

"We're famous!" Cal said. "Come on, let's try a Talaska!"

"Those sandwiches are eight bucks," Mr. T. said. "We're not the Moneybag family, buddy."

"I got this one," Cal said, shaking his piggy bank, which he had brought from home. It sounded a little lighter than he remembered. "Well, we might have to split it, but it will be fun. Come on."

As the Talaskas went into the diner, Alison Mangan's dad walked out. Cal said hello, and Mr. Mangan nodded. From outside the big window, Mr. Mangan watched the Talaskas and quickly pulled out his cell phone before heading down the street.

Cal looked for James, but he was out with Ms. Donegan in the food truck. The Talaskas did run into the MacGuires, who yelled, "Why, hello!" as if real heroes had just entered the diner. And there was Mrs. Moylan sitting at the counter. She shook Mr. and Mrs. T.'s hands, smiling and wishing them luck with the contest. She didn't seem worried about supporting them now.

A few minutes later, the Talaskas took a seat in a booth, and a waitress came to take their order. Her name tag read MELINDA.

"We'll have five Talaskas, please," Cal said, counting his change on the table. "No, wait. Better make that *three* Talaskas, please."

"Talaska? What's that?" Melinda asked in a bored voice. "I don't think we have that."

Mrs. T. smiled. "We're friends of Ms. Donegan's," she said. "She named a sandwich after us. It's out on the sign."

Melinda leaned back to look outside. "I don't see that, sweetie," she said. Cal half stood so he could see the sign. And it was true—someone had wiped the name of the Talaska sandwich off the board.

Then he saw a man walking up to their table, clapping his hands together and sending clouds of chalk dust into the air. Cal could guess whom Mr. Mangan had been calling in such a hurry.

Mr. Wylot.

"Hello, Nelson," Mr. Wylot said to Cal's dad. He was a little out of breath, like he had hustled over to the restaurant. "I see you have time for lunch, but not work."

"It's Saturday—" Mr. T. started to say.

"Oh, Nelson, I'm just joking," Mr. Wylot said. He put his chalky hands on the table. "In fact, I'm here with good news that couldn't wait until Monday. I'm giving

you a job in the new plant we're building on the out-
skirts of the Mojave Desert."

Cal gasped, and Imo sputtered, "What?"

People at other tables looked their way.

"I was inspired to make the decision by something
my beautiful daughter Leslie told me," Mr. Wylot said,
and winked at Cal. "The job is scheduled to start immediately. I have a ten-year contract right here." He took
a stack of papers out of his shoulder bag and smacked
them down on the table. "Nelson Talaska, this contract
will keep you in accounting for the rest of your life! Isn't
that amazing?"

Mr. Wylot spoke loudly, as if he was showing off. A few other diners clapped lamely.

"Dad, say something," Cal said.

Mr. T. wouldn't look at him. Still, something changed in his face. "Mr. Wylot, this is too much," he said quietly. "That's something my family and I would have to think about and such."

Mr. Wylot smiled down on him. "There's nothing to think about. The job starts in three days. Until then, don't bother coming back to the factory here. Your work in Hawkins is over."

Cal couldn't take it. He asked his mom and dad, "But what about our house? James? Our other friends? The town?"

Bug barked. Imo guessed who he was talking about. "Yes," she said. "What about Sarah?"

"Who's Sarah?" Mr. Wylot asked.

"Our babysitter," Mrs. T. said.

"Hmm, I know Sarah," Mr. Wylot said. "Here's a fun fact. Did you know her college scholarship comes from the Wylot Foundation?"

"Wait," Cal said. "Do you mean she might get kicked out of school if we don't leave?"

"I never said that!" Mr. Wylot pretended to be

shocked. "Only that I control who gets money to pay for college. But let's talk about happier things, like your big move to the Mojave Desert."

This was all too much. Cal was dazed. "What about the contest?"

"What contest?" Mr. Wylot asked innocently. "Oh! You mean the Wish Shoppe Great Grab Contest? I'd forgotten all about that. I guess you'll miss out."

"Why are you doing this?" Cal asked, his face burning again, but this time because he was angry.

"Cal . . . ," his mom warned.

"No, let the boy ask," Mr. Wylot said. And he patted Cal on the head. "Do you know what a boss is?"

"I'm eleven, sir," Cal said.

"Good," Mr. Wylot said. "Then you know a boss is in charge. What would happen if the people who worked for him were suddenly beating him at contests? And everyone was watching, just as they are right now?" He gestured toward the other tables. "That wouldn't make him the boss anymore, would it?"

Cal got it. That was why Mr. Wylot was doing all this now at the diner. He wanted everyone in town to know he was running the show. And it was working. The faces of the few people who were still looking their way seemed to have changed. The hope Cal had seen in Mrs. Moylan's face had faded.

Mr. Wylot's smile was gone, too. His eyes burned like lasers into the Talaskas. Bug growled. Then Mr. Wylot clapped and waved over the waitress.

"Melinda, bring these folks a Wylot sandwich," he said. "They need the best in the house. And that's always a Wylot!"

Cal felt like a volcano that was about to blow. He struggled not to explode as his dad drove them home to Piedmont Place.

As the Flying Monkey pulled into the driveway, Cal saw the mailman trotting away down the sidewalk. The mailman spotted Cal and put his hands over his ears, singing "La la la" as if to block out anything Cal might say. Cal knew he was only half kidding. Cal had once persuaded him to do the chicken dance while delivering the mail.

As the family went into the house, they found a slip on the front door that the mailman had left. It said the Talaskas had a package waiting for them at the post office. Mrs. T. shouted after the mailman, "Thanks, Henry!"

In the kitchen, Butler and Bug had their spectacular reunion. If they were separated for more than three minutes, it was as if they'd been apart for weeks. Butler rolled on his back and wiggled, crying happily, and Bug did the same.

Finally, Cal couldn't keep it in anymore. "We CANNOT move to the Mojave Desert!" he blurted out. "How can that even be an option?"

At the kitchen counter, Mrs. T. was opening the gallon of chocolate ice cream they had picked up on the way home. She took bowls out of the cupboard, but no one seemed interested in ice cream. The contract from Mr. Wylot sat in front of Mr. T. on the table, blocking the spot where Cal's dad played his invisible keyboard.

"You're right, Cal, it's not an option at this time," Mr. T. said, flipping through the contract. "Mr. Wylot's new factory will be a couple hundred yards from the actual desert line."

"Dad!" Cal shouted. How could Mr. T. joke about this? Imo was watching everything, but she wasn't helping, either.

"This could be an opportunity for us, Cal," Mrs. T. said. "Life might be easier for everyone this way."

"But we'd still be under Mr. Wylot's thumb, just really . . . hot." Cal didn't know what to say or where to start. What about their house? They'd have to leave it.

Guessing what Cal was thinking, Mrs. T. said, "Yes, we'd have to leave this house and Hawkins."

Her face seemed to droop like she couldn't believe what she'd just said. And the rest of the family was quiet for a minute, too.

It was Imo who spoke first. "I'm with Cal on this one," she said. "In my opinion, this stuff *does* matter. What the Wylots are doing is just way too . . ."

"Unfair!" Cal cried.

"Exactly," Imo agreed. "It's as unfair as when Lando Calrissian tricked Han Solo in Cloud City!"

"Nothing's been decided," Mr. T. said. "I told Mr. Wylot we needed more time than he's provided."

If only we had a real piano, Cal thought. His dad would be able to play, and that would let him think. He would see how bad this moving idea was. They needed the Great Grab more than ever.

"Can't we wait until after the contest?" Cal asked.

Mrs. T. turned away to put the ice cream in the freezer. "Cal, this is way more important than some contest."

"This isn't just any contest," Cal said.

His dad held up his hands. "Okay, I can see how you kids feel," he said. "I'll wait to sign the contract as long as I can. Deal?"

Cal knew it was probably just to get him to stop arguing, but he'd take it for now. "Thanks, Dad."

★ ★ ★

Later that afternoon, Cal was doing homework on his bed. Or trying to. He couldn't keep his mind on algebra.

Why were his parents giving up so easily? It was driving him crazy. He needed to do something. He rushed to the phone. He made three calls and sent three emails about what was going on, all to the same person— Grandma Gigi.

Gigi was famous for being slow to respond to messages. She liked to think about what to say. Cal thought of the time he'd sent her a silly joke about a giraffe on a train. He waited for her to email back. She did. But three weeks later and with only one word: *ha*.

Today, luckily, she didn't take as long to get back to

him. He checked his email and found that she had written more than one word this time. There were two.

Cal thought of the slip the mailman had left on their front door. He jumped to his feet and ran to his bike in the garage. Imo was there, staring into space and tugging one ear. She had started to clean her wrenches but stopped. She was as distracted as he was.

"Where are you going?" she asked. "If it's to do something about all this, count me in. People like Mrs. Moylan and Alison Mangan need us to stand up to the Wylots!"

"All right, you can come," he said. "But hurry."

She hopped on her bike, and together they pedaled down Piedmont Place.

"Where are we going, anyway?" Imo asked.

Cal answered using the two words from Gigi's email: "Post office."

★ ★ ★

An hour later, Mr. and Mrs. T. were waiting on the front steps as Cal and Imo pedaled into the driveway. Mrs. T. had the phone in her hand and was talking to one of the neighbors.

"They're back, Denise," Mrs. T. said into the phone. "Thanks. I'll call you later."

"Looks like we made the wrong call," Mr. T. said. "The Wylots didn't kidnap them after all."

Cal was alarmed. "Is that what you thought?"

"We were kidding with each other," Mrs. T. said with a shrug. "Kind of. Anyway—" She shook her head, getting back on track. "Where were you?"

"At the post office," Cal said.

"Why?" Mrs. T. asked as Butler and Bug circled Imo and Cal, bouncing up and down. "Let's go inside and you can explain."

A minute later, they were settled around the kitchen table. The contract from Mr. Wylot sat at one end and they huddled at the other, like it was an animal that might bite them.

Mrs. T. put her hands on the table. "Look, guys," she said. "I know you're upset about the contest and everything."

"But you can't go that far without telling us," Mr. T. chimed in. Cal knew scolding them was hard for him. He hated being the adult. "You're creating too much fuss."

Imo and Cal both nodded, and Cal said, "Grandma Gigi sent us things she's been holding on to. Things to help."

Mrs. T.'s eyebrows went up. "Help do what? Your grandmother doesn't keep anything."

"She did," Cal said. "She has things for both of you." He put a cardboard box on the table. "There was a note inside saying we should give them to you now."

Mr. T. opened the flaps of the box. He reached inside and took out a limp piece of fabric. He peered at it. "Is that . . . ?" he asked.

Mrs. T.'s hand covered her mouth. "Oh," she said softly.

It was a faded yellow sweatband.

"There's a school yearbook in the box, too, Mom," Imo said. "We looked at it. You were the best athlete at our school . . . in the state . . . in almost every single sport."

"That's why you're always looking at the old school trophies," Cal said.

Mrs. T. nodded. "This was my lucky sweatband. No

one could stop me when I wore this." She took the band carefully out of Mr. T.'s hand, as if she couldn't believe it was real. She gave the faded material a little stretch. "I guess I've gotten a little out of shape since then."

Mr. T. touched her arm. "I think you're beautiful, no matter what."

"Thanks, honey." Mrs. T. wiped a tear off her cheek and stared at the sweatband.

"Gigi kept something for you, too, Dad," Imo said. She picked up a plastic box with his name on it and held it out to him. Through the clear lid, they could see a fancy pen.

"That's . . . that's the pen my uncle gave me for my high school graduation," he said. "I wasn't going to open the box until I signed my first big music contract."

"What else does Gigi's note say?" Mrs. T. asked.

"Nothing, really," Cal said. "Just that no one messes with this family."

"No one has 'messed' with the family," Mr. T. said. "I wouldn't let that be—" He stopped. His eyes took on a new spark.

"I'm wrong," he said. "Mr. Wylot has taken our jobs. Made our friends' lives difficult. That family has laughed at us and stolen our sandwich. This is where it ends."

He opened the plastic box and took out the pen. Cal thought he looked like a future king pulling a sword from a stone.

"Dad," Imo said, "the ink might not work after all these years."

Mr. T. smiled. "One way to find out. No more doubts."

"Rabbo!" Butler and Bug both barked from beneath the table. They must have been there the whole time.

Mr. T. pulled Mr. Wylot's contract closer. He uncapped the pen and held it to the paper. He looked at them with his glasses slanted on his face. "No one messes with my family."

As his pen scratched across the contract, writing *NO DEAL,* Mrs. T. slid the sweatband onto her head. *BAM!* It was as if she grew a foot taller. She picked up Mr. Wylot's contract and tore it into small bits.

Mrs. T. looked at each of them and then said in a strong, clear voice, "We have to win this contest."

The rules of the Great Grab were clear.

Mr. Vance called to make sure the Talaskas knew to be at the brand-new Wish Shoppe in seven days, at exactly nine AM. They and the Wylots would be the first visitors allowed in the Wish Shoppe. Until then, both families were to keep clear of the store, even the parking lot.

"We don't want anyone getting an unfair advantage," Mr. Vance said. For some reason, the Vice President of Fun sounded less perky than usual. "You must also agree to the legal document I just emailed you. Don't be scared of words like *death by shopping cart, hopelessly marooned,* or *mysterious vomiting.* The document is for everyone's good and super fun!"

Before Mr. Vance hung up, he reminded them there would be a final elimination round on the day of the contest. Only one family would be allowed to keep everything they could grab in the store.

"How will they make the decision?" Imo wondered out loud after Mr. Vance's call. Cal was sitting with her and their mom in the living room. Mr. T. was out back with Butler and Bug.

"Good question," Mrs. T. said. She had put the headband away for now and was perched in front of her computer. "These contests always have some kind of wild twist."

"Then we better get set for anything they can throw at us," Cal said. "The good thing about you and Dad not having work is that we can train for the contest."

"That's the only good thing," Mrs. T. said. She glanced at the stack of bills next to her keyboard.

"We just have to make it for another week, until the Great Grab," Cal assured her.

Mrs. T. didn't seem convinced. But maybe she saw the worry on Cal's face, because she said, "You could be right."

To change the subject, Mrs. T. tapped her computer screen. "I did a quick search on the Wish Shoppe," she said. "Check out this news story."

Cal and Imo leaned in to read it.

Michigan Teen Lost in Wish Shoppe for Three Days
By Park Ridgefield for the *Hawkins Herald*

Alex Dante, thirteen, of Grand Rapids has been found after going missing on April 22. Alex had last been seen near the entrance of the Wish Shoppe Circles of Dreams in East Lansing, Michigan.

"I dropped Alex off at the bridge that leads across that River of Low Prices," his mother told this reporter. "By the time I parked the car, he was gone."

Alex vanished without a trace. For three days, his parents and friends searched the area around the store. All with no luck. No one guessed that Alex was actually *inside* the store the whole time.

"I got lost in the Clothing Circle," Alex said after being rescued by an equally lost eighty-five-year-old woman looking for garbanzo beans. "I wandered into the Appliance Circle. I made a tent out of a big cardboard box and drank water from a floor-sample refrigerator. My biggest wish was to get out of Wish!"

How could a straight-A junior high school student get lost in a store for three days? Simple. All fifty Wish Shoppes are jammed with five acres of every kind of product on the planet. Shoppers complain that there is no rhyme or reason to the stores. Aisles branch out from different departments—or Circles of Dreams—and lead nowhere or spiral into dead ends.

The founder of the stores, King Wonder, has often said, "Wishes can lead you anywhere! So our Wish Shoppes have Circles of Dreams and aisles that lead to other Circles and aisles and so on and so on and on and on and on. What's so confusing about that?"

Cal had read enough. "Okay, that can't be true!" he said. "The writer's totally making that up! We would have heard about that kid getting lost."

"Maybe King Wonder is covering it up," Imo said. She leaned closer to the computer. "The rest of the article says Alex and the eighty-five-year-old got lost again. They had to be re-rescued by a toddler who stumbled into the Appliance Circle."

"A toddler wandering the store alone?" Cal rolled his eyes. "Come on!"

Imo shrugged. "Could be true. All those Circles and aisles make a pretty confusing maze. I mean, have you ever been in one of those stores?"

"Uh, yes," Cal answered. "Maybe three or four times . . . *with you.*"

"And how many of those times did we get lost?" Imo countered. "Three or four?"

Secretly, Cal admitted Imo had a point. "I still think that story's a lie."

"Just because *you* make everything up doesn't mean other people do," Imo fired back.

Mrs. T. held up her hands. "Okay, okay. It doesn't matter if this stuff is true. We just need to figure out a path through the store that will take us to the things we want."

"I'm on it," Cal said. He ran up to his bedroom, grabbed his whiteboard, and brought it back to the living room. The board was where Cal came up with some of his best ideas—like the master plan to convince his parents they needed a swimming pool. (That plan had failed in the first stage: "Persuade parents to wear sweaters during a heat wave so they get really, really hot.")

Cal uncapped his marker and got ready to write down ideas from Mrs. T. "Okay, shoot," he said.

Now that his parents were on board with the contest, Cal figured he would have to give up a little control. But his mom shook her head.

"We'll all come up with ideas," Mrs. T. said. "But mostly it's got to be you, Cal. Think of your dad and me as the team owners, and you're the quarterback. Okay?"

"Better than okay," Cal said. "Thanks, Mom."

Imo didn't seem as enthusiastic about this way of thinking. But she finally nodded. "All right, all right," she groaned. "What should we do first, oh, mighty QB?"

Cal wrote one word on the board: MAP.

Because they weren't allowed to visit the store before the contest and they couldn't find a map of it online, Cal came up with a plan to make their own map. That way, they could plot their course.

He asked Mrs. T. to hunt for pictures online from other Wish Shoppes—and she found quite a few. Most were of people goofing around, holding up a compass or scratching their heads as if hopelessly lost. A few held up wish lists that included things like "I wish I could find my way out of here!" Mrs. T. printed out the photos, and the family pieced them together into a weird kind of map.

Imo and Cal taped it to the living room wall and stood back to take a look.

"Holy Aristotle," Cal breathed. "That map is huge."

"Just like the store," Mrs. T. said. "After all, it covers more land than downtown Hawkins."

To train their brains to find what they wanted, Cal asked Imo to invent scavenger hunts around the house. He timed family members as they darted in and out of rooms, up and down stairs, looking for the strange items on Imo's lists.

"Here, Dad," Imo said, and handed Mr. T. a checklist. "You have to find old floss, a green feather, and a toy army figure."

Cal was pretty athletic, but no one in the family had ever prepped for a competition quite like this. They were sloppy at first, tripping over their own feet and panicking when time started to run out.

When Bug ran into Imo carrying a bucket of sand from the sandbox and it fell into the dishwasher, Cal was struck by a bad thought. The chaos would be three

million times worse at the Wish Shoppe. With so many amazing possibilities of things they could put in their carts—like toys, TVs, or tennis racquets—plus the time pressure, Cal realized they would be a mess.

"One thing," he said that night at the dinner table. The family was exhausted and just about to dig into Bug's second-favorite meal, meat loaf.

"What one thing?" Imo asked, pouring ketchup on her meat loaf.

"That's the answer," Cal said. "We need to stick with the *one thing* that each of us wants on the day of the contest. Otherwise we're going to get distracted and make mistakes. After we get that, we can grab whatever else we want if there's time."

"Excellent advice," Mr. T. said. When everyone agreed, he added, "Please pass the rice."

The next day, the family spent hours plotting routes on the map. They stuck with just the Circles that had things they wanted: gym equipment, musical instruments, science gear, video games, and . . . Bug still wasn't clear on what he wanted.

"We can forget about this whole side of the store," Cal said, pointing to the map. "All the Circles we want to hit, like the Fun and Games Circle and the Fitness Circle, are over here."

"But what if we get lost?" Imo said. "And wind up on the other side?"

"We won't," Cal said. "We're going to be too prepped for that."

Cal decided they should get ready for any possible tricks Mr. Vance might throw their way at the final elimination. Like doing everything backward, including talking.

"No emoc!" Cal said. "Nuf s'ti!"

Imo threw a couch pillow at him. "Bmud s'taht!"

They kept practicing, pretending to shop while skipping, singing, and spinning. The Talaskas trained all day, every day.

The night before the contest, Cal studied the map of the store . . . for what felt like the billionth time. He barely noticed that his dad was behind him and had his glasses on a slant.

Mr. T. was mumbling something about "memorizing the entire store." But Cal was too busy staring at the map and didn't really hear him. He focused on the Fun and Games Circle. That was where he would grab the

Wonder World Video Game System. Once Cal had that, he would toss into the cart anything else that would fit.

But there was one thing he dreamed of grabbing tomorrow more than anything—and that was respect. Cal wanted the Wylots and everyone else in Hawkins to treat his family like the winners he knew they were.

In fact, Cal wanted it so deeply, he imagined he could see the word *RESPECT* floating over the map.

"I'm coming for you," Cal said, tapping the map, and then he went to bed.

On the morning of the Great Grab Contest, the Talaskas woke up and brushed their teeth, as they always did. But Cal noticed something different.

There wasn't fighting over who was next in line for the bathroom. No frantic search for a missing sock. No BTAs. Cal's family was like a well-oiled machine.

We're just like the Rivales, he thought. Then Bug smeared toothpaste in Imo's hair, and Cal thought, *Well, not exactly.*

Cal, Imo, and Bug came downstairs to the kitchen, where their parents were waiting. Mr. T. started ringing the family bell like crazy.

"Surprise!" Mrs. T. said. "If we're going to be a strong

team today, we should look the part. Your dad and I made costumes!"

Mr. T. pointed to six piles of clothing on the table. Five of them had a purple velvet belt and a purple velvet shirt with a family member's name on the front and TALASKA on the back. There was even a new purple collar for Butler.

"Hmm," Cal said. Was this a good idea? But Imo had already pulled her shirt on top of her overalls, and Bug was putting the collar on Butler.

Why not? Cal thought. He slid the belt through the loops in his pants and reached for his shirt. It was baggy in places and tight in others, but he loved it. He felt like a superhero.

"Thanks!" he said to his parents. "We've got forty-five minutes to get to the Wish Shoppe. Plenty of time, but we should hit the road right after we eat."

They wolfed down a breakfast of pancakes and, feeling pumped, hustled out to the driveway. But when they got there, it was as if someone let all the air out of their balloon.

Or tire.

"Oh no," Cal said.

The Flying Monkey's front-right tire had finally collapsed. The car was hunched over to one side, the tire rim resting on the gravel.

Imo crouched and touched the tire's gaping hole. "I can't patch it. The hole's too big. The Flying Monkey is grounded."

"And so are our hopes of getting to the Wish Shoppe on time," Mrs. T. groaned. Then her eyes went to Mr. T.'s face. "Honey, are you okay?"

As Cal watched, a vein on Mr. T.'s neck popped out and his cheek started twitching. Mr. T. opened his mouth, and Cal thought about when he poured soda too quickly into a glass—how the fizz would overflow and go everywhere. That seemed to be happening with his dad.

As Mr. T. stared at the deflated tire, he looked like everything inside him was about to overflow.

"Honey?" Mrs. T. said again.

Mr. T. clamped his mouth shut in a tight line. Then he stomped toward the house, counting to ten. Actually, he went way past ten and just kept going and going.

This can't be the way things end, Cal thought. His mind raced through possible solutions.

"We could walk," Cal said.

Imo shook her head. "Way too far."

"Bikes?"

Imo shook her head again. Cal remembered that their mom didn't have one and she couldn't ride double.

"Let's get a lift from someone," Cal said. As if on cue, a van started up in the driveway next door and backed into the street. It was the Rivales! *They must be heading out to the Wish Shoppe,* thought Cal.

"Wait!" he shouted. Waving his arms, he ran with Imo to the sidewalk. But the Rivales must have thought the Talaskas were just saying hello. They waved back in perfect unison and drove down the street.

Imo looked at the other houses. "Everyone else is gone!" she said miserably.

She was right. Cal thought about calling James's sister for a ride. But she didn't have a cell phone. And James and his dad were already at the Wish Shoppe with the Donegan Diner food truck. "Can we call a taxi?" Cal asked Mrs. T.

His mom smiled and shook her head. "This is Piedmont Place, honey!"

Cal kicked the ground. His mom was right. There wasn't a taxi within an hour of them. By then, the Talaskas would be disqualified from the contest and the Rivales would take their place.

"Rabbo!" Butler barked while spinning around and around. Bug joined in. "Rabbo! Rabbo! Rabbo!"

Cal turned to see what Butler and Bug were so excited about.

Holy Aristotle.

"Wait a second," Mr. T. said from near the house. His face looked almost calm again. "Is that a . . . ?"

"I think it is," Cal answered.

A car tire was rolling down Piedmont Place.

"What the provolone is going on?" Mrs. T. asked.

Like a homing pigeon, the tire angled toward the Talaskas' driveway, but it missed and bounced off the curb. The force sent it wobbling for a few more feet, and then it fell over.

Mr. T. trotted into the street and turned the tire upright. Imo joined him, and they rolled the tire to the Flying Monkey.

"Does it fit?" Cal asked.

Imo nodded, dumbfounded. "It's perfect, in my opinion. Where did this come from?"

That was when Cal noticed the writing along the inside rim of the tire. "The Butler did it!" had been scrawled in purple ink.

"Someone really wants us to make it to the Wish Shoppe," Cal said. "But who?"

No one had an answer, and the family had to get moving. *Right now!*

Imo and Mr. T. put on the new tire, and the Talaskas climbed into the Flying Monkey. When Mr. T. turned the key, the song "We Are Family" boomed out of the busted CD player. It had never sounded so good.

"Are we going to make it, Dad?" Imo asked.

Mr. T. nodded. But the way he gripped the steering wheel made it clear he wasn't sure.

When the Talaskas pulled into a parking space at the Wish Shoppe and poured out of the car, it was 8:58 AM. Two minutes to spare. The first thing Cal noticed was the hundreds of butterfly-shaped balloons that formed a wall between the parking lot and the store. They floated and flapped in the wind, tugging gently on the strings that tied them to the ground.

Three news vans and a crowd of about two hundred people, including the Wylots, the Rivales, and Mr. Vance, were already gathered next to the balloons.

Like the Talaskas, the Wylots were in costume. They had on the long fur coats from their video and wore bandanas around their necks. Cal and his family hustled over to them. Leslie glanced at her watch and frowned, clearly upset the Talaskas were on time.

Cal spotted James and his dad behind the Wylots. James and Cal exchanged thumbs-ups. "Go get 'em, Captain!" James called.

"Um, what's he doing here?" Leslie pointed at Butler. Bug stepped in front of him, as if trying to protect the dog from lightning that might fire out of her finger.

"Family members who were in the videos get to be in the contest," Cal said. He wasn't sure if that was a rule. He had just never thought about leaving Butler home.

Leslie opened her mouth to say something nasty or challenge him when—

Bug looked up into her eyes and softly barked, "Rabbo." He wrapped his arms around Butler's neck, and Butler pressed his head against Bug's.

"Aw, how adorable!" Mrs. MacGuire cooed from the crowd. Cal had to admit that it was pretty darn cute. And even Leslie couldn't resist.

She seemed torn. Finally, she held up her hands and said, "Whatever! Let Butler do it!"

"I thought the Butler already *did* it!" someone said, and the audience laughed.

Cal nodded his thanks to Leslie, who was already back to her usual nasty self. She rolled her eyes at Cal just as the butterfly balloons were pulled back like a curtain. They revealed something—no, make that *someone*—amazing. . . .

King Wonder!

The owner of Wish Shoppe was here, in the flesh. With a gold crown perched on his silver head, King sat

upon his Throne of Savings. The chair was made of giant
dollar signs, and he waved a gold scepter with a butterfly on top.

Mr. Vance tapped his shoulder, and King's dreamy
eyes came into focus. "Oh good-good-good!" King said
in a high-pitched voice. "Now we can begin!"

He waved to the news cameras, and they all pointed
in his direction.

"Welcome, one and all!" King announced. "Welcome
to the Great Grab Contest at the Wish Shoppe Circles of
Dreams, where shopping is so easy, you'll forget where
you are!"

There was a snicker or two from the audience. King

cleared his throat. "It's a beautiful day here along the River of Low Prices, the largest man-made river in the world!"

The "river" was six feet wide and three feet deep and ran all the way around the store. The water was clear, as in a swimming pool, and dollar signs had been painted along the bottom—as if high prices had tried getting into the store and sunk to the bottom instead.

Mr. Vance leaned in to whisper in King's ear. "Fine, fine . . . make that the largest man-made river in the general area!" King said. He smiled warmly at Mr. Vance. "What would we do without our trusty Vice President of Fun?"

Cal noticed that the Wylots grinned at each other.

"Our two finalist families, the Wylots and the . . ." King paused. "We're sorry, but we're having trouble saying this other name. . . ."

Why does King say we *when he's talking about himself?* Cal wanted to ask, but his dad responded before he could. "We're the Talaskas," Mr. T. said.

"It rhymes with *Nelson, you're fired,*" Mr. Wylot said, as if trying to be helpful.

"It does? Really?" King asked, appearing confused. Then he continued, "As you know, there will be one final elimination round, and only one family will get to keep what they grab today. At first, we thought we might ask a trivia question to eliminate one family. Maybe a question about the rarest purple flowering plant on the Apalachicola River."

"That's the Florida skullcap," Mrs. T. said instantly.

The crowd gasped as people checked her answer on their cell phones. "She's right," Maisy Franklin, the librarian, said in awe.

We won! Cal thought.

But King was still talking. "Then we decided no, no, no. We should do something physical. You know, really get the old blood pumping. Like walking on your hands for a hundred feet."

Bug flipped over. And darted around the concrete on his hands.

We won! Cal thought again.

"But . . . we thought no," King said. "That's not right, either. We figured it should be more interesting. We decided the elimination should happen *inside* the store *while* the Great Grab is taking place."

"Here comes the twist," Mrs. T. said.

King sat back and waved his scepter at Mr. Vance, a signal for him to take over.

"Thanks, King," Mr. Vance said. "Our shoppers know there are nine Circles of Dreams inside every Wish Shoppe. But do they know how to find them fast? To prove you're the perfect shoppers we love, you must visit each Circle in the store and take the ribbons with your family's name. You'll find them in the center of the Circles. You're not allowed to touch the other family's ribbons."

Panic seeped into Cal's body. And he could feel the rest of his family tense up, too. They had planned on going only to the Circles where they wanted things, not *all* the Circles in the store!

"Of course," Mr. Vance said with a chuckle, "you can grab whatever you'd like along the way and put it in your cart!"

When he said *cart,* two men in Wish Shoppe uniforms appeared, pushing two jumbo-sized shopping carts. They rolled one over to each family. Cal could see a digital timer, set to twenty minutes, stuck below the handle.

As Imo examined the cart, Mr. Vance asked her, "Are you excited, little girl?"

The cameras pointed at her, and Imo suddenly looked like one of the Rivales. Her face went blank and she froze.

"Awesome!" Mr. Vance said, as if Imo had just said something very interesting. He turned back to the other family members. "You have twenty minutes to grab what you want and get back to the starting point. Everything you grab must be in your cart, and everyone in your family has to cross the line together. If you don't return within twenty minutes with all nine Circle ribbons, you get nothing."

"Oh, and one last thing . . . ," King said with mischief in his eyes.

"Here comes another twist," Mrs. T. whispered. Cal braced himself.

"There is no talking allowed inside the store," King said with a wink. "If you speak, your family will be disqualified and you will lose." He took a breath and asked, "Are you ready to make all your wishes come true?"

"Yes!" Cal shouted, and the rest of the Talaskas nodded. The Wylots pulled their bandanas up over their faces, making them look like bank robbers. Their eyes bored into the Talaskas, and then they, too, nodded to King Wonder.

"Go grab your dreams!" King shouted.

A starter cannon fired and, after all the nuttiness of the past few weeks, the last round of the Great Grab Contest had finally begun!

With a loud *tick tick tick,* the timer on the Talaskas' cart started counting down from twenty minutes to zero.

"Let's go!" Mr. T. got behind the cart and pushed it. Or tried to. Maybe he shoved too hard, or maybe the cart was just ready to break. But the second Mr. T. put pressure on it, the cart toppled over.

"Whoa," Mrs. T. said.

Mr. T. flipped it back upright and tried again. The cart skittered onto its side. The crowd started chuckling.

"Do you need an instruction manual?" a teenager asked. The audience laughed again, and it stung Cal a little. People had already figured they were going to lose to the Wylots.

Ignoring the laughter, Imo spun the wheels of the flipped cart. "The wheels are fine, but the balance is all out of whack," she said. "If we push it, it will keep flipping."

"We need a new cart, Mr. Wonder!" Cal shouted.

King started to get to his feet, but Mr. Vance leaned in to whisper in his ear. Sitting back in the throne, King said, "You get only one cart."

"That's not fair!" Cal called back.

"Fair?" King asked, as if he had never heard of the word. "We're sorry, but those are the rules."

As the Talaskas stood looking down at their wounded shopping cart, the Wylots had already sped across the bridge over the River of Low Prices. Leslie glanced back and gave Cal a nasty wave as they disappeared into the store.

"This is a nightmare," Cal said.

The other Talaskas weren't listening. They were all talking at once and kept lifting the cart and trying to push it, but it just wouldn't stay upright.

"*Ting ting ting!*" Cal said, imitating their family bell, and they quieted down. "We can't panic, guys. It's just a matter of figuring it out, right, Imo?"

While Cal and Mrs. T. held the cart upright, Imo took a closer look.

"We can't push it," she said. "But that doesn't mean we can't pull it. We just need to do it from the right angle." She got down on her knees and pulled the front of the cart. It moved toward her smoothly with no sign of tipping over. "See, this works!"

"We can't crawl around the store in twenty minutes!" Cal said.

"Give me your belts," Imo said. "Quick!"

Without asking what she was up to, everyone slid off their purple belts and handed them over. Imo moved fast, like a one-girl pit crew at a NASCAR race. In thirty seconds, she had knotted their belts together into a small harness and tied it to the front of the cart.

"Come here, Bug," Imo said.

"I don't know, honey," Mrs. T. said, guessing what she was up to.

Imo shrugged. "We're too big for the harness, and so is Butler—but Bug isn't."

Bug stepped into the loop, and Imo tightened it snugly around his waist. "You okay?" Imo asked him.

Bug barked happily. And Cal knew why. He probably felt like a sled dog!

As if Butler had never been more proud, he barked, "Rabbo!"

Now that the Talaskas had a cart that barely worked *and* they had to visit all nine Circles in the store, Cal needed to come up with a new plan on the fly. "Okay, listen up," he said. "I'll grab the ribbon from the Television Circle on the way to the Fun and Games Circle. You guys get the ribbons from your Circles, and we'll meet at the Pet Circle, okay?"

Imo did the math in her head. "That leaves four ribbons."

"I know," Cal said. "They're on the other side of the store. The side we didn't study."

He held up a hand before she could say *And whose fault is that?*

"We'll have to grab the other ribbons after we meet at the Pet Circle," Cal said. "Bug, you'll pull the cart with Butler in one big loop around the store until you reach the Pet Circle, and we'll meet you there with what we grab. We can run faster if we're on our own. Okay?"

All agreed, and with that, the family was off and running across the River of Low Prices.

The glass doors of the Wish Shoppe slid open—

"Remember, no talking inside!" Cal warned them.

—and then the doors closed behind them with a *whoosh.*

In the future, a Well Wisher wearing butterfly wings would be waiting at the entrance to shout, "Welcome to Wish Shoppe, where your wishes come true!" Today, of course, it was as quiet and creepy as an empty school—a giant, seemingly endless school. Perky dentist-office music drifted down from the speakers. Cal imagined he could hear the rattle of the Wylots' cart somewhere in the acres of aisles and products.

And, of course, there was the ticking of the timer on the cart. They had already lost four minutes!

Cal held a finger up to his lips. *No talking, remember?*

he said to Bug with his face and eyes. And Bug made the same gesture to Butler, who twirled his tail in agreement.

But Imo was looking at Cal, not Bug or Butler—as if she knew that Cal would have an even tougher time with the no-talking rule. After all, talking was one of Cal's greatest talents.

The Talaskas stood in a circle, put their hands in the center, and pumped them up and down three times. They couldn't say it, but Cal knew they were all thinking it: *Talaskas together!*

Then, with one last wave from Mrs. T. to all of them, the Talaskas split up. Bug and Butler headed off along the outer wall. The rest of the family chose different aisles and dove into the heart of the store.

Cal sprinted toward the Fun and Games Circle. Or where he remembered it was from the map they'd made. It should be just past the Television Circle. His shoes slapped on the shiny tile as he raced past clay knick-knacks shaped like famous skyscrapers and through displays of canned peas. He was starting to get worried when a giant circular wall of TVs rose all around him.

Yes! The Television Circle!

The thousands of TVs had the sound turned off but

flickered with color. Some were tuned to the local TV station and showed King Wonder talking to the crowd outside.

The rest of the sets displayed Cal.

Wait . . . what?

As Cal ran by, he could see himself running on the screens—or at least his hair. Who was taking video of the top of his head? He looked up and spotted security cameras whizzing along tracks on the ceiling. The TVs showed what the cameras saw!

Distracted and still moving fast, Cal caught his foot on something and tripped. He opened his mouth to shout—and then, remembering the rules, clamped it shut again.

Somehow Cal got his balance before he wiped out. He looked back, trying to find what he had tripped on. And the answer was obvious.

A rope had been strung across the aisle, close to the ground. This was just the kind of thing Emma Wylot would do.

Little did she know she had done him a favor. The rope had forced Cal to slow down—and remember the ribbon! He would have kept running like a madman without getting it.

A purple ribbon with TALASKA printed in block letters sat on a glass table in the middle of the Circle. The Wylots must have taken theirs already. Cal stuffed the purple ribbon in his back pocket and kept moving.

He knew he was just seconds away from the next Circle and the Wonder World Video Game System!

When he arrived in the Fun and Games Circle, it was empty, but the air buzzed as if someone had just been there. Before Cal could forget again, he went to the center of the Circle and picked up the second Talaska ribbon.

Then he let himself take a good look around. Suddenly, his feet wanted to move in every direction at once. The shelves were filled with marvels such as robots that made lunch, smartphone earrings, hologram Ping-Pong, and a Clap-n-Gro plastic tree, which grew and danced when you clapped. It was dizzying, and Cal knew why people could get lost so easily. He wanted to GRAB it all, and he couldn't remember which direction he had come from.

This is what we trained for, Cal told himself. He closed

his eyes for one second to get a grip. It would cost precious time on the clock, but it was worth it.

Calmer now, Cal opened his eyes . . . and there!

How had he missed it before? A giant blinking sign under a shelf read:

WONDER WORLD VIDEO GAME SYSTEM!

But the shelf was empty.

Cal didn't panic. He searched the Circle until he spotted just the edge of a box dangling over a top shelf. It was a Wonder World Video Game System!

Someone—more than likely, someone with the last name Wylot—must have tossed all the Wonder Worlds up there. How was Cal going to get his hands on that one?

Tick tick tick. Cal didn't need the cart's timer in front of him to feel the seconds ticking down.

Should he give up on the Wonder World? Grab something else? What about that dancing plastic tree? It was pretty cool and all set to go—he just had to drag it to the Pet Circle and toss it in the cart.

No, Cal thought. He wasn't going to let the Wylots stop him from getting what he wanted.

Cal looked around for a ladder, a trampoline, or a giant pogo stick—anything that might help him reach the high shelf. Nothing. Just the toys, the electronics, and that drooping plastic tree.

Desperate, Cal started climbing the shelves. Not easy. Each shelf jutted out slightly over the one below it. Soon the angle made it almost impossible to hang on.

This wasn't working. He jumped to the ground with a thud.

Where was Bug? Cal could have used the shopping cart as a stepladder. No, he realized, it wasn't Bug he needed. It was Imo. Or at least he needed to think like Imo.

What would Imo do? She'd use the stuff around her like tools to solve the problem.

Cal's eyes darted around the Circle again. *Yes!*

He grabbed the Clap-n-Gro plastic tree in its pot and dragged it to a spot under the Wonder World.

He looped an arm around one of the top branches and started clapping. The tree rose slightly, lifting his feet off the ground. It was working! Cal kept clapping, and soon he was five feet in the air. He was nearly five feet tall himself, so he just might be able to stretch and reach the Wonder World.

But it was no good. Whenever he stopped clapping

to reach for the box, the tree would droop slightly and he'd drop down. Cal tried clapping with one hand. But that didn't work. He thought for a second.

Of course! With his arm still looped around the branch, he slapped his forehead a few times.

Whap! Whap! Whap!
Ow! Ow! Ow!

The tree didn't know the difference between his clapping his hands or his head. It danced and swayed to the rhythm. His feet slammed into the toys on the shelves below him. Boxes of electronic musical toys and calculators went flying.

Cal held on and stretched. . . .

His fingers grazed the Wonder World box. He grabbed one

end and pulled it toward the edge. It was too heavy, and gravity yanked it out of his hand. The box fell end over end and hit the floor with a plastic-crunching crack!

Uh-oh. That didn't sound good.

Cal could be next—only it wouldn't be plastic that would crack.

"Greetings, dearest Wish Shoppe shoppers!" King Wonder's voice boomed over the speaker system. "We wish to let you know that time is flowing quickly. You have thirteen minutes left to fill your carts with dreams and ribbons, and return to the finish line!"

Cal didn't have time for another clapfest with his forehead. He had to keep moving.

He made a quick decision. Cal eased up on the slapping, and it was like lifting his foot off the pedal of a go-kart. The tree ran out of gas. The dancing stopped, and it slowly drooped toward the floor.

Halfway down, Cal let go of the branch, and he landed on the hard tiles. He grabbed the box at his feet and started running.

With the box clutched under one arm, he sprinted out of the Circle and down an aisle of Styrofoam coolers and beach umbrellas. He was sure it led to the Pet

Circle. But he was wrong. He suddenly found himself facing the outermost wall of the store.

As the seconds ticked away, Cal struggled to remember the details on the map.

Which way should he go?

And where was that mooing coming from?

M *oo!*
    Baa!
Cock-a-doodle-doo!

Animal sounds came from the next aisle. On a hunch, Cal followed the noises. He wasn't sure what to expect when he came around the corner, but it definitely wasn't what he found.

Hundreds of stuffed toys shaped like a farmer were scattered in a knee-high heap on the floor. And in the center of them all were Butler and Bug. Cal's brother was still in his harness and struggling to pull the cart through the heap. Butler's paws were digging at the toys like he was trying to create a path for Bug.

Cal recognized the Friendly Farmer toys from TV

ads. They were supposed to help little kids learn about animals.

A giant canister filled with Friendly Farmers had collapsed on top of Bug and the cart. It was as if Bug were stuck in a ball pit, but instead of balls there were chattering farmers, complete with straw hats and pitchforks. The farmers' touch screens must have clicked on when they fell, because they were all making strange farm noises.

The cows' mooing was so weirdly high-pitched, it hurt Cal's ears. And the chickens' clucking reminded him of a teakettle at full blast.

Cal had to hand it to Bug and Butler. They weren't freaking out. They were just determined to get loose. Butler started clamping down on the toys with his mouth and throwing them to the side. Bug tried to pull the cart free, but there were just too many of them. Cal waded through the toys, throwing aside each squawking, cackling, quacking farmer, until he reached Bug.

Cal gave Butler a quick scratch, and then he put his hands out as if asking, *What happened?*

Bug's lips parted to say something. Then, remembering the silence rule, he used his face and hands to say, *I don't know!*

Cal almost laughed. For the first time, talking with Bug actually made sense!

Under all the toys, Cal discovered that a rope had been strung across the aisle, just as in the Television Circle. One end was tied to the canister that had been overflowing with Friendly Farmer toys. Bug and Butler had tripped on the rope, and the canister had fallen over.

Cal had zero doubt this was another trap set by the Wylots. Why were they more concerned with stopping the Talaskas than with getting stuff in their cart?

In a flash, Cal realized the answer: The Wylots didn't care about getting more things today. They already had all the expensive junk they could ever wish for. They wanted to grab the one thing they couldn't put in their cart: to win at any cost and show the town and the world that they were the boss.

Right now, the Wylots were scattered throughout the store, making sure of just that. They were probably setting other traps. *If only I could see what they were up to,* Cal thought as a security camera whizzed overhead.

But, of course, he could. He knew what he had to do.

Cal, Bug, and Butler finished clearing away the Friendly Farmers—except for one that Butler kept in his mouth. Cal tossed the box he'd grabbed in the Fun and Games Circle into the cart. The weight of the box restored the cart's balance. Cal could now push it without tipping it over.

Bug shook his head and pointed at himself. *No, I want to pull!* Then he opened his mouth as if he would yell if he didn't get his way.

Cal held up his hands. This wasn't the time for a BTA. *Fine! Knock yourself out! But go this way! We're making a detour.* Cal jabbed his finger toward where he had just come from.

Bug and Butler took off. Cal hustled to keep up. He reached them just in time to stop them at the Television Circle.

Many of the TVs still showed what was happening

outside the store. But that wasn't why Cal had wanted to come back here. His eyes searched for the TVs tuned to the security cameras.

Bug pointed at a TV above Cal's head. *Mom!* Bug mouthed silently.

Cal followed his brother's finger to the screen. It showed Mrs. T. in the Fitness Circle. She was sweating and taking a moment to catch her breath.

From this angle, Cal could see someone his mom couldn't.

Mrs. Wylot.

Leslie's mom was on the other side of the Fitness Circle. As Cal and Bug watched helplessly, Mrs. Wylot took down a sign that read THIS WAY TO THE PET CIRCLE! and replaced it with one that said THIS WAY CLOSED!

When Mrs. T. tried to meet up with the rest of the Talaskas, she would get hopelessly lost!

Pulling Cal's arm, Bug pointed at another TV. *Imo!*

Imo was in the Hardware Circle. Why was she just standing there? Cal looked more closely. She was straining to move, but her feet were stuck to the ground. Literally.

As ridiculous as it seemed, Imo had stepped into a pool of glue that companies used to make furniture.

It poured out of a bucket that had been tipped over on the floor. Cal felt like he was watching a cartoon. But this was all too real. Even if Imo took off her shoes, she would have to step in the pool of glue and would still be stuck.

He watched as she struggled to reach a bottle on a nearby shelf—and grabbed it. Cal hoped whatever was in the bottle would help her get free, but he couldn't read the label.

He could see Leslie Wylot, though. She was sneaking out of the Hardware Circle, carrying something that looked like a fishing net. Cal swore he could make out an earbud in her ear, and her mouth was moving under her bandana. She was talking!

So that was why the Wylots had chosen costumes with bandanas that hid their faces. They were wearing headsets to communicate with each other. They must have grabbed them in the Fun and Games Circle.

Bug tugged Cal's arm and pointed to the TV that showed the Pet Circle, which looked quite pleasant. Fake tree branches tangled over the Circle, creating a home for the Butterfly of Savings. But their dad was there—and he was in big trouble. At the bottom of the screen, Cal could see Mr. Wylot opening animal cages in the Pet Circle. He was releasing all the snakes, including the giant boa constrictor.

The families weren't allowed to talk, but that didn't mean Cal couldn't communicate. A store microphone was glued to a display case of remote controls. For years, people had been saying Cal wanted to be a puppet master. Now was his chance to see if he had what it took.

Cal picked up the mike and tapped it with his palm.

BANG! The sound echoed through the overhead speakers all around the store. On the screens, the Wylots and Talaskas looked up.

Cal signaled for Butler to drop the Friendly Farmer in his mouth. Butler cocked his head as if saying, *Why?* But he did it.

Cal flipped the toy over and lifted a flap to reveal the touch screen. He pressed START and held the farmer up to the microphone.

"The sheep says . . . ," the Friendly Farmer announced. The toy paused, waiting for Cal to type in what a sheep said. Cal hit a series of letters on the touch screen.

"*Moo?*" the farmer said. "No, no, NO! That's just SILLY!"

There was a reason these toys were on sale. The

farmer sounded like an annoying know-it-all with a singsongy voice.

Cal typed more letters. "The cow says . . . *Fitness!*" the farmer blathered. "No, no, NO! That's just SILLY!"

Bug covered his ears. And Cal nearly did, too. The voice was getting on his nerves. But it was working. In the Fitness Circle, his mom looked up at the camera. Her face said, *What the Swiss is going on?*

"The chicken says . . . *Sign!*" Before the farmer could say "No, no, NO!" Cal pulled it away from the microphone. He watched as his mom thought about the message. She pointed at the sign that said THIS WAY CLOSED!, and Cal pushed buttons again. This time, the farmer proclaimed, "The goose says . . . *Wrong!*"

His mom touched the fake sign and it came loose, revealing the real sign underneath.

Cal's fingers pressed the toy again. "The rooster says . . . *Yes!*"

His mom gave a thumbs-up. She got it. She was heading the right way now.

Bug tapped the timer on the cart.

The numbers 10:23 blinked at them. Just over ten minutes left!

Cal didn't have time to go through the same thing with Imo and his dad. It would be faster if Cal, Bug, and Butler went to them.

★ ★ ★

With Bug pulling the cart behind them, Cal and Butler raced down the aisle. Cal imagined the map. He knew they had to run through the Sporting Goods Circle to reach the Hardware Circle, where Imo was stuck.

The aisle suddenly opened up into the Sporting Goods Circle—and *WHAP!* Something flew out of nowhere and struck Cal's shoulder. The force spun him back into the aisle next to Bug and Butler, but he kept his balance.

What the heck was that?

Bug picked up the foam dart that someone had fired at Cal. It was the size of a loaf of bread. Butler grabbed it in his mouth and started tearing it up.

Cal poked his head around the edge of the aisle. In the center of the Sporting Goods Circle, a display of three tennis ball–serving machines sat on a steel table. A sign read: THE ENDLESS SERVER—RETURNS TENNIS BALLS FOR HOURS!

He could just barely make out her face, but Cal could see Emma Wylot crouched on the table between two of the serving machines. She must have snagged a foam-dart gun from the Fun and Games Circle. She aimed it at Cal and fired again.

Cal ducked back into the aisle. He and Bug were safe where they were, but they couldn't get across the Circle. Cal couldn't risk Bug's getting pegged by a dart. His parents would never forgive him. They would have to go back and hope they could find a different route to the rest of the family. They could get the ribbon from this Circle later.

Even as he thought this, Cal knew they'd never have enough time.

Before they left the Circle, he couldn't resist giving Emma a piece of his mind. He poked his head out again and pointed his eyes at her. *I see you! This isn't fair!*

Emma didn't even bother to give a nasty wave, as Leslie usually did. She just shrugged.

Cal turned to pull Bug along with him when he spotted Imo on the other side of the Circle. She had freed herself from the glue pool and was jumping up and down to get his attention. Then she kicked the ground. It reminded Cal of a little kid pouting.

I know it stinks that we can't get through! Cal said by shaking his head and throwing up his hands.

No! That's not it! Imo pointed again at her kicking foot. Frustrated that Cal still wasn't getting what she meant, she turned away.

Tugging her ear, she looked at the shelves around her, and Cal could almost feel her brain buzzing. Even Emma stood up a little to see what she had planned.

In a blur of movement, Imo grabbed a ski helmet and put it on her head. She put four skateboards on the floor and laid a surfboard on top of them. She put one foot on the surfboard and pushed back and forth, back and forth, with the other. When she had enough momentum, she stood on the surfboard and shot across the Circle.

Emma had been waiting for this. She stood all the way up and raised the foam-dart gun.

The force of the dart would knock Imo off the board. And, helmet or no helmet, the fall would sting.

Emma fired—

But Imo must have been waiting for her opponent's move, too. She dropped to her knees and then lay on her back on the rolling surfboard. The dart sailed over her. Imo reached up and snagged the Talaskas' ribbon as she slid under the display table. Before Emma could reload, Imo had rolled past Cal and into the safety of his aisle.

Grinning, Imo jumped off her surfboard "lawn luge" and handed Cal her ski helmet and the ribbon. Without hesitating, she walked back to the aisle opening.

Cal reached out to pull Imo back. She shook her head and pointed at her kicking foot again and then behind Cal. He turned and finally got it. *Oh!*

A display of kickball launchers lined the shelf. They were plugged in and loaded with red rubber balls, like the ones from gym class. They were facing the center of the Circle.

Imo moved to switch them on. Once again, Emma knew what she was up to. Emma had turned the tennis ball–serving machines toward their aisle. She gave Imo a little salute. Imo returned the salute, and the two girls shared a look of grudging respect.

Then they both started switching on the different machines. The tennis balls fired across the Circle at the Talaskas, and the kickballs shot toward the center of the Circle.

As if her work here was done, Emma slung the strap of the dart gun over her shoulder and climbed off the display table. With one last look at the Talaskas, she quickly left the Circle.

Cal saw they could get across the Circle now. Each time a tennis ball fired out of a machine toward them, a flying kickball was there to block it. Just in case, he put the ski helmet on Bug. Then, with Cal and Imo leading the way, Bug pulled the cart under the colliding balls to the other side. One tennis ball was knocked free and hit Cal square in the forehead. *Smack!* Right where he'd been slapping his forehead earlier. Cal wondered if he had a bull's-eye painted there.

We did it! he said silently, and the three kids shared a high five and a quick snuggle with Butler. In a flash, Imo shoved a box she'd grabbed onto the bottom of the shopping cart.

Cal didn't take time to see what it was. They took off sprinting toward the path that ran around the entire store. Up ahead, Mrs. T. was waiting.

She was breathless, but she was standing like a relay racer ready to run a lap. She tossed her box into the cart and handed Cal the ribbon from the Fitness Circle.

Cal pointed to the timer, then toward the Pet Circle. *We don't have much time to meet Dad!*

Even though she was wearing her sweatband, sweat poured down her face. But she nodded. *Let's go!*

The timer read 7:34.

Unlike the other Circles, with their tons of aisles, the Pet Circle had only two ways in. Sliding glass doors opened and closed on their own as people entered and left. That kept the Butterfly of Savings and any of the slithery critters from escaping.

The air in the Circle was heavy and humid, as in the birdhouse at the Grand Rapids zoo. The shelves were filled with dog food, cat litter, squeaky toys, and cages and tanks of animals and bugs.

To keep from distracting shoppers, Wish Shoppe sold only creatures that didn't make much noise. There were plenty of fish, silent insects, and, of course . . . snakes.

Butler's mouth had popped open, and he was looking

around as if he were in heaven. Mrs. T. looked intently at Bug and put her hands on his shoulders. *Stay with Butler,* she mouthed.

The wide trunk of a fake tree rose out of the center, sprouting branches and leaves that wove across the ceiling. Cal knew from a security camera that his dad was stuck against the wall on the other side. They found Mr. T. there, holding a huge object wrapped in what looked like a dog blanket. Cal could see the Pet Circle's ribbon poking out of his pants pocket.

Mr. T.'s face lit up when he saw them, but he stayed frozen. Why wasn't he moving?

Mrs. T. made her *What the cheddar is going on?* face.

Mr. T.'s eyes darted around the room, as if telling his family to follow where he was looking. Cal did and discovered that the Talaskas were not alone.

All four Wylots were in the Pet Circle, too. Emma was actually on the ceiling, swinging from branch to branch, the foam-dart gun in her belt. Mr. and Mrs. Wylot were looking under crates. Leslie had the net on a pole, and she was also scouring the room for something.

What are they looking for with a net? Cal wondered. Then it hit him.

The butterfly! The Wylots were going to grab King Wonder's butterfly!

It was worth the world to King Wonder. And Cal imagined how Mr. Wylot would use that to get what he really wanted. Maybe he would demand to be part owner of Wish Shoppe and have even more people working for him.

No matter what the Wylots were up to, the timer was still ticking. The Talaskas had to get out of there.

Come on, Dad, Cal said with his eyes. Then he made squiggly motions while shaking his head. *There are no snakes. They're all hiding.*

Mr. T. shook his head. *It's not the snakes! It's this!*

Careful not to let the Wylots see, Mr. T. turned very slowly. *Holy Aristotle.* With fluttering purple wings the size of dinner plates, the biggest butterfly Cal had ever seen was perched on his dad's back.

It was King Wonder's Butterfly of Savings.

Mr. T. raised a finger to his lips and looked up. Cal understood. His dad didn't want to move because he was scared of revealing the flying insect to the Wylots.

The Talaskas needed to get the butterfly back into the branches without the Wylots' seeing it.

Mrs. T. raised her hand. *I know what to do!* She made

a typing gesture, like she was sitting in front of an invisible computer.

Cal wanted to shout, *Are you sending an invisible email?*

She held up a finger, as if she had just discovered something.

Oh! Something you found online? Cal mouthed.

Mrs. T. nodded. She hurried to the wall and reached for the light switch. The Wylots saw it and stamped their feet. Emma dropped to the ground, rushing to stop Mrs. T.

No! No! the Wylots seemed to be saying. Cal wanted to join them.

Trust me, Mrs. T.'s face said, and then she flicked the light switch.

The Pet Circle plunged into darkness. The Wylots and Talaskas were suddenly rushing about the Circle. No one was talking—at least that

Cal could hear—but there were grunts of surprise and what sounded like a struggle.

Cal felt something slither up his leg. Being unable to talk was probably a good thing. He wasn't sure the Friendly Farmer was allowed to say what was running through his head.

Cal spun away from the spot. He felt the creature on his leg shake free and launch into the air.

Click! The light came back on. Mrs. T. put her hands together on her cheek and tilted her head as if she were sleeping, and pointed up.

Cal got it!

Mrs. T.'s research had paid off again. The butterfly thought it was nighttime and had flown to the safety of the branches to rest.

The Wylots had been on the move, too. While the room was dark, the entire family had rushed out the door that the Talaskas had used. It was sliding shut.

Just as it was about to close, Emma noticed what the Talaskas were looking at. She lifted her dart gun and aimed up at the Butterfly of Savings. Her eyes said it all. If the Wylots couldn't have the butterfly, no one could.

NO! Cal thought.

Even Leslie looked shocked. She shook her head at Emma. But Emma pulled the trigger anyway. The dart shot through the air.

Cal had a choice. He could leap forward to keep the door from shutting, or he could jump up to stop the dart.

He leapt and swatted the dart down.

The door slid shut. Through the glass, Cal saw Mr. Wylot pop Leslie's net into the outside track of the door. It was locked, with the Talaskas stuck inside the Circle.

Emma pointed out the butterfly to Mr. Wylot. His eyes lit up, and he reached to lift the net so he could open the door—

In a flash, Imo's hand shot out. She turned the lock on the inside of the door.

Now the Wylots couldn't get in, but the Talaskas still couldn't get out. They faced off in two lines on either side of the glass door.

Mr. Wylot shrugged, and Cal guessed what he was thinking. It was too bad Mr. Wylot couldn't capture the Butterfly of Savings, but he'd still show the Talaskas and the world who was boss.

Leslie held up the Wylots' ribbons and fanned them

out so Cal could count them. Nine. The Wylots had gathered all the ribbons. They just needed to get to the finish line first.

Cal spun around. At least the door on the other side of the Circle was open. For now.

Emma jerked to one side. Cal's heart bumped. Was she going to race around the outside of the Circle and get to the open door first? But she just threw back her head and laughed silently.

Leslie gave a nasty wave, and the Wylots sauntered off, pushing their empty cart, as if they had all the time in the world.

But for the Talaskas, time was running out. Their cart's timer blinked:

3:56.

It was impossible. There was no way the Talaskas could run around the store, gather the last four ribbons they needed, and beat the Wylots to the finish line.

That was when Mr. T. pulled the Pet Circle ribbon from his pocket and handed it to Cal. Something felt different about it. Cal looked down and saw he was actually holding five ribbons stacked on top of each other. That made a total of nine.

The Talaskas had all the ribbons!

How? Cal asked, stunned.

Mr. T. smiled and acted like he was studying an invisible wall. *I memorized the map. All of it!*

He must have been running all over that side of the store before going to the Pet Circle. Imo, Mrs. T., and Bug were jumping up and down. Cal didn't care if it wasted time. He gave his dad a hug.

Then Cal clapped his hands. *We have to get out of here.*

Imo nodded furiously. *Go! Go! Go!*

Mr. T. threw his wrapped bundle into the cart. It was heavy, and there was no room left in the overflowing cart. Cal didn't take the time to wonder how it had gotten so full.

Bug was pulling away like an unstoppable sled dog, with Mrs. T. pushing behind the cart. Mr. T. was running in front with Butler, and Imo and Cal ran on either side, just in case the cart tipped or something fell out.

On this side of the Pet Circle, they were in uncharted territory. Only Mr. T. knew the way, or at least Cal hoped he did. Cal was starting to worry when he spotted a big sign with an arrow:

THIS WAY TO EMPLOYEE EXIT
Employees only! All others, please use main exit!

Yes! An exit! The family picked up speed and ran in the direction of the arrow.

Fifty yards later, they slammed open the exit door and burst out of the maze into the sunshine. The non-air-conditioned breeze felt incredible. With his ears free of the store's perky music, Cal could think more clearly.

But that sound was replaced by the roar of the crowd.

The Wylots were nowhere in sight, but the spectators were a hundred feet away, still gathered on the other side of the River of Low Prices. A sidewalk ran from the store to the river. The Talaskas needed to race down that sidewalk, cross the bridge, and reach the finish line.

"No way they're going to make it in time!" a man in the crowd shouted.

"I'll bet you a dollar they give up right now," a woman shouted back. "The Wylots never lose!"

Cal wasn't the only one who heard them. Bug's head snapped up. A look of determination came over his face. He slowed down and reached out to scratch Butler behind the ears.

"What's that kid doing?" a little boy asked.

Cal knew. Bug and Butler were choosing this moment to finally perform their B&B Scooter Madness Stunt in public.

Bug took off running. Cal grabbed for his shirt, but missed as the cart whizzed away.

No, Bug!

A kid and a dog on a mission, Bug and Butler ran toward the River of Low Prices. Cal knew that Bug imagined himself sailing over the river with the cart, landing dramatically on the other side. Then the finish line would be just a short trot away.

What happened instead was a catastrophe.

Butler made a wide turn before coming to the two-foot-high concrete ledge that ran along the river, since they had always practiced avoiding the "target" at the last moment. But Bug jumped over the ledge. The cart rammed into it and didn't budge as he sailed through the air. The harness went tight and yanked Bug back, slamming him against the ledge with a *whap!*

Someone in the crowd groaned sympathetically. "Ouch!"

Bug dangled over the side in the harness, his feet submerged in the River of Low Prices.

As fast as her body would move, Mrs. T. scrambled to kneel on the ledge. She pulled the harness and hauled Bug up like a fish. He wasn't crying and hurt. He just looked angry that his stunt didn't work after all. Mrs. T. hugged him and put him down on the other side of the ledge. Butler was there immediately, nuzzling Bug worriedly.

Mrs. T. stood so she could step off the ledge, too. That was when all the running caught up with her. She started to lose her balance. For one awful moment, she tottered on the edge of the River of Low Prices.

Cal reached for her. *Mom—*

And then she slipped.

Mrs. T. spun in the air and hit the water on her belly. *Smack!* She came up on her knees, soaking wet, just her shoulders and head above the water. She had lost her headband, and her hair was matted to her face.

There was a burst of laughter from the crowd, with a few hoots and cruel jeers, as the news cameras rushed over to capture the moment.

"How's the water?" a high school kid asked.

Mrs. T. didn't seem able to move. In fact, none of the Talaskas did.

Except Imo.

With a nod to Cal, she took a step forward, and Cal could almost hear the cameras zooming in on her. The attention would normally make her shy, but not now. Imo climbed on top of the ledge so everyone could see her. She raised her eyes and her head, and then in a loud, clear voice, she said, *"In my opinion,* you're a winner, Mom."

Imo jumped down into the waist-high water. She fished around for something near her feet. It was the headband, and she tossed it to her mom. Mrs. T. pushed her hair back and put the wet headband around her head.

Her eyes were shiny as she mouthed, *Thank you, Imo.*

"No problem," Imo said, helping Mrs. T. out of the river. "And we only have eighteen seconds."

Cal's gaze went to the timer. It was true. Now just seventeen seconds. Make that sixteen. Fifteen.

In a flash, Cal thought of all the things he could say to convince his family they could do this. They *could* reach the finish line on time. All the bottled-up words from the past twenty minutes wanted to pour out at once.

Cal opened his mouth and this came out:

"Ahhhhhhh!"

It felt so good to yell after being silent for so long that Cal didn't think he could stop.

And he wasn't alone. Soon his whole family was shouting and barking. They raced toward the finish line, suddenly the world's loudest family.

"AHHHHHHH!"

Just then, the Wylots came out of the main entrance. They had ditched the bandanas and the headsets. And they were taking their time, as if winning the contest were the easiest thing in the world.

"Hurry, Mr. Wylot!" Alison's dad shouted. "They're coming!"

The Wylots spotted the Talaskas. It was as if a giant, invisible hand goosed all the Wylots. They leapt in the air, and then they were off and running.

The Talaskas' stuffed cart was shaking so hard, Cal

thought it would collapse. Mrs. T. was managing to keep up, but her wheezing was getting much worse.

The two families reached the bridge at the same time. The carts slammed into each other like chariots in an action movie, and the wheels bumped and collided. The Wylots shoved and pushed, and the Talaskas struggled to keep their cart upright.

The crowd counted down the last seconds.

"Three!"

The families raced across the bridge.

"Two!"

They were just a few feet from the finish line.

"One!"

The crowd roared. The Talaskas and the Wylots—
and their carts—had all crossed the finish line in
time.

"It's a tie!" an old woman shrieked.

Exhausted, the Talaskas fell on top of each other in
front of King Wonder's throne. Once again, they were a
rolling ball of arms, legs, a tail, and giggling. Cal felt as
hysterical as he'd been while making the video weeks ago.

"Don't find the missing *P*, Cal!" Coach Eaton yelled.

Cal just laughed. When he looked up, he found the
Wylots standing in a line watching them and laughing,
too.

"Congratulations, Wylots! Looks like we're all winners!" Mrs. T. said. The Talaskas climbed to their feet,

and their hysteria died down to chuckles. But the Wylots kept laughing. Even the normally silent Emma was guffawing like crazy. It was creepy, and Mrs. T. asked uncertainly, "Pretty funny that we're all winners, right?"

"Oh, that's not why we're so happy," Mr. Wylot said. "We're not laughing *with* you. We're laughing *at* you."

Leslie grinned at Cal, then pointed at Imo. "You broke the rules, *Jessie*," Leslie announced with glee. "We weren't allowed to talk during the contest. But you said, 'In my opinion, you're a winner, Mom.' We're the winners. Not bragging. Google it."

The Wylots must have been listening in on their headsets just before they tossed them.

"What this little girl did was very, very sweet," Mr. Wylot said, gesturing at Imo. "But a clear violation of the rules. Don't you think, King?"

King Wonder hesitated. Mr. Wylot cleared his throat loudly twice until Mr. Vance met his gaze. Mr. Wylot made a signal with his hand. Mr. Vance ducked his head to whisper to King, who nodded as he listened.

"The Wylots are correct," King said. "The Talaskas must be disqualified."

No! Cal thought. *Imo managed to stop being shy, and now this? Has her bravery cost us the contest?*

King held out his hands as if there were nothing else he could do. "We are going to declare the winning family to be—" he started to say.

"Wait?" a voice shouted. It was Sarah!

Bug's babysitter was rushing through the crowd toward them.

"You can't let the Wylots win this time?" Sarah said to King when she reached the Talaskas.

Mrs. T. touched Sarah's arm. "Thanks, sweetie," Cal's mom said, and then lowered her voice. "But remember, Mr. Wylot controls the money you need for school. He could take it away from you."

"It's not much of an education if it keeps me from doing what's right?" Sarah responded.

"Here's a little education for *you*," Mr. Wylot said to the Talaskas. "Even with nothing in our cart or if we barely try, the Wylots will always beat you. We'll always win."

This was too much for Mr. T. "I . . . I . . . ," he said.

"Oh, this should be good," Mr. Wylot said. He looked like a cat about to toy with a mouse. "Come on, Nelson.

Use your words. Maybe a rhyme about being jobless and having a family you can't feed?"

At the mention of *family,* Mr. T.'s face changed. His eyes narrowed and he stood up straighter. "This is wrong, Mr. Wylot," he said, "and you know it."

"Dad, that doesn't rhyme," Cal said.

"Because I'm not nervous," Mr. T. said. "Because I'm right."

Mr. Wylot shot a look at Mr. Vance, who whispered into King's ear again. When he pulled back, King frowned and said, "We need to declare the winner. And, well, we—"

"Please, can I say something?" Cal asked.

King nodded absently, and Cal stepped forward. This was going to take all his skill. At the front of the crowd, Ms. Graves nodded at him. "Go for it, Cal," she told him quietly. "Talk him over to your side!"

But Cal had figured out something while running around the store. He didn't always need to talk. Sometimes it was just all about listening.

He took a breath and said to King, "Excuse me, sir, but didn't you say there was no talking *inside* the store?"

"My goodness, the boy is right!" James called,

copying the mayor's voice. Then, in Leslie's voice, he said, "Why, I think he might be onto something!"

Leslie clapped a hand over her mouth as if words were escaping her lips.

Ms. Donegan nodded. "Cal's right. King did say that." A few people murmured, as if they remembered the same thing.

"When my sister spoke, she was *outside* the store," Cal said.

Mr. Wylot snapped his fingers angrily at Mr. Vance, who leaned toward King Wonder's ear again. This time, though, King held up a hand to block him.

"You know," King said, "we like it when people *listen* to us." He gave Mr. Vance a look. "And when they aren't always *telling* us what to do."

King's eyes went from Mr. Vance to the Wylots' empty cart and their angry faces and, finally, to Cal. He seemed to like what he saw, and he nodded.

Turning to the cameras, King said, "The Tal . . . Tal . . . this family is correct. The ban against talking was only inside the store. We declare a tie! Both families are winners!"

The crowd cheered, mostly fueled by Sarah and the

Talaskas' friends. Alison joined in the clapping. Her dad instantly pulled her away, toward their car. She gave Cal a last smile over her shoulder.

Leslie's braids were shaking with anger. "How can we both be winners?" she asked her dad. "Does that mean the Talaskas are our equals?"

"Bite your tongue!" Mr. Wylot snapped.

"Not to worry, my friends," King Wonder told the Wylots. "Both families are winners. They can keep whatever is inside their carts."

"But there's nothing in our cart!" Leslie said. "All we have are these ribbons!"

"Oh, we see," King Wonder said, as if trying to keep a straight face. "Too bad. We guess we were wrong about the *winners* part." He rose from the throne and walked to the Talaskas' overflowing cart. "This cart tells a different story, though, doesn't it?"

Now that King Wonder was standing closer, Cal saw how red his cheeks were and how excited he was about the contest. "Let's see what we have here," he said, like a little kid about to unwrap a present. "What did you grab for yourself, Mrs. Tal . . . Tallulah . . . ?"

Cal's mom smiled. "It's Talaska. But Mrs. T. is fine."

He smiled back. "Well, what did you get for yourself, Mrs. T.?"

"Oh, we all know," Mr. Wylot said. "She got herself home gym equipment. The rest of them grabbed a keyboard, a laboratory, a video game system, and . . . that one?" He pointed at Bug. "I don't know, candy or something. Their cart might as well be filled with nothing, too."

Cal couldn't believe it. Mr. Wylot remembered everything Cal had said the Talaskas wanted on the day of the first elimination.

"I'd like to show you what we got, Mr. Wonder," Mrs. T. said. She took out the small box she had grabbed. "I don't know why this was in the Fitness Circle, but I do know where it will find a good home. It's for you, honey."

Mrs. T. gave the box to a surprised Imo.

"But what about something for your home gym?" Imo asked. "Or something for your trivia?"

"I'll get the trivia organized later," Mrs. T. said. "Right now, I want to work on the big stuff."

Imo opened the box and removed a smaller one, shiny silver and about half the size of a toaster. She put it down and flicked a switch on the side. *BLAM!* A parachute fired out of the box, creating a kind of ceiling over the family. Light shot up from the box and reflected off the parachute, filling the surface over their heads with stars, planets, moons, and zipping comets.

The crowd oohed and aahed.

"It's a mobile planetarium, which normally only museums can afford," Mrs. T. said. "Now you can start planning trips for the spacecraft you're going to invent."

Imo tugged her earlobe as her eyes wandered across the stars above, and then she smiled at Mrs. T. "Thanks, Mom," she said. "I got something for you, too."

It took both hands, but she pulled a large plastic bundle out of the box she had picked up at the Sporting Goods Circle. She put it at Mrs. T.'s feet and said, "It's a giant inflatable pool. Not quite a home gym, but it's a start."

"I love it," Mrs. T. said. "Thanks, honey."

King Wonder, giddy, was clapping. "And, Cal, what about you?" he asked. "What did you get? My Wonder World Video Game System?"

Cal nodded. "For a second," he said. "But then I decided on this." He reached into the cart and pulled out the box he had grabbed in the Fun and Games Circle. He gave it to his dad.

"I knew you wouldn't get something for yourself, Dad," Cal said. "You can finally put that talent for music and words to good use."

It was a sound-effects keyboard. Instead of notes, the keys produced *BLURP, SPLOOSH, SPLAT,* and *PFFFFT.*

Mr. T. laughed. He handed Cal a box from the Music Circle. Inside were a mallet and a gong that was as tall as Bug. "It can replace the small bell at home," Mr. T. explained. "Use it to call family meetings whenever you have another big idea."

"Oh, that's . . . awesome," Cal said. "Thanks, Dad." Actually, he wasn't sure what to make of the gift.

"What?" Mr. T. asked. "You don't like it?"

"No, I'm sorry," Cal said. "Sure I do."

Mr. T. said, "You know, all those years as an accountant rubbed off on me. That mallet is pure gold and probably the most expensive thing in the store!"

Cal liked the sound of that and gave the gong a whack with his hand. *ZWONG!*

"If you decide to sell the mallet," Mr. T. said, "it won't solve all our problems. But it will pay the bills for a couple of months—and give us some time to figure out our next step as a family. Maybe even help Sarah with school if she needs it."

"Amazing," Cal said. "But what about Bug?"

"Rabbo," Bug said to Butler. And then he added, "Don't worry about me, Cal."

KA-BLAM! The words were like a lightning bolt. Cal was stunned. His little brother had just said real words!

Cal could tell that his dad was trying to keep calm, as if he didn't want to scare Bug into only barking again. Mr. T. gave Bug a high five.

"This is what I really wanted!" Bug said, pointing at his family around him. "But I got other stuff, too."

Bug started pulling things out of the cart. Most of them had probably been buried under the other boxes, unless Cal had been too distracted to notice.

There was a napkin dispenser from the café, a

doorstopper from the entrance of the store, a robotic beaver from the River of Low Prices, a Friendly Farmer, a plastic *B* from a sign inside the Wish Shoppe, and a huge dog bone for Butler.

"Rabbo!" Butler barked, and ran circles around Bug.

Cal had to admit that it was a pretty good haul. And Bug wasn't done yet. He held out a foot-long screw.

Crash! Something fell inside the store.

King Wonder cringed, then laughed. "Are the winners ready for their picture?"

"Will it appear all over the country?" Imo asked.

King nodded. "Yes, young lady, it will."

"Good," Imo said. "I want everyone to see what a perfect family we have."

Cal couldn't have said it better himself.

Mrs. T. reached over to hug Imo. The cord of her inflatable pool got tangled around her ankle. In an explosion of air, the pool inflated.

At that instant, a photographer snapped the family's picture for the Wish Shoppe ad campaign.

Cal could imagine what the photo would show: Mr. T. standing behind the sound-effects keyboard, Bug holding up the *B*, Cal banging the gong—with the whole family in the inflatable pool under the planetarium's stars, next to the grinning King Wonder. In the background, Cal dreamed, people could see the Rivales stacked in a crazy human pyramid as the Wylots slinked off to their limo.

The cameras zoomed in on the Talaskas. Imo was too excited to be nervous as she answered reporters' questions. "Well, first," she said straight into a camera, "I want to say hi to Grandma Gigi. In my opinion, she should be here with us."

Cal felt the weight of the mallet in his hand. He

couldn't wait to try it out on the new family-bell gong thing.

He hadn't told his family about the other contests he'd been checking out. He had his eye on one at an amusement park. But from the loopy grins on their faces, Cal didn't think he would need to scheme too much to convince them to enter.

After all, they were now the Prizewinners of Piedmont Place.

"*Angel Thieves* is a literary Texas jewel that tantalizes with its unusual construction, fascinates with its symbolism and imagery, and encourages deep thought of humankind's motivation either to help others in need or ignore them or even submerge them deeper into despair. Because sometimes, those who struggle to survive and be free have no one else except an angel, a bayou, and a kind person with an unselfish heart."—LONE STAR LITERARY LIFE

Angel Thieves

Angel Thieves

A NOVEL BY

KATHI APPELT

A CAITLYN DLOUHY BOOK

Atheneum New York London Toronto Sydney New Delhi

atheneum

An imprint of Simon & Schuster Children's Publishing Division
1230 Avenue of the Americas, New York, New York 10020

For information about special discounts for bulk purchases, please contact Simon & Schuster Special Sales at 1-866-506-1949 or business@simonandschuster.com.
The Simon & Schuster Speakers Bureau can bring authors to your live event. For more information or to book an event, contact the Simon & Schuster Speakers Bureau at 1-866-248-3049 or visit our website at www.simonspeakers.com.
Also available in an Atheneum hardcover edition
Book design by Debra Sfetsios-Conover
The text for this book was set in Adobe Jenson Pro.
Manufactured in the United States of America
First Atheneum paperback edition March 2020
10 9 8 7 6 5 4 3 2 1
The Library of Congress has cataloged the hardcover edition as follows:
Names: Appelt, Kathi, 1954– author.
Title: Angel thieves / Kathi Appelt.
Description: First edition. | New York : Atheneum, [2019] | "A Caitlyn Dlouhy Book." | Summary: The lives of four characters, including cemetery thief Cade Curtis, a runaway slave, and an illegally captured ocelot, flow together across time through their connections to the Houston bayou and an angel carved from Georgia marble.
Identifiers: LCCN 2018017994 | ISBN 9781442421097 (hc) | ISBN 9781442339668 (pbk) | ISBN 9781442484665 (eBook)
Subjects: | CYAC: Robbers and outlaws—Fiction. | Fugitive slaves—Fiction. | Slavery—Fiction. | Ocelot—Fiction. | Statues—Fiction. | Bayous—Fiction. | Houston (Tex.)—Fiction.
Classification: LCC PZ7.A6455 An 2019 | DDC [Fic]—dc23
LC record available at https://lccn.loc.gov/2018017994

TO ANNE BUSTARD FUSILIER,
SWEET BELIEVER

Angel Thieves

The Bayou

HOUSTON, TEXAS
BUFFALO BAYOU

The bayou giveth and the bayou taketh away. You can't trust her, not for a minute. Give her the sun and she'll blind you. Give her the rain and she'll swallow you. Give her a storm and she'll claim your highways and your bridges. She'll breach your shiny new buildings, your waking nightmares, your broken heart.

The bayou's no angel, that's a fact. But who's to say she hasn't seen one or two, their tattered wings, their tangled hair.

Pay attention.

Listen.

Pray if the spirit moves you.

Cade Curtis

Cade Curtis doesn't know so much about praying, but he does know about angels.

Heads bowed, hands held together in prayer, or maybe, palms toward the sky. Carved out of stone.

Cade's heart beats fast, like it always does whenever he's out like this, with his father, Paul. Just the two of them.

This is what they do, isn't it? Wait for starless, moonless nights, rain-soaked or foggy, and together, father and son, make their way to hallowed ground. Churchyards. Graveyards. Bone yards.

From their seats in the cab of their Ford F-150 pickup, they take note of the dilapidated church, so faded that it's only barely visible in the glare of their headlights, a ghost of a church.

The steeple is knocked askew, maybe the victim of a huge gust of wind or a fallen tree. Or maybe, Cade thinks, it simply collapsed of its own emptiness, slumping into itself like a crumpled paper bag. Abandoned buildings do that.

His father parks the truck on the side away from the road, out of sight of anyone who might pass by. Unlikely, thinks Cade. The route they took to get here was as deserted as this church, even though it was barely an hour's drive north from the center of bustling Houston. Together they step out of the warmth of the cab and into a cold mist that quickly turns to rain. Cade zips up his jacket. His dad rests his hand on Cade's shoulder. Cade leans against him, but only for a second. They need to get on with it. Cade reaches into the back of the truck for a blanket, soggy from the rain, and Paul gathers his backpack. In it are the tools of his trade—a chisel, a hammer, a rope.

The two make their way among the scattered headstones, square concrete blocks with barely visible names etched into them. Cade notices one monument that looks like a carved tree up next to a rusted fence.

"Woodmen of the World," says Paul.

Cade has seen others like it, in other cemeteries. They mostly look like stumps, with the occasional ax leaning against them, as if the person buried there simply chopped a tree down, leaned their ax against it, and died. There are also a few crosses, some toppled onto their faces. Those aren't what Cade and Paul are after, even though some, he's sure, are carved of marble and could bring a fair price.

He sweeps the grounds with the beam of his flashlight, paying attention to the monuments, the trees, the fence posts along the edges of the yard, the things he can see above the ground, and tries not to think about what is below the surface.

"Just bones," says Paul. "Old bones."

Nevertheless, Cade's careful where he steps, especially among those graves where the ground has sunk like a shallow dish. It means that the coffin below has rotted and caved in. What's to keep an old skull from floating to the surface?

He pulls his jacket a little tighter beneath his chin. He's never actually seen any bones. But it doesn't keep him from imagining them rising to the earth with each passing day.

Finally they find the angel, all alone in the far corner away from the road. "Texas granite," says Paul. Cade knows that this makes her worth the trouble.

She stands beneath a small grove of trees, draped in

a curtain of vines that hang from their limbs. He and Paul pull the vines away. She's taller than most of the angels that they've found, and the pedestal she stands on is anchored to a solid slab of concrete. Even in this darkness, he can tell how lovely she is. Mrs. Walker will say that she is "full of grace." Cade hopes so. They need some grace. He shifts from one foot to another. Mostly they need the money this angel will bring.

It's obvious to Cade that the church, the graveyard, the angel—especially the angel—have been neglected. "I don't think anyone will miss her," says Paul. Cade doesn't doubt his father. It's clear, despite the dark, that no one has tended this cemetery in a very long time.

He points his small flashlight toward the base of the statue while his father chips at the old grout with a hammer and chisel. The thin beam shatters into watery pieces before it can reach the angel's feet.

At last, Paul says, "Okay, I think she's loose now." Cade pockets the flashlight, throwing them into deeper darkness. They stop to get their bearings, and together, they wrap the statue in the wet blanket and snug the rope securely around her. Father and son stand on either side and rock her back and forth, to break her loose. Then, on the count of three, they lift her off the pedestal. Despite the blanket and his leather work gloves, the statue's iciness penetrates into all ten of his fingers. She's heavy. Solid granite. The dead weight of her pulls at his shoulders.

"Careful," Paul says. So much rain seems to add weight to the statue, and Cade feels it slipping from his grip. He leans over a bit, stumbles.

"Hold up!" his father whispers. Cade freezes.

The sound of tires on wet pavement is unmistakable. As gently as they can, they lower the angel onto the ground, then squat down beside her.

Whoever is driving is slowing down; the light from the headlamps bounces off the trees above them, throws broken prisms against the headstones. Cade is sure he can feel the shards of light prick the back of his jacket.

Who would be out on an old road at this hour? His mind races. A sheriff? A hunter? Cade knows it's not anybody he'd want to meet while stealing from the dead, in the dead of night.

He tries to keep from falling backward into the mud, tries to keep from thinking about the bones below his boots. He hates this. The rain. The mud. The drumbeat in his ears.

At last the car passes. Paul straightens up, gives Cade his hand, pulls him up. They're almost the same height, these two, nudging up against six feet, and they look so much alike, they could pass for brothers. Same sandy-blond hair. Blue-green eyes. Broad shoulders. Built for lifting heavy objects. Like this angel.

"Let's just take it slow," Paul says. Cade's legs are stiff from squatting down, so he shakes them out. He knows that if he slips on the muddy ground, he or his father or both of them might wind up being crushed by their quarry. Killed by an angel. How ironic would that be?

He takes a step forward without noticing the invisible vine that stretches from a shaggy oak tree down to the ground. Its stinging nettles grab his face and bite into the tender skin beneath his right eyebrow.

"Fuck!" he says, lurching forward. The statue slips, pulling both of them with her. It takes all their strength to keep from tumbling to the ground.

"Take a second," he hears his dad say. Once more they set the statue down, and Cade pulls off his glove, cups his hand to catch the freezing rain and splash it on his burning eye.

"You okay?" asks Paul.

Cade nods. "Yeah, I'm fine," he lies.

Paul pauses. "Let's hope she's worth it." Cade hopes so too. Finally they manage to push and pull her into the truck's bed and slam the tailgate shut.

"Good work," says Paul. But for Cade, the job is not quite done. He digs the flashlight out of his pocket. Paul lifts his chin, nods. "Hurry," he says. Cade knows it's unlikely he'll find what he's looking for, but he can't get back into the truck until he at least takes a look.

If only, he thinks.

He aims the beam of light across the scattered graves.

It only takes a moment to see that what he's looking for isn't there. But before he turns back to the truck, he shines the light on the base of the angel they've just removed.

The dates on the marker read *b. 1878–d. 1899.* Cade does the math. The woman who was buried there was twenty-one when she died. The angel is so much older. Stone outlasts people, after all.

Just below her name are the words *Beloved Wife, Mother, Daughter.* She must have mattered, else why put an angel on her grave, especially one carved out of Texas granite? Once the angel was cleaned up, once the multiple coats of soot and resin and algae and bird droppings were washed away, she would recover her original color, a shade known as "sunset red," which wasn't so much red as golden pink. Take a good look at the Texas State Capitol building, or the Galveston Seawall, and you'll see. Better, take a look at a Texas sunset.

Cade glances at the truck's bed. Anyone else might think there was a body back there. Cade clicks off the flashlight, pockets it again, and climbs into the truck with his dad.

"It's almost like she didn't want to leave," says Paul, rubbing his hands together to warm them up. *Beloved Wife, Mother, Daughter.*

Unbidden, an image of Cade's mother appears. Evie. Cade's met her only once, but she stays in his head all the same, like a firefly, flicking on and off. There, not there. He pushes his wet hair back and wipes his face on his wet sleeve as Paul turns the heat up full blast. The sting from the scratch has gone from burn to simmer. Cade pulls the visor down and looks in the mirror. It looks like someone has taken a fine-point marker and drawn a line underneath his eyebrow.

"Lemme see," his dad says.

Cade turns toward him. "It's just a scratch."

His father switches on the running lights, puts the truck in gear, and weaves his way from behind the broken-down church; he eases back onto the road.

As they near downtown Houston, Paul is extra cautious, careful to stay under the speed limit, mindful of traffic lights; he keeps his distance from other cars, to avoid any attention from the police. Because how do you explain an angel in the back of your truck at four o'clock in the morning?

How do you explain an angel at all?

Finally they pull into the garage behind Walker's Art and Antiques. Paul puts the truck into park and turns off the heater. The quiet rolls over them, and for a moment, neither moves.

Maybe it's the simmering scratch, so close to his eye, that gives him some clarity, but Cade can see the cost etched onto his father's face. Mrs. Walker calls the two of them "angel hunters." That's the euphemistic term for their profession.

Nevertheless, call it what you will. A thief is a thief.

In the sudden quiet, Cade gets it—this is not what he wants to be. And as if the angel herself was whispering into his ear, he realizes he needs to do something else. Something he can do in the light of day. Something Good.

And once again, he wishes they had found a different angel, one that began with *if only*.

Soleil Broussard

Come Sunday morning, walk up the broad steps of the Church on the Bayou. Enter through its graceful carved doors, doors that are over a hundred years old, and right there, head bowed, you will see Soleil Broussard, sixteen years old, sitting beside her parents. She wears a small gold cross on a thin gold chain around her neck. There's a tiny honey bear jar tattooed on the inside of her left wrist.

This church is like Soleil's second home. Her mother is the chief administrator, which is the second most important job after the minister. Soleil knows it as well as anybody and better than most—every crack and cranny, every inch of this old building, including the courtyard.

This church. Every year she attends summer Bible school, and every Christmas she plays a shepherd in the annual Nativity scene (except when she was three, when she was a lamb). When you are the daughter of the chief administrator, you are expected to *participate*.

She listens while the handbell choir, dressed in their red-and-white robes, rings out a version of John Lennon's "Imagine." Their lovely notes hover in the sanctuary long after the song is done.

Soleil closes her eyes and breathes in the familiar smells—beeswax from the candles; roses that have been clipped from a climbing bush in the church courtyard; her mother's Aveeno hand lotion; the remnants of her father's Camel cigarette, the one he smoked that morning with his coffee. The combination means Sunday.

But this Sunday is not like past Sundays. Soleil sits up straight, back against the pew. She turns her face directly toward the minister. "Let us rejoice in this happy day," the minister, Reverend Clara, says.

Soleil? Mostly she loves to rejoice. If she could stand up in the middle of the service, she would shout, "Rejoice, for heaven's sake!"

Instead, she grabs her hair in her right hand and twists it over her shoulder, like she's wringing it out, as if she could squeeze some rejoicing out of her hair. Her mother taps her on the arm to make her stop.

Standing on the broad platform next to the altar is the Byrd family. Two parents and little Tyler, who is nestled in his father's arms. The three of them are beaming.

This family has been through so much, and now they are embarking upon a new life, but rather than starting that new life here in Houston, where Soleil could see them regularly, they are moving to California . . . and taking Tyler with them. New jobs and a family full of aunts and uncles and cousins are waiting for them. Waiting with open arms.

So rejoice, okay? The thing is, Soleil is happy for them. She is. But she is not so happy for herself.

She hears the minister's familiar words: *Let us be the heart and hands of Jesus.* Soleil is fairly certain that Jesus would not be having His own nonrejoicing moment in the midst of all this happiness.

She knew this day would come, when Tyler and his parents would leave, but knowing that and living it were two different things.

And now, this persistent rain makes it all the worse. It was rain, after all—buckets of it—that had brought the Byrds to the Church on the Bayou in the first place.

Soleil feels a lump in her throat. The Byrds lost

everything in that storm. They were rescued from their rooftop by a neighbor with a flat-bottomed boat. When they arrived at the church, exhausted, Mr. Byrd was holding on to Tyler, and Mrs. Byrd was holding on to a plastic shopping bag with everything they owned. All that was left: a few disposable diapers and a bag of puppy chow.

Tyler, clinging to his father's neck, would not stop crying.

The Byrds spent days on cots in the broad hallway of the church, days and days of rain and wind, and more people seeking shelter. And Tyler, crying.

But that was a year ago. And now, here they were, with enough money to move back to California where they have family who can help them rebuild their lives.

The honey bear on Soleil's wrist is tender. The newness of it still surprises her.

"Brothers and sisters," says the minister. "Let us pray." Soleil leans into the minister's voice. She closes her eyes again and holds her hands together.

"Let us call on the traveling mercies," says the minister. "To carry this family safely all the way to Los Angeles, into the arms of their kin."

In the middle of the prayer, Soleil looks up. There is Tyler, safe in his father's embrace, next to his mother.

As she looks at him, he twists around and spots Soleil. His little face lights up, and he waves, his tiny fingers flashing open and shut like a warning light, his toddler smile as big as the moon.

Just in time, the choir begins to sing. "*This little light of mine . . . I'm gonna let it shine . . . this little light of mine . . .*" Her mother leans over and whispers, "Your signature song, Lay-Lay." Soleil winces at her nickname. The sound of it doesn't make anything better.

The choir keeps singing. . . . "*Let it shine, let it shine, let it shine.*"

But how, Soleil wonders, can she get her light to shine with all this blue coming down? And yet? *And yet?* There's this honey bear tattoo on the inside of her wrist. And it seems to hold a message: Rejoice!

Zorra

People come and people go. That is the way of things. The bayou knows this. It's the same with the animals. Once there were ivory-billed woodpeckers, Carolina parakeets, red wolves along her course. They came. They went. But what about the ocelot? A young one, not fully grown, born in the Laguna Atascosa, four hundred miles south. What about Zorra?

She presses herself as far toward the back of the pen as she can, but it doesn't keep the pouring rain from seeping through the leaky roof of her enclosure and drenching her golden spotted coat. Despite its thickness, she shivers, tucks her paws underneath her chest. Where is her bright yellow sun, the warm dirt beneath her feet? Where is the cry of the nearby coyote, the one that sang her to wake every night in time for the hunt, and then sent her to sleep before dawn?

These memories buzz all around her like a nest of hornets.

She isn't even sure how she got here. Only that she felt a piercing sting in her left shoulder, followed by darkness too deep to see. Next thing she knew, the only light came from a narrow window in the door of her cage. She curled into a tight ball.

An ocelot is not a company keeper. Like most of her kind, she stays to herself, unconcerned about companions. But here in this small container, her aloneness digs into her spotted fur. Not even when she slept in the arms of the jacaranda tree, on those nights when the moon disappeared and the thicket turned as black as a grackle's wing, had she felt so solitary. Still, other creatures are trapped here with her. She hears their snuffles, their whines, their scratchings against the wooden floors and sides of their cages, cages on either side of hers. She knows they are there, but she doesn't know their smells, doesn't understand their cries.

Her cage fills up with other sounds too, sounds that aren't animal. Had she grown up in a city and not in the dense thicket of the Rio Grande along the Texas-Mexico border, she might have recognized them for what they were: the passing of cars on asphalt and cement, the wailing sirens of ambulances and fire trucks, the rocking roll of the freight trains, and the constant hum of wires carrying electricity from one tower to another. All these noises are new to her. Not at all like the busy cooing of doves and the hissing chirr of rattlesnakes. Nothing like her Laguna Atascosa, her ancient territory.

The only familiar noise is the sound of a nearby river. But unlike her river, which tumbled and swished on its way to the sea, this one sounds deeper, slower. Maybe, she thinks, it's not even a river at all.

Her stomach rumbles. It's been days since the human, the one she thinks of as the Caretaker, has fed her. She can tell when he is near because he emits a thin, high-pitched sound, something like a bobwhite, but not at all the same. Ever since the rain began, he disappeared. She doesn't miss him, or his whistle. But she does miss the smelly food that he puts inside the metal bowl.

The food reeks like carrion. Something dead. Some animal she doesn't recognize, something that's been ground and mashed and stripped of fur or feathers and bones. For the first few days after she arrived, she refused to eat it, but then she grew so hungry that she finally couldn't help herself. She lapped it up, her sides heaving as it slid down her throat. It hardly had any taste, but it filled her stomach.

And the next thing she knew, it began to rain. Day became night became day and still the Caretaker never came. The snuffles and scratches and whines from the adjoining cages grow more urgent.

Something else—the river. She can tell by its sound that it's gaining speed. Moreover, it seems to be closer, rising. She stands for a moment and shakes her soaking coat. The only thing the rancid metal bowl holds now is water.

She nudges it with her nose. There, just underneath the scraping sound of metal against wood, she thinks she hears her name.

Zorra. A whisper.

Zorra. From the water, she hears it.

Zorra. So soft it hurts to listen.

Buffalo Bayou

HOUSTON

She's not really a river. She's a bayou, and long ago, after the sea pulled itself back and back and back, oh, fifty miles or so to the south, she started gathering water upstream in a salt-grass prairie, where the rain ran off and pooled underground, then bubbled back up and rambled her way to the Gulf of Mexico.

She's been called many names. Mother River. Buffalo River. Buffalo Bayou. And surely there are more besides, names not written down in books or maps. But the bayou, she remembers all her names, every one, in every language.

Akokisa. Bidai. Atakapa. Patiri. Karankawa. Caddo. Gullah. Creole. Spanish. French. Hebrew. German.

She never forgets. That's the God's honest truth.

Other names too, not only her own, she holds in her brackish currents.

Like Achsah.

Pronounce it like this: *Axa*.

The bayou remembers Achsah.

Achsah

The morning the rooster crowed, just after midnight, and the Captain finally died, was the morning that Achsah was set free. It said so in the Captain's will, right there in his own hand on clean white vellum, and testified to by the lawyers. Free.

Achsah rolled the word around in her mouth, not quite willing to say it out loud. Then the rooster crowed again and she shook the Captain's body to make sure he was well and truly dead.

Free. Achsah was free. And the Captain was free too, free from the yellow jack, from the rattling cough and the screaming fever that had lit up his old body like a nest of charcoal. Achsah had tried to cool him down with water from the river. The doctor had told her to keep him cool, and the water from the river was the coolest water there was. No such thing as cold water in Houston.

But no amount of river water could stop the fever's rampage or the coughing that ate away at him. Achsah knew that. The doctor knew that. The Captain knew that. Which was why he made sure that his will was written and signed, the will that set Achsah free.

Not too many freed Negro women, not in Texas. Not in the year of our Lord 1845. Not a Negro woman of childbearing age, the most valuable kind. The trouble was, the Captain had tricked her.

He set her free, all right. But not her little girls. Her Mary Ann. Her Juba. He didn't set them free.

Achsah left the side of the Captain's bed, but before she did, she stared at him hard, to make sure that he was gone. She waited several long minutes, hardly daring to breathe herself, and walked to the window. It would be hours before the sun rose, hours before anyone else would know about the passing. If she was lucky, it would be a full day, or days.

How long had she waited for this moment? Her whole life. Her *whole* life. But especially these last six years. That was how long the Captain had owned her. She realized right then that the old wet air should have felt different now that she was free. Should have felt like new air. Such a word, wasn't it? *Free?*

She knew she only had this small moment to think about it. Down the hall, her daughter-girls slept, their arms and legs knitted together atop their cot, their little-girl chests rising and falling in the quiet country of Sleep. She turned back to the window.

All these years, almost a third of her life, the Captain had promised to set Achsah free upon his death, and he did, ignoring the remonstrations of his friends, all of whom had fought against Mexico so they could keep their slaves. The Captain himself had served in the Texian Army, right next to the general, Sam Houston. Moreover, the Captain had lent the army his ship to use for moving troops along the coast, in and out of Galveston, the same ship Achsah had sailed on when he bought her at the Forks of the Road Slave Market.

The market sat at a crossroads near Natchez, the old Spanish town on the banks of the Mississippi. The Captain bought her when she was barely twelve years old. "Big for her age" was what the slave dealer said, with a wink toward the Captain.

Six years ago, and that was the last time she saw Natchez or the Mississippi or the thin boy who had been chained to her as they walked up the old Indian path from Alexandria, Louisiana, away from her mama, away to the Forks of the Road, tethered to a boy whose name she never knew, didn't want to know because then she knew she'd miss him. That's what a name does: makes this empty place where missing goes and stays.

This she knew because she missed her mama, whose name was Happiness. Achsah had missed Happiness over and over and over since she left Alexandria and walked, chained to a thin boy whose name she didn't know, to the Forks of the Road. And it was the last time she sailed on that ship, too, sailed in the Captain's own cabin, locked there where he treasured her, night after night, relieving herself in a copper jug, heaving into it too, her arms shaking, blood running down her legs. Barely twelve. Big for her age.

Achsah. The bayou remembers you.

Mother River Church of God's Blessings

HOUSTON, REPUBLIC OF TEXAS
1845

First there was only a brush arbor, set a ways back from the homesteads and up the road from Kleinfeldt's Sawmill. It was close enough to the Mother River for the occasional baptism, when the Reverend Phillips called his parishioners to follow him down the wooden steps of the banks and into the cool waters, tilt their heads backward toward the sky, and pray for salvation while the water closed over their faces. And they also prayed that the water snakes and alligators might let them be, at least for those few moments that they were submerged.

So this was the Mother River Church of God's Blessings. A fine name for such a godly gathering. And the Reverend Phillips, who came to Houston all the way from Georgia with his wife, Celia, couldn't have loved them any more.

The Phillipses were an attractive crew, the reverend with his auburn hair and his broad face, a light-skinned face that burned easily and that bore a smattering of freckles across his nose. Mrs. Phillips stood barely five feet tall and was what folks'd call "sturdy" in polite company. As for Major Bay, he stood a foot taller than the reverend, and his skin was as dark as Phillips's was light. Both men wore broad-brimmed hats to keep the ever-present Houston sun out of their eyes.

The brush arbor was fine for a time, but Houston grew, and so did the number of churches. There was a large Catholic church that rose up right in the center of town, and just across from it was the Lutheran congregation, complete with a bell tower. Soon enough, the members of Mother River Church of God's Blessings decided to build a chapel, not so fancy as the Catholic and Lutheran churches. Rather, a small whitewashed clapboard building situated a ways from the docks and tucked behind a grove of burr oaks and hackberry trees. Inside were several rows of pews, which were set toward the front, near the altar. These were for the white folks, and even though their Negroes were welcome, they had to stand in the back, in a large space behind the pews, including the reverend's own slave, Major Bay, whose towering height was a fact they were both aware of.

No matter what, there was always Miss Celia at the piano. Every Sunday the chapel filled up with praise music. And anyone visiting might be amazed at the sound of that piano. It was said that you could hear it all the way to the Brazos River to the west, and the small village of Harrisburg to the south, the notes slipping through the walls and bouncing on out atop the currents of Mother River. One visitor even said, "I wouldn't be surprised if the seagulls could hear that piano all the way to Galveston." It was almost as if the piano itself was filled with so much spirit that its very keys created a heavenly chorus.

And while Miss Celia played, the reverend exhorted, "Sing out, brothers and sisters, for the Lord is listening. Sing out!"

And they did, each and every one, including Major Bay, whose deep baritone voice filled the bottom register and made the windows vibrate.

"Sing out," called the reverend again, so the brothers and sisters, white and black, young and old, of Mother River Church of God's Blessings did. And at least a few of them, let's say two or three, sang as if their very souls depended upon it.

Soleil Broussard

It's surprising, if you want to know, how many versions of honey bear jars you can find. They come in both glass and plastic. They can be clear or opaque. Big or small, holding their thick golden contents, robbed from the bees, added to tea and oatmeal and Greek yogurt.

When the hurricane had dumped a record-setting fifty inches of rain on parts of Houston, thousands of people were forced out of their homes. Lucky for Soleil and her family, their house had stayed dry. But lots of others weren't so fortunate.

The Church on the Bayou had opened its doors for people to shelter there. Row after row of cots filled the hallways and the classrooms. Some in the back of the sanctuary, too, and probably a dozen people, at least, slept on the hard wooden pews. No one complained. People even stayed in the basement despite some water that seeped in through the old brick walls.

Soleil volunteered to help. "Tantos bebés," said Sra. Zapatero, the lady who ran the nursery. And it was *so many babies*. For days, everyone did their best, but there weren't enough laps to sit on, not enough arms for holding, no bathtubs for soaking, so many dirty diapers and runny noses and hungry tummies.

Then there was the chain-reaction crying. One baby cried and set off another and another and on and on. Especially Tyler. Eighteen-month-old Tyler Byrd, who could not quit crying, not even for a moment. He cried in his sleep, when he was awake—nonstop. Soleil held him in her arms until they ached. Rocked him for hours until she felt dizzy. She offered him cookies and milk and jelly beans. She took his hand and walked him all over the church. Up and down the stairs. Through the hallways, the kitchen, the playroom. She even took him to the covered porch to watch the rain. He cried.

His father, having been rescued himself, left during the day to help with rescue operations. His exhausted mother tried to calm Tyler down, but she was so weary from rain and wind and loss, Soleil could see that she needed to rest. Thus Soleil kept Tyler close. And Tyler cried.

Soleil sang to him. She danced with him. She held on to him.

And somehow, amid all the donations that arrived, along with scores of hot meals and new socks and travel toothpastes, someone dropped off a couple hundred jars of honey.

Whoever it was lined them up along the altar rail in the sanctuary, a small battalion of honey bears, so that when Soleil, carrying Tyler in her arms—Tyler who couldn't be consoled at all—walked into the sanctuary, she found the little army of honey bear jars caught in a rare beam of sunshine that slipped through the high windows above the balcony. Tyler reached out with his tiny hands and picked one up, held it in front of his round little face, set it back down, picked up another identical honey bear jar, set it down, too, until finally, he picked up the one, *the one* that said *Tyler* among all the others. Soleil set him on the floor, and he hugged the honey bear jar close to his chest, sucked in an enormous sniffle, curled up on the carpet next to the altar, and fell into a deep, deep sleep.

Soleil waited, watched, then lifted him up and carried him to his mother, asleep on an air mattress in the hallway. There she tucked him in next to her. After that, Tyler rarely set the honey bear jar down.

Even when he waved to her from the altar that Sunday, it was in his hands, still full because it wasn't the honey he wanted. Soleil knew that Tyler's honey bear was a trophy, won for being *best crier ever*.

Thus the tattoo, a reminder that miracles sometimes look like the right honey bear jar for a small boy.

Cade Curtis

Walker's Art and Antiques is old. It's been in the same location on Washington Avenue for more than a century. It's constantly in need. A new windowpane. An updated computer. A part for the air conditioner.

Paul and Cade and Mrs. Walker also have needs. Groceries. Clothes. Dental work.

The sales from the shop are brisk, but not brisk enough. Cade knows this. Mrs. Walker calls the extra funds that the angels bring in a *comfort*. "As angels are wont to provide," she says. "Besides, I have it on great authority that they're going to very fine homes where all their needs will be met."

This one is valuable. Carved out of Texas granite, sunset red.

But as they take her out of the truck and carry her into the shop, as they unwrap her from the soaking-wet blanket, Cade notices a thin crack. It runs from the corner of her eye, down her cheek, past her chin, and into the collar of her robe, as if a tear traced a path along the side of her carved face.

Beloved Wife, Mother, Daughter.

It's almost as if she didn't want to leave.

Paul Curtis

"We all write our own histories, don't we?" Paul has told that to Cade so many times. In the collective history of Cade and Paul Curtis, they didn't set out to be angel hunters. Paul never set out to become a father at the ripe old age of sixteen. It'd be pressing it pretty hard to say that *any* sixteen-year-old boy sets out to become a father. But that was the case with Paul. Cade's mother, Evie Nelson, was just as young, sixteen.

The day came, and Evie handed their baby, only a few days old, to Paul while he stood on her doorstep and begged her not to close the door.

Evie, his Evie. *Don't close the door.* Every ounce of him shook, as if his bones might rattle his entire being to pieces. Then she handed him the birth certificate, the space for the baby's name still blank because she couldn't bear to fill it in, wouldn't fill it in. The baby in his arms. His baby. In his arms.

His Evie. No other Evie.

"Don't come back here again," she said, her words so thin, like strands of a spiderweb woven between them, a web he couldn't pierce. And there were more words. "You promised. You promised," she said.

The web grew thinner.

He'd made a promise.

Then she closed the door and left him there, his tiny baby in his arms, a piece of paper in his hand, a blank for a name.

Paul knew what was up; he knew that her parents would never tolerate this baby, especially her father. After all, he'd never tolerated Paul. Never tolerated Evie, either, for that matter.

Paul would never forget her father's hand on the back of his neck, squeezing him as he shoved Paul down into the grass of their front yard. "You worthless piece of shit!" he swore, smashing Paul's face into the dirt, pressing his knee into his back, until Paul was sure his spine would crack. And all the while, Evie stood so still, the horror skittering across her face. That was four months into her pregnancy, just as she began to show.

He didn't see her again until that moment that she handed him their baby, the sound of the door closing an echo in his ear.

And then it was Paul's parents' turn. "If you're old enough to be a father, you're old enough to make your own way in the world," and they too turned their backs with a silence that blasted through him, made him hold his baby tighter. His baby.

He hadn't meant to fall in love with Evie. He hadn't meant to take her in his arms and let the whole rest of the world slip away. He hadn't meant for it to be only Evie and the sky and the sun and his heart meeting hers, as if it had been made to do just that. He hadn't meant for any of that to happen. He especially hadn't meant for her to get pregnant, not then, not when they were still in high school, still so young. Sixteen.

It wasn't the way he'd intended to write his history.

At first, he didn't think she would go through with it. They even met with the school counselor, who was no help at all. She simply gave them a handful of pamphlets. "Here are your options," she told them, as if pamphlets were the same thing as options. Paul handed them to Evie, who burst into tears.

"I love you," she told Paul like that explained everything. It explained it all, didn't it? At least it did to Paul.

But as it turned out, all of them . . . his parents, her parents, Evie—especially Evie—all turned away. No one even said good-bye.

They chose their options.

Paul Curtis

But Paul Curtis, sixteen years old, looked at his baby boy and knew: he had an option too. It was how the history of Paul and Cade began. "By loving you up," he had told Cade about a million times. "It was the only real thing I knew how to do."

Soleil Broussard

Shortly after the storm finally unloaded its last crazy inches of water, the families who had taken shelter at the Church on the Bayou one-by-one began to leave, headed to stay with relatives, headed to try to clean up and reclaim their flooded homes, headed to different shelters, until eventually, there was only one family left: the Byrds.

The hurricane had taken everything: their car, their house, the swing set in the backyard. Even the trees along the front walk had been swept away. There was only a shattered mountain of debris where their home had once stood.

And that is when Mama, chief administrator of the Broussard family, announced: "They're coming home with us."

"It's only temporary," Mama had told the Byrds. "Until you can get back on your feet. Then you'll move to California."

Of course Soleil and her dad agreed. Wasn't giving shelter to those in need exactly what their reverend meant by *being the heart and hands of Jesus?*

Just like that, Soleil became Tyler's de facto big sister, babysitter, and dancing partner. But who knew that keeping up with a toddler would take so many hearts and hands? Who knew that he would be so madly crazy about Soleil? Who knew that she would feel the same? Who knew that he would call her Yay-Yay because he couldn't pronounce the *L*s, and that would seal the deal forever?

Zorra

Zorra. Trapped in a cage barely large enough for her to spin in a circle, a cage that is leaking like crazy from the pouring rain. Her stomach growls and all she has to fill it with is water. She hasn't eaten in days, not since the rain began. She can hear the invisible animals snuffling and chuffing, and one, a bird of some kind, has been screeching for hours.

Zorra's legs are built for speed, but they are cramped here in this leaky cage. She needs to run. She needs to find the thorny mesquite trees and rub her soaking coat against their rough, gray trunks. Mostly she needs to chase down a fresh rabbit or a chapparal. Soon.

The bird sends its terrible song into the humid air. Every nerve underneath Zorra's spotted skin hums.

Finally she uses her front paws to scratch against the door. She scratches and scratches and scratches, peels the soaked wood off in strips, until her claws begin to tear and bleed.

Zorra. Creature of the brush thickets. Native of the Rio Grande. Isn't there a song for Zorra?

Soleil Broussard

Soleil spreads her homework out on the kitchen table and listens while her dad plays his favorite song, "Jole Blon," on his accordion. It's an old Cajun tune that he said he was born knowing. Soleil can't understand all the lyrics, and she's not sure that her father does either, a mishmash of French and Creole, something about a blond woman who was the prettiest of all.

In 1927, a massive flood covered more than twenty-seven thousand square miles of Arkansas, Mississippi, and Louisiana with thick, muddy water, water that defied the levees. It took down bridges and swallowed roads. It gobbled up acres of corn and cotton and sugar-cane, stripped the paint off the barns. It drove Soleil's ancestors, the Broussards, from Point Coupee Parish in

Louisiana to Houston, where they settled in the Fifth Ward in a section called Frenchtown. *Creoles of Color*, they were called. None of them were blond.

And neither was Soleil. Instead, her hair was amber and flew away from her face in thick curls that tumbled down her back. Her skin was light brown, like her Creole ancestors who arrived in Houston with their jumbled-up bloodlines of Spanish, French, African, Caribbean, and Taensa, none of whom lived in French-town anymore either, since Highway 59 pretty much sliced it all up with its multiple lanes of steel and concrete.

Her father's inherited accordion came with them. "Pretty sure it was strapped on the back of a mule," he says. "Which is why it's never in tune."

Soleil's not sure what the mule had to do with the accordion not being in tune. More likely it had to do with the river water.

"Join in, Lay-Lay," her dad says. *Just like that*, she's reminded of Tyler's name for her: Yay-Yay. A reminder that *just like that*, the Byrds were gone, and even with her father's accordion filling up the air, the house feels eerily quiet. It's amazing how noisy a toddler can be, she thinks.

She closes her eyes, and under her breath, she prays,

"Keep them safe, please." And from the other room, she hears her mother's voice, joining her father's. It's a familiar sound, her parents' voices, twined like a braid, filling the house with song.

Soleil sometimes joins in, but mostly she doesn't. She loves to sing, but more than that, she loves to dance.

What Soleil knows is that when she dances, it makes her feel as if she isn't actually connected to the ground. Her two best friends—yes, she has *two* best friends, Channing and Grapes—told her that sometimes they feel the same way.

"It's like I just can't help myself," says Channing, twisting a strand of kinky hair around her forefinger. She's going for full-on locs, but it's taking some time.

"Me too," says Grapes, talking about dance, not locs. She couldn't grow locs if she wanted—her hair isn't thick enough, and it's way too straight.

Of course, Grapes is not her real name. Her real name is Grace. But somewhere around the third grade her little brother, Jordan, who was three at the time, accidentally called her Grapes, and instead of being mad or upset, she thought it was funny. And since Grace is a fairly common name, she decided to just roll with it.

As for Soleil, it's pronounced *so-lay*, which in French means "sun." "So full of light," her mama always tells her.

But now, with the sun itself missing in action, Soleil doesn't feel full of light at all. She presses her elbows on the table and rests her chin in her hands. She never knew she would miss the Byrds so much, like an ache she never knew she could feel.

Her father sings the last of the lyrics in "Jole Blon." "*Jole Blon, Delta flower, you're my darling, you're my sunshine. . . . I love you, and adore you . . . and I promise to be true.*"

Soleil doesn't know any other fathers who play old waltzes on old accordions. He squeezes the bellows closed, with a whoosh that sounds like a sigh.

He must've seen something in her face because he set the accordion on the floor, pulls her into his arms, and gives her a gigantic hug, just like he has every day of her entire life.

"Lay-Lay, ma cherie. It'll be okay. You'll see." And Soleil, named for the sun, prays that he is right.

Because on top of everything, there is someone else who has entered the picture.

Just like that.

Cade Curtis.

Taking up space.

Cade Curtis

What Soleil doesn't know:

Cade thinks about the way her name opens in the middle and doesn't end, like there's no stopping it.

He notices the way her hair swishes from side to side across her back as she walks down the halls.

Admires the honey bear tattoo on her wrist.

He would like to hang out with her, maybe meet her for a cup of coffee or invite her to play pinball at the store. He bets she is good at pinball, with absolutely no evidence for that whatsoever. Why would she play pinball at all?

But then again, what about the angels? What would she think, if she knew?

Soleil Broussard.

Taking up space.

Buffalo Bayou

HOUSTON

The bayou loves her some stars. For thousands of years, she's been catching them. Straight out of the sky. Stars falling from the Milky Way, sizzling as they hit the water and sink into her bed, safe at last from their journey through space.

Make a wish. Then make another. Don't tell a single, solitary soul.

Achsah

Six years was how long Achsah belonged to the Captain. Since she was twelve years old. Since she was sold away from her mother, Happiness.

When the slave dealer showed up at their cabin, with orders to chain Achsah to the coffle, to take her to the Forks of the Road, Happiness had stepped in between her and the dealer, begging him, pleading with him, "No! You can't take my girl. No, sir. Don't take my baby girl."

Achsah, hearing her mama's words, *baby girl*, her words for her youngest child, Achsah thought her whole body might fly apart right there, bits of her hanging in the cabin air. She tried to scream, but the terrors had jammed into her face, rendered her mute, while it seemed like more and more pieces of her flew away. The slave dealer pushed Happiness aside and jerked Achsah by the arm, pulled her toward the door. Happiness lunged for him, but the dealer shoved her again. Achsah heard the thud of his fist against her mother's rib cage, saw her mother slump to the ground.

"Don't get up," he ordered. Achsah knew, from the way her mama groaned, that she couldn't get up, even if she wanted.

"She's my baby," her mama cried. "My baby girl."

And that was the last time Achsah saw Happiness, her mama, all those bits and pieces of herself still back at that cabin door.

She had missed Happiness every single day.

But now she was free. The Captain was dead. And she wanted, more than anything, to take her papers, to take a mule and ride to Alexandria and find her, to fall into her mama's arms, to hear her say *baby girl* again. That was what she wanted.

But what she needed was to bundle up Juba and Mary Ann and run. Run to Mexico, where no one could take them away from her. "Not my baby girls," she said. "Not mine."

Juba and Mary Ann

HOUSTON, REPUBLIC OF TEXAS
1845

Juba knew, stay quiet, as quiet as a flower on a stem, so quiet. She was good at Quiet. All her life, all five years, she had practiced Quiet. Quiet sharpened her eyesight, so she could notice things like the gray-and-white cat that hid in the brushy space between the main house and the privy. Quiet allowed her to overhear the voices of the grown-ups when they didn't know she was listening. Quiet showed her how to slip from one spot to another without being seen. She wore Quiet like a shadow.

Not Mary Ann. At three years of age, she didn't like Quiet. She liked birds, especially their songs. Her mama told her more than once, "Daughter, you're like a whole flock of chickadees!"

Mary Ann liked being a whole flock of chickadees. If she could, she'd climb a tree, maybe every tree, and she would flit from one branch to another, and then she would burst into the sky in a noisy explosion, right into the mighty blue of it all.

Quiet—Juba.

A flock of chickadees—Mary Ann.

Achsah's daughters.

Cade and Paul Curtis

Imagine a sixteen-year-old father, with a brand-new son and no place to go. With a warning from his parents to leave and not come back, Paul stuffed his backpack as tightly as he could with clothes, took the old stroller from the garage, the very same stroller his parents had used for pushing him around the neighborhood. He packed Cade into it and struck out on foot, up and down the streets of Houston.

He passed a hospital. He passed a fire station. He passed a twenty-four-hour emergency room. He paused in front of each one. Then moved on.

"Thirty-two dollars," he told Cade. "That's all the money I had."

Cade had heard the story a million times, heard

about how his dad eventually walked his way to the park that straddles both sides of the Buffalo Bayou, connected by several long bridges high over the water. Next to one of those bridges was a concrete bench, where Paul stopped long enough to give Cade a bottle of formula and change his diaper, and also to eat half a box of Raisinets, a last-minute grab from his mother's pantry. Then he gathered up his pack and the stroller and walked across the bridge, up Washington Avenue, one of the oldest streets in Houston, into a neighborhood called the Heights. Did Paul know that the neighborhood had a name? Hardly, but it was a name that made sense, as it was nestled on a bluff that overlooked that bayou. It was higher than most sections of Houston, which wasn't saying a lot. Truth is there is hardly a metropolitan area in the world that is flatter topographically than Houston, Texas.

The Heights was originally called Germantown, because so many German settlers landed there in the early days of Houston. The Heights was old and new all at once.

"That was us," his father told Cade, "an old kid with a new kid."

Now Cade is exactly the age his dad was when he was born. Did that make him an "old kid"?

Of course, Cade didn't remember that long walk when he was just a baby. Didn't remember pausing in front of the hospital or the fire station or the emergency clinic. Didn't remember crossing the bayou. His dad told him that they hadn't gone too far when Paul saw a sign in a shop window. HELP WANTED. His dad had never had a job, never had a baby, never been so tired. Suddenly he didn't even care what the job was, the need for it gripped him like a glove. He looked at the sign above the door: WALKER'S ART AND ANTIQUES STORE.

"I'm telling you, Li'l Dude. It was a sign." Okay, Cade didn't love being called "Li'l Dude," but he did love hearing the story. He looked upon it as his and Paul's very own creation myth, like their personal beginning of the world-as-they-knew-it. The first chapter in their collective history.

At any rate, Paul pushed Cade through the door and walked directly to the counter and asked Mrs. Walker for an application.

When Mrs. Walker saw Paul and baby Cade, she somehow knew what was going on, and even though the garage apartment she had in the back of the store lot was old and rickety and didn't really have reliable heating or air-conditioning, she knew it would serve this weary boy and his baby, so she offered it to him, and without even seeing it, Paul hugged Mrs. Walker and said, "Yes, ma'am," followed by, "Thank you, thank you, thank you." And that was followed by a wail from Cade.

"It was like you were telling us, 'In the name of all that is right and holy, please change my diaper and give me something to eat,'" said Paul, beaming while he said it.

Mrs. Walker gathered up some old sheets and towels from her apartment on the second floor above the shop, and an ancient electric fan from the store, and showed them their new home. The old garage had probably once served as a barn. It still housed a midcentury Packard, one with fins on the back and a bumper that hung down on one side. There was a FOR SALE sign on it, but it was dusty and hard to read. It seemed like the sign might have had a red background at one time, but now it was a dull shade of pink. It was obvious the sign had been there for a while.

"Everything here is for sale," said Mrs. Walker. Then she added, "But not everything has found the right owner yet." Somehow Paul knew what she meant. As he followed her up the rickety steps toward the apartment, he realized that if he believed in fairy tales, he would say that she looked just like what he imagined a fairy godmother might look like. Her hair was white and poofy, and her pink glasses set off her blue eyes. Her skin was so light it was almost translucent. Not only that, but she was tiny, barely reaching his chin. The only thing missing was her magic wand.

When she unlocked the door and stepped aside, he looked at the ratty apartment with its coating of dust and cobwebs, looked at his brand-new son, and took in a huge, deep breath, as if he had never inhaled before.

Mrs. Walker told him she'd see him in the morning. He could start his new job then. He hugged her again and put his hand on his chest. "You can count on me," he said, and watched her walk back down the rickety stairs. Then he pounded the old mattress to loosen some of the dust, threw the sheets on it, gave Cade another bottle, and changed his diaper again. Finally he softly rocked his little son in his arms. "You and me, Li'l Dude," he said, "we're going to be okay." And he kissed Cade's face from top to bottom and then tucked him back in the stroller. The stroller would have to serve as a crib for now, at least until he could save a little money, more than thirty-two dollars anyway.

With his tummy full, and his diaper dry and his face all kissed up, Cade didn't mind. The stroller was comfy and safe. As for Paul, he finished off the box of Raisinets, and without even taking off his shoes, he fell onto the mattress and into a deep, deep sleep. Cade too slept as if he knew that he was home. And he was. And he has been for these past sixteen years.

Of course, he doesn't sleep in his stroller anymore, and over time he and his dad fixed the place up so it isn't so ratty. His dad hung old posters of baseball pitcher Nolan Ryan, one in his Houston Astros uniform and another with his Texas Rangers uniform, on the walls, along with a red-and-blue neon Budweiser Beer sign that features a cart being pulled by the Budweiser Clydesdales. Paul doesn't drink Budweiser, but he loves Nolan Ryan and the Clydesdales and so does Cade, and they both like the way the legs of the horses run and how the wheels of the carriage turn whenever the sign is turned on.

"Just look at us," Paul said. "We've got us a bachelor pad." Cade didn't care what his dad called it. To him, the only name that mattered was *home*.

And Mrs. Walker? She has loved him all his life— his father, too—loved them both, in the fierce way that fairy godmothers, related or not, tend to do. Paul and Cade would do anything for her. They'd even go out in the driving rain in old cemeteries in the darkest dark of night.

Paul Curtis

Dear Evie,
I hope this letter gets to you. It's the only
one I'll ever write. You made me promise
not to ever return. I won't. But in case you
want to find me, I'll be at Walker's Art
and Antiques Store. When you're ready,
that's where I'll be.
Love,
Paul

The Marble Fields

LONG SWAMP, GEORGIA

CHEROKEE NATION

1837

Count the years in millions. Count the tiny sea creatures in billions or more. Count the massive weight of water and sand and heat and fold it together in layers, press it down, down, and down, and fuse it into calcareous beds that grow and grow. Then let the ocean rock itself back and forth, to and fro, over millennia until at last she finally pulls herself back, exposing mountains so white they make the moon look pale, showing off the ridges of pink and gray and blue.

Let those mountains and ridges catch the sparks from falling stars, let them sing back to the howling wind, and sink down, farther and farther toward the center of the Earth.

Then cover it all with clay and sand and watch the

grasses grow and the trees rise tall and thick, hiding the moonlit, star-struck stone.

Count the breezes that blow, and the rains that fall, exposing an outcropping here and there. Count the Etowah, who turned the stone into statues and buried them in their mounds taller than trees, mounds that they built over hundreds of years.

Count the Creek and Cherokee who carved the stone into bowls, and chimneys, and sturdy steps for their cabins. Carved it into animals and figures small enough for a pocket or a pouch. Smooth, translucent, warm to the touch, holding moonlight, holding star-dust.

Pink, gray, blue, white marble. As beautiful as the marble of Tuscany and Greece and Macedonia.

Count the people between 1838 and 1839. Creek. Cherokee. Chickasaw. Choctaw. Seminole. Houses burned. Crops destroyed. Families ripped from homes.

Count the ghosts, count them in thousands, numbers impossible to reckon, who died along the trail. Elders and children were the first to go. But not the last.

Go ahead.

Count them.

First, they were coralled into stockades. Then they were forced to march away, away from their homelands.

Count the army troops, atop their horses and mules. Count the betrayals, the broken treaties. Count the fevers, the frostbite, the broken hearts, the starving bellies. Don't stop counting.

Not until you count a tall, thin boy who carried the marble with him.

Until he didn't.

Buffalo Bayou

HOUSTON

If it's marbles you want, the bayou has them. She loves their different names: aggie, tom, bonker, clam, hogger, toe breaker, onion skin, bumblebee, jasper, tiger eye.

Made of glass, made of clay, made of alabaster.

Made of marble.

Yes, some marbles are made of marble.

You could make a bet. You could have a tournament.

The bayou doesn't need any games. She's happy with the marbles just the way they are, the way they capture the light as they fall through the water, the way it splits into thousands of shards.

Soleil Broussard

Cade. He sits behind her in Mrs. Franco's American literature class at Henrik Brenner High School, and it's as if he's brand-new, this Cade-right-behind-her. This Cade-who-smells-like-wintergreen. The Cade-who-is-living-and-breathing-in-the-same-world-as-her.

What is she supposed to do with all of this *Cade*? Maybe she could tell Channing and Grapes? Maybe she should ask her mom? Or dad? But how? How is she supposed to say all the things she wants to say, especially if she doesn't really know what those things are?

Major Bay

Major Bay, he kept his ear to the ground, he knew the schedules of the steamboats that came up and down the river from Galveston. He knew the hiding places where a body could wait for a passing barge.

He knew how to get the word out, when it needed to get out. Someone want to cross that river into Mexico? He knew how to get them there.

Don't call him Moses. He'd never stand for that. Don't call him friend. He doesn't have time. Don't call him at all.

He'll find you when you're ready.

Just before the Captain died, he knew. . . . Achsah was ready.

Achsah

Her name meant "locket," from the Hebrew Bible. "Something to be treasured," said the Captain, slamming the Bible shut. And he had "treasured" her over and over, her first baby arriving barely a year later, followed soon by another who didn't live, and one more who did. A pair of daughters, the only sweetness she had known since she left Happiness in Alexandria and the thin boy at the Forks of the Road. Now here she was, a free woman, with the papers to prove it. That should taste sweet, shouldn't it?

But then the Captain went and tricked her. He signed away their daughters, her little girls, to the wife of his old friend James Morgan. Five and three years old. Just signed them away. Like that.

"Only till they're twenty-one," he had told her. Twenty-one! That was too long. Achsah knew that by the time her girls turned twenty-one, no one in the Republic of Texas would remember that they should be freed, no one would remind them, not one person would vouch for them, especially not James Morgan.

Achsah clenched the thin fabric of her nightdress in both of her fists and tugged hard until the collar of it dug into the back of her neck. She felt the burn of it. In the other room, her daughters slept. Just down the road, she knew that Mrs. Morgan waited.

"What's she need with two little girls?" asked Achsah to no one at all. "What's Mrs. Morgan need with my girls?"

From the window, she could hear the quiet water of the river, the sun still hours away. Mother River. Some called it Buffalo River. Why, she didn't know. She hadn't seen a real buffalo, though she had seen the skins stacked up on the docks waiting to be loaded onto ships and headed for the markets. Those weren't the only skins. Cowhides. Wolves. Beaver. Bobcats. Plenty of wildlife in Texas. Plenty of hunters to bring their skins to the docks.

There were other kinds of hunters too, the kind that tracked a person down with dogs and ropes and long rifles.

What else? Achsah had seen the slaves who were arriving by the hundreds, by the thousands, from the southern states to the east and the islands of the Caribbean. Unlike the skins, they weren't being shipped out. They were being shipped in.

For a second she thought she heard the raspy rattle of the Captain's breath, but when she looked toward him, there was nothing, nothing but his body, which had once seemed so enormous, but now looked so small. Like a shell, she thought, and she was reminded of the empty shell of a crab, cracked open and fragile, so thin that sunlight could seep through if you held it to the sky. She listened again, but all she heard was the lap of the cool, muddy water as it beat against the banks, just below her window. A thin wisp of fog floated over the river's glassy surface, a haint, barely visible in the thin glow of stars.

Achsah, it seemed to say, *run while you can*. Achsah crossed her hands over her chest. The haint hovered over the water. *Find the Lady*, it whispered.

How easy it would be now, to just take her papers and go. To Mexico. Or California. Or any place except here. Since Texas was severed from Mexico, nothing could keep the Texans, along with the Americans who were pouring into the republic daily, from owning slaves. They even named the settlement after the general, Sam Houston, the man who defeated Santa Anna. The man who signed the deal. Unlike Mexico, slavery was the official law in Texas. Texas won the war. Slaves were the prize.

She should get herself on the Captain's ship while she could, the ship that carried cotton from the turning basin in Harrisburg, down the dark brown river into the Gulf of Mexico and off to sea. She knew exactly where it was docked in Galveston, knew the port there, the same port she'd arrived in six years earlier. She and the Captain had lived on the old island before he moved them to Harrisburg, just south of the new city of Houston. Both of the girls had been born on that narrow strip of sand between the mainland and the sea. She knew that the ship sailed to Mexico from time to time, loaded with cotton for sale in the Mexican market.

"Mexico," Achsah said aloud. If she could get to Galveston, she could get to Mexico. She had gotten word, one whispered word to another, that Major Bay had made arrangements.

Run, the haint on the river whispered as it floated above the water. And she should, she should run like the river, run to the sea, run to the boat that she arrived on.

And then in her mind's eye she saw Mrs. Morgan's sour eyes, her mouth a straight line that cut across her pale face, as if she had a constant toothache. Achsah rubbed the side of her own face. If she could, she'd rub Mrs. Morgan's face until she couldn't see it anymore. Just rub it away.

Free. The Captain had promised, and he had kept his promise. But how could Achsah be free without her daughters? Instead of heading south, she would go north, against the river's currents, to Houston. That's what Major Bay instructed. It was her only chance to keep her girls away from Morgan.

The cock crowed, the Captain died, she had to go. As fast as she could, because she knew that the Morgans could walk through the front door anytime—maybe as soon as the sun rose, maybe in a day or even two. No matter. Whenever they arrived, it would be too soon. They wouldn't knock. They wouldn't wait. They'd take her baby girls.

Achsah hurried to their room, nudged them right out of their bed, all sleepy eyed and dreamy, pulled them onto their feet, their hair like soft brown clouds around their little girl faces, stunned into waking.

Who could be free with all that trickery swirling over her? Not Achsah. And not her girls. Mary Ann and Juba. Quickly they all three changed into their day clothes. Achsah reached into the pantry and grabbed some potatoes and biscuits and dried ham. Then she picked up a cast-iron kettle, the one she had boiled water in for the Captain's tea, maybe a thousand cups of tea, maybe more, tea imported from South Carolina. He wouldn't be drinking any more cups of tea, would he? She put the provisions inside the kettle and slid the lid over it.

Finally she patted the pocket of her skirt to make sure that the tiny figurine was still there, a chunk of pink marble, carved in the shape of a woman, a round circle for her mouth wide open as if it were breathing in the entire world, given to her at the Forks of the Road by the thin boy whose name she never knew. It was the only thing she had ever owned, including her very own self.

No more. She was free. Almost.

Only a few days earlier, Reverend Phillips had visited the dying Captain, to pray for healing and salvation. Achsah had stood in the dark corner of the room, in the shadow. Seen, but not. She listened. "I've brought you the Word of the Lord, brother," said the minister. But the word that came to Achsah wasn't from the Lord. It arrived the next day, and it came from Major Bay, instructions passed to her from one slave to the next, whispered in brief exchanges at the fruit stand, spoken in quick passings at the stable, sung while walking between rows of corn on a hot summer morning. She had memorized them. She knew where she had to go.

Then, with steps as quiet as a fox, Achsah and her daughters disappeared.

And the haint on the river slid into the glassy water, whispering. *Run, Achsah. Find the Lady and run.*

Juba and Mary Ann

Juba held on to her mother's cotton skirt with one hand and on to her little sister's hand with the other. She was in the middle, and that was not where she wanted to be. She was more used to being on the edges, where she could watch and listen.

It was so early, the sun was still tucked away, but it felt as if she had been up for hours. In fact, it felt as if she had been awake since before she was even born. Every nerve ending, every cell, was on watch, and Juba was good at that, watching. She had watched as the Captain had grown weaker and weaker, while his once-booming voice waned to a raspy whisper, crowded out by the hideous, hacking cough.

It had scared her, to see the Captain, such a large

man, become so small in such a short time. It scared her to be caught in the middle like this, between her mama and little sister.

Mary Ann was scared too. So scared. She wanted to cry so bad her face hurt from holding it in.

Achsah had told them, "Got to be quiet." She said it underneath her voice, so low only the three of them could have possibly heard her. And she said it especially to Mary Ann. Juba had no problem being quiet. But Mary Ann, every bit of her wanted to make noise. Noise was her bailiwick.

Even the Captain, stern as he was, always let her sing. Sometimes he even clapped while she sang, especially to "The Starry Crown." It was her favorite, and she knew every verse by heart. Maybe, she thought, if she could sing about the starry crown, she wouldn't need to cry. She started to open her mouth, but Achsah looked at her hard, the hardest way she'd ever seen her mama look at her.

"Not now," said Achsah. "Not now." So Mary Ann gripped her big sister's hand as hard as she could. She held on. She was quiet.

Soleil Broussard

WHAT MATTERS

Prayers. For a long time, Soleil didn't know that she was allowed to make up her own. Instead, she thought that the only people who could make them up were preachers and nuns and the Bible figures, like King David with all his psalms. People who had credentials.

Then one day her mother told her, "Lay-Lay, all a prayer needs is a 'Dear Lord' at the beginning and an 'Amen' at the end. What you put in the middle depends on you." Then she added, "Just make sure the middle matters."

Right now, there is so much that matters. There is Tyler and his family, hoping to find their way in California. There is the persistent rain that never seems to stop. And now there is Cade. Cade-right-behind-her.

Pray, Soleil. Pray.

Cade Curtis

Cade didn't meet his mother, Evie, until he was six years old. Actually he was six years, five months, and twelve days. It was a moment carved into Cade's psyche, a moment not to be forgotten no matter how hard he tried. Until then, Evie was just a kind of shadow that Cade could once in a while see out of the corner of his eye, a sort of mental cricket that created a low-frequency hum in his head. She was always there, but not really.

Whenever he asked Paul about her, the response was always "She'll show up when she's ready." And all Cade could do in the face of that statement was wait.

And then the day came when she was. Ready.

One afternoon, at the back of the store, in the midst

of a furious pinball frenzy between Cade and his dad, Cade happened to look over his shoulder. Normally he didn't take his eyes off the silver ball, bouncing from one chiming bumper to another, only barely looking to see the score numbers add up, but for some reason, he stepped back and took a quick glance, and that was when he noticed the woman standing behind them. She was looking from Paul to him, him to Paul, and all of a sudden she became a crying woman, with short, spiky blond hair, a color not too different from his own. He also noticed that her fingernails were painted a pale, pale blue color that reminded him of Easter eggs.

And the next thing Cade knew, Paul had his arms wrapped around her, holding on to her, like if he let her go, she might fly apart. The silver pinball rolled right down the center of the machine and into the gutter. *Ding, ding, ding. Game over!*

They stood like that for a long time, wrapped tightly together, the woman and Paul. Cade watched in stunned silence. Here was someone he'd never seen before, and his dad was hugging her as if he'd known her forever.

And all at once, she pushed Paul away and rubbed both of her eyes with the backs of her hands. Her face was a hot mess of tears.

Then she pushed Paul again, shoved him back on

his heels. "You promised!" she said, at first only barely audible.

"Evie," said Paul.

Evie. A name carved into Cade's memory. And it seems like he might have laughed or cried or something, but actually he was bewildered, especially when she stepped forward, both fists raised, and shoved Paul yet again, her face knotted with anger. "You promised me! It was a promise!" she cried. Which just added to Cade's bewilderment.

Here he had wondered and waited for his whole life, all six years of it, and Evie had finally shown up, just like his dad said she would. She was apparently ready. After all this time of *not* being ready. But she was also furious.

He watched as Paul tried to calm her down. "Evie," he said. "I'm sorry." And that just seemed to set her off even more.

"Sorry?" The word seemed to explode in the air. "Sorry?" *Boom!*

Sorry sorry sorry flew through the shop, bounced against the walls, the windows, the pinball machines. *Ding! Ding! Ding!*

"I trusted you! It was a promise. You promised. . . ." Her voice thinned into a low wail of *promise, promise, promise.* Over and over, until she wrapped her arms around her own waist and sank onto the floor. While Cade watched, his father knelt down beside her. "I'm sorry, Evie. I'm so, so sorry." His voice was so soft Cade could only barely hear it. But he *could* hear Evie. Loud. Shouting. Filling up the universe.

And then Cade's head went into overdrive, as if his thoughts were a silver pinball, banging into the sides of his brain. *Ding!* So many words, spilling out. *Ding! Ding!* Crazy hard words. *Ding! Ding! Ding!*

And the more words he heard, the more scared he felt, until finally he couldn't breathe. Panic filled his chest, his arms, until *whoosh*, a warm liquid streamed down his legs and filled his favorite sneakers, the ones with the blinking red lights, the ones that Mrs. Walker had bought for him, the ones he loved beyond compare. *Ding! Ding! Ding!* And all at once, starting from the very bottom of his gut, a furious high-pitched, "NOOOOOOOOO!!!!!" came screaming out of his mouth.

Dingdingdingdingdingding!!!!!

Cade took off, leaving a puddly trail behind him. He scrambled through the store, out the door, and all the way to the bachelor pad atop the garage. There he shot into the bathroom and slammed the door. *Wham!*

For the next several moments he paced back and

forth, two steps forward, two steps back. Forward. Back. Forward. Back. Finally he sat on the edge of the tub and panted. He sucked huge gulps of air in through his mouth, but it didn't help. The smell of urine filled his nose.

His cheeks burned. He stood up and stripped his soaking shoes and pants off and threw them into the bathtub. And suddenly he couldn't help it. Standing there in only his T-shirt, his wet clothes piled in a heap, he burst into tears. Ever since he was born, he had waited for his mom to be ready.

But as it turned out, *he* wasn't ready for her.

He turned on the shower, then stepped in, stood on top of his soggy clothes, and let the water run down his body. He couldn't tell where the water began and his tears ended. They were all mushed up together.

After a long while, he heard his father knock.

"Cade," said his dad. "It's okay, Li'l Dude. She's gone."

But knowing she was no longer there didn't help. Seeing her in person had made her real, and the reality of Evie changed everything he knew. He heard his dad open the door and stand outside the shower curtain. Cade was thankful that Paul didn't pull it open, thankful that his dad somehow knew that he needed his privacy. "When you're done, we'll make a pizza," said Paul. "Sound good?"

Cade nodded. Pizza sounded good, especially Paul's pizza. Obviously Paul couldn't hear him nodding, but he seemed to understand anyways, and his father said, "I'll be right here, kiddo." And that was followed by the best words Cade had ever heard: "I'm here for you."

Cade Curtis

And the reality of Paul is that he has been true to his word. He's never stopped being right here. It's a promise he's kept. Now Cade is sixteen, exactly the same age his father was when Paul broke that other promise, the one to Evie.

In the history of Paul, there were options. There was one he had promised Evie he would take. But he didn't. He couldn't.

And Cade knows that his father still thinks about Evie. He knows this because *he* thinks about her too. He can't help it. Because right before Cade had bolted, he heard Evie tell Paul, "If my husband ever found out, he'd take my kids away from me, and I could never live with that."

Even amid the chiming of the silver pinballs in his head, Cade heard those worst words ever. In fact, he's never stopped hearing those words. But now, when he thinks about them, he also thinks, *Fuck you, Evie. Fuck you.*

Achsah

There had been a boy for Achsah too. Between Juba and Mary Ann. He had curled up low in her belly, tugging on her back, weighing her down. Her feet outgrew her one pair of shoes, he pressed down that hard. From the start, Achsah knew something was wrong. He was too quiet, too low to the ground.

The Granny Woman confirmed it. "This baby's scared. He's not good for this world." And so he stayed inside her for too long, and each day, he grew quieter and quieter, until at last, the Granny Woman gave her a dark tea of black cohosh and slippery elm, boiled up with ginger root.

Three days. Three nights. That's what it took for the scared boy to finally make his way out. Achsah could tell straightaway that he wasn't going to stay.

As if they had heard the news, the nighthawks started screeching, their cries ringing the moon like a collar. Achsah felt her knees buckle out from under her, and the Granny Woman lifted her up and helped her back to the sodden bed, where she rolled onto her side and pressed her face into her hands.

"Night birds feel it," said the Granny Woman. "They know when sorrow's about." And soon as she said it, the Granny Woman wrapped the baby up in a plain cotton cloth and covered his small, wrinkled face, and all Achsah wanted to do was carve out a hole in the black dirt beside the river and bury herself in it.

"Take me," she cried. "Take me!"

It's the prayer of every parent. *Dear God, take me.*

But don't take her now. Now she held on to her baby girls. Juba. Mary Ann. No one was taking them from her. Especially not sour-faced Mrs. Morgan. Not if she could help it.

Run, Achsah. Run.

Find the Lady.

Cade Curtis

THE HISTORY OF ASSHATS

It was Cade's best friend, Martin Noriega, who originally dubbed Evie with the nickname "Asshat." Same for
Cade's grandparents, only plural. "Asshats."

Cade never forgot the first time he heard that
word. He and Martin were examining the myriad of
marbles in the store's collection.

It was a Saturday afternoon and Mrs. Walker had
told them they could each choose ten to keep for their
own, the number ten being symbolic for their ages at
the time. So there they were, two ten-year-old boys,
sitting on an ancient wool rug with dozens of marbles
between them.

While Cade sorted his marbles into groups by
color, Martin held a dark brown marble, with tiny gold

flecks running through it, up to the light. It was called a galaxy.

"Look," Martin said, holding the marble in front of his right eye. "If I ever lost my eye, I could use this as a replacement." It was true. The marble was exactly the same dark brown as Martin's eyes, except that Martin's eyes didn't have the gold flecks. Still, Cade thought it'd be cool to have a marble for an eye. It made him want to find a blue one, just in case.

He turned to his blue group, and just as Cade grabbed a deep blue Neptune, Martin asked, "So, is Mrs. Walker your grandmother?" It caught Cade off guard. He hadn't meant to keep his family history from Martin, but until that question, it had never come up. Mrs. Walker had always seemed like the quintessential grandmother, even though he had never called her anything except Mrs. Walker.

No one had ever told Cade *not* to share the information, had they? So while he continued to separate the blue marbles from the red ones, and the red ones from the agates, and the agates from the cat's-eyes, and so on, taking care to set each one in its respective group, making sure that he didn't misplace any, the whole History of Paul and Cade spilled out of him, including the part about Evie and her horrible words. And just as he finished, both the story and the sorting, he stopped and sat back on his heels.

Martin didn't look up. He kept right on sorting. A huge worry fell over Cade. What if the truth was too much? What if Martin stopped being his friend? *What if, what if, what if?* He stared at the marbles, and for a second, they all looked the same. Same color, same size, same everything.

He watched as Martin picked up a red marble, with white threads running through it, rolled it between his thumb and forefinger. Without taking his eyes off the marble, Martin Noriega, best friend ever, held it up to the light, pushed his black hair away from his face, and said, "Asshats." Then he stuck the marble into his pocket and continued sorting.

And five seconds later, maybe ten—who was counting?—both of them fell onto the wool rug, laughing. They laughed so hard that tears rolled down their cheeks.

Asshats. Exactly the right word.

Soleil Broussard

Soleil slips into her seat in her junior American literature class, and there is Cade-right-behind-her. They are reading *The Things They Carried*, by Tim O'Brien, a book about soldiers in the Vietnam War.

Soleil's grandfather fought and died in that war, and the book makes her think about him, even though she never met him. It's a collection of short stories, and the title story is about the things that the soldiers took with them, like one soldier carried his moccasins, another kept his girlfriend's panty hose in his backpack. "For luck" was his reason.

Thinking about things being carried reminds her of the Byrds, the way they arrived at the church with only a plastic bag containing diapers and puppy chow, and the way they left with Tyler holding on to his honey bear. When they left they were driving an old car, a 2002 PT Cruiser that had at least two hundred thousand miles, or as Dad called it, a "beater." It wasn't the most reliable car on the road. And California was a very long way from Texas.

Soleil clasps her hands on her desk. *Please look after them,* she whispers.

Her prayer is interrupted by Mrs. Franco, their teacher. She has given them an assignment: *write an essay about an object that you would carry, and why it matters to you.*

But it is not the unread book, or the unfinished essay, that Soleil concentrates on, because in this moment, in the history of Soleil, Cade-right-behind-her is drumming his fingers on his desk.

And she can't figure out what to do about any of it—the breathing, the drumming—except that she knows she wants more of him than just the fifty minutes of class, Monday through Friday. In fact, what she really wants is to dance with him. And this thought is a surprise because she has just now thought it. Just now realized that yes, dancing with him is what she wants. She knows that if they were dancing, she would fit just underneath his chin. So perfect! And thinking this new thought, she can almost feel that Cade chin resting on the top of her head, which makes her feel all buzzy, like she might actually light up from all that buzzing.

She has gone out with other boys. She has kissed other boys. She even let one boy slip his hand up her shirt while she kissed him, an action that left both her and the boy a little embarrassed, a little like *that was weird*. But those other boys weren't Cade-right-behind-her.

All the drumming and buzzing and hand up her shirt makes her feel a little stupid. So she does the one thing that she knows how to do for sure. *Dear Lord*, she prays, *don't let me be stupid*.

Amen.

Buffalo Bayou

HOUSTON

If words could sink like stones, there would be millions of them resting in the bayou's bed. As it is, they hover just above her surface, high-pitched whispers. You could mistake them for mosquitoes.

Careful.

A word here. A word there.

You never know when one might sidle into your ear and tell you something you've never heard before. It might be true. It might not be wrong. It could be a bald-faced lie.

Achsah

About that baby boy. No one ever told her where they took him. Didn't say where his body lay. But she gave him a name anyways. Named him True. Because that's what he was, and don't go telling her that True wasn't good for this world.

The truth was, the world wasn't good for him.

So he couldn't stay.

And Achsah missed him every single day.

Mrs. Trudy Walker

If it hadn't been for the price of oil, it's likely that Mrs. Walker would never have dealt in stolen angels.

Walker's Art and Antiques was a family-run outfit that she became part of, having fallen in love with and married the son of the son of the son of the original Walker family. Her true love's name was Hans. They met back in 1960, when she was seventeen and he was thirty.

One day, approximately eighty years after the original Walker first opened the shop doors, Trudy walked through those same doors, looking for a piece of jewelry with a single pearl that she could give to her mother for her birthday. Her mother had always wanted pearls, but Trudy didn't have enough money in her clutch to buy too *many* pearls, so she was hoping to find something pretty that perhaps had *one* pearl. She figured that maybe something old would be less expensive than something new.

Thus, Walker's Art and Antiques. Instead of a pearl, she found her oyster. Hans.

Straightaway, they got married and went to Cuba. "That was before the embargo," she told Cade and Paul. "Cuba! Can you imagine it?"

Theirs was a marriage of such tenderness and joy. "I loved every minute of our life together," she told them. And bit by bit, she told them about the many adventures in living that she and Hans had shared. The only sadness was their inability to have a baby.

"We tried," she'd said. "But eventually we decided to enjoy what we had, not what we didn't." And she almost always followed this up by looking straight at Cade and declaring, "And then here you come! Right out of the blue!" She would pause. "It's almost as if you and your daddy knew that there was an open space here for you, like you were the baby who was meant to be here."

And of course, that was followed by "Hans would have loved you!" She had said it so often that Cade was fairly certain that Hans *would* have loved him. And from what he had heard about Hans, Cade knew he would have loved him right back.

Sadly Hans died way before his time. He was only fifty years old, a young age for a seemingly healthy man.

"It was such a shock," said Mrs. Walker. "I thought I'd never get over it." And that was always followed by "we always wanted to go back to Cuba."

The other person who couldn't seem to get over it was Hans's mother, Mrs. Walker the Elder. She was still alive when Hans passed, and she took it so hard that after her son was buried at the old Mother River Cemetery, she ordered a special monument for his grave, a carved angel made of Italian marble, beautiful Carrara marble, the finest in the world. It was a pale shade of gray and had a vein of dark black swirling through it. She'd never seen anything so beautiful. She had it installed at the head of Hans's grave.

Trudy loved the angel. She loved her mother-in-law, too. Both women were glad to have each other, and also glad to have the angel to keep the departed Hans from being lonely in his solitary grave.

Only a couple of years later, the elder Mrs. Walker passed. But our Mrs. Walker managed to keep the art and antiques store running. And she was a discerning businesswoman, maintaining the shop as a cornerstone of the commercial side of the neighborhood.

The thing about an art and antiques store, especially one that has been in the same place for a long time, is that it serves as a resource. Not every antique is priceless. So young folks just starting out can sometimes find just the right old chair for the corner of their new living room, one that isn't too expensive, but has a sheen of living on it. A cozy spot to rest.

On the other end of life, relatives of the departed can find a repository, a place to take items that no one in the family needs or wants, but that they can't bear to throw away. If you've ever bought a whimsical set of salt and pepper shakers from an antique store, maybe in the shape of Dutch windmills, they've likely come from either the estate sale of the newly deceased or from some family member just dropping them off in hopes that they will eventually find a new table to sit upon.

And then there are the wealthier patrons who drop in from time to time to see if there is anything of value to possess, like a set of French crystal champagne glasses for their daughter's wedding, or a carved cherrywood buffet from Pennsylvania to set in the foyer of their new mansion. These last are the bread and butter of the antique business. No one, after all, can survive by selling salt and pepper shakers in the shape of Dutch windmills.

That was the way the Walker family had always seen it. Mrs. Walker saw it that way too.

However, running a business alone is not an easy undertaking, especially in Houston. With all its shiny buildings and its Space Center and its noted universities and medical research facilities, Houston is very dependent upon the oil industry. When oil prices are high, Houstonians spend. When oil prices take a dive, things like French champagne glasses and cherrywood buffets turn out to be not so essential. Retail businesses, even old established ones, tend to suffer. Which is what happened in 1985.

Mrs. Walker did everything. She lowered prices. She held big sales. She kept the air-conditioning set at seventy-six degrees, which is not very helpful in hot, humid Houston. Nevertheless, it was clear to everyone, including her accountant, that Walker's Art and Antiques was knee-deep in financial troubles. After a hundred years plus some, it was on the brink of closing its doors.

And then a miracle happened. Well, Mrs. Walker called it a miracle. A well-dressed man wearing a pair of Tony Lama ostrich-skin cowboy boots, boots that cost in the range of five hundred dollars, walked through those almost-closing doors and strolled up and down the aisles. Of course, Mrs. Walker hoped there was something in the store that he wanted. She stood at the counter, watching his every move. Finally he walked up to her and asked, in a voice almost too quiet to hear, "Do you have any carved angels?"

Sadly she didn't. But he gave her his phone number and said, "If you come across any, let me know. I have some clients who are collecting them." Then he said the magic words, "They'll pay top dollar."

It took Mrs. Walker about thirty whole seconds to lock the doors of the shop, climb into her old Oldsmobile Rocket 88, jet down the road to the Mother River Cemetery, walk up to Hans's grave, and say, "Honey, I'm so sorry, but I've got to put this angel to work for us." So she called the church that ran the cemetery and let them know that she was removing the angel from her husband's grave. When the woman on the other end of the line said something like "Isn't that like stealing from the dead?" Mrs. Walker didn't miss a beat. She said, "Nope, more like giving to the living."

She knew that Hans would agree, and she didn't consult with her mother-in-law, Mrs. Walker the Elder, who was buried two graves over, next to Hans's father.

No need to anger the dearly departed, she figured, when what she needed was this angel.

And the angel, carved from the finest Italian marble, provided.

In the thirty-odd years since the Cowboy walked through those doors, other angels have done their part as well, especially when the price of oil drops below, say, fifty-five dollars per barrel, give or take a dollar or two.

The Angels

Ever since that first angel, Mrs. Walker has given each one a title, depending upon its saving grace.

There was the Angel of the Leaking Roof. Unlike Hans's marble angel, she was small and unassuming. "But she got the job done nonetheless," says Mrs. Walker.

Later came the Angel of the Replaced Truck, after the old truck completely wore out.

There were two named for Texas Children's Hospital. Cade spent almost a week there with pneumonia. He was only four years old. "Thought we were going to lose you, Li'l Dude," said Paul. Cade doesn't remember the hospital or the angel. But he is told that it took both of the angels to settle the bill, and that was after the hospital forgave part of it.

There was a small angel named Crown, which was for Mrs. Walker's broken tooth.

And another was named for a break-in that happened one Sunday afternoon while they were out for a picnic. She was called Silver, for the several sets of silver that were taken.

There was, among these angels, one that brought in more cash than anyone anticipated, so Mrs. Walker used the extra funds to make a donation to the Sisters of Mercy. "There's no reason to take more than is needed," she said.

Only a year ago, there was the Angel of the Hurricane, which helped to replace the shop's front glass that blew out with the winds.

Cade isn't sure what the weeping angel is for. Mrs. Walker hasn't said, and neither has Paul. All he knows is that she is different from all the rest.

Beloved Mother, Daughter, Wife.

Even so, she is not the statue he wishes they could have found.

Zorra

Can't someone find an angel for a small, rain-soaked ocelot?

Her bloated belly hangs low, pulling the skin tight along her bony spine. Her legs ache from being so cramped. And all around her are the voices of her fellow captives. She hears their cries. Zorra cries too, until her throat is so swollen she can't cry at all.

At last, she lays down on the floor of her wooden cage and closes her eyes. The steady rain slips through the cracks above and drips onto her face.

Zorra, Zorra.

Sleep through the night.

Sleep through the day.

Sleep through the driving rain.

Soleil Broussard

Soleil walks up the front steps of church; the mist in the air creates tiny rainbows in the lights on either side of the doors. It's Wednesday night. Bible study. She hesitates, and when she does, the rain picks up again, and the slender prisms dissolve. She tucks her chin and steps inside.

She pauses at the nursery. The room is full of babies and toddlers. She searches for the familiar presence of Tyler. Of course, he's not there.

She hurries to the high school room. In the middle is a circle of old sofas with a large round coffee table in the center, its edges worn smooth from years and years of shoes resting on them. She squeezes in between Channing and Grapes, their knees bump against one another's.

Lenny, the youth minister, calls them together and offers up a prayer of greeting.

After the amens, Lenny announces: "Okay, campers!" For some reason, Lenny calls the group "campers." Soleil has no idea why, and she suspects that Lenny doesn't either.

He continues: "Remember, this Sunday night— yes, that's this weekend—we'll be having our fall pizza party."

That's right! Soleil had forgotten. Last year the pizza party was canceled because of the hurricane. But thankfully, despite the copious amounts of current rain, there was no hurricane brewing up in the Gulf of Mexico. So, why not a pizza party?

"Look around," Lenny says. "We have plenty of room here, right?" Soleil nods, yes, there is plenty of room.

"Isn't welcoming people what Jesus would have done?" asks Lenny. "No matter who they are, or where they're from, or what their story is?" He pauses. "Isn't that *ultimately* what love is all about?"

Ultimately?

"And hey," Lenny says. "Look at this." To everyone's surprise, Lenny holds up a vintage—we're talking 70s era—disco ball. And while he holds it, he says, "We can add dancing to the menu."

In a split second, Soleil's heart begins to race.

"Sunday night, bring a friend." Then Lenny adds something about ice cream and root beer to go with the pizza, and he passes out a stack of flyers. They're copied on bright purple paper, a color that feels both cheerful and serious. Soleil takes one. *Just one.* She tucks it inside her jacket pocket.

Here was a way to ask Cade out. She didn't even have to talk to him; she could just hand him the flyer, as if she was handing them out to everyone, so it wouldn't seem personal, not at all like asking him out for coffee or to go to a movie or something.

She checks the purple flyer in her pocket. The top of her head buzzes.

The next morning she grabs her backpack and heads out the kitchen door, just in time to catch the bus to school. Once there, the day stretches like a lazy cat. It's as if time has slowed in some exponential way, every minute taking an hour, until finally, *finally*, the bell rings, and she has landed in the desk in front of Cade-right-behind-her, without even touching the ground between her last class and this one.

Maybe, she thinks. *Maybemaybemaybe* . . .

She hesitates. A sinking feeling comes over her. What if he says *no*? What if he already has a girlfriend?

Or a boyfriend? What if he's not into the Bible? Or Jesus? Or God, even? She really doesn't know a single thing about him, other than he drums on his desk and smells good.

But then she hears Lenny's voice in her head, *room to spare. Yes*, she thinks. She has room to spare. She pushes the what-ifs aside, takes a deep breath, and reaches into her pack for the purple flyer, but then it hits her: she has left it in her jacket pocket, which is in her locker. Now what? *Is this a sign?* she wonders. She considers abandoning her plan.

It is stupid anyway, she thinks.

But then she remembers, *love, ultimately, dancing.*

She can do this. She can take a big, fat chance.

Quickly she pulls a piece of paper out of her notebook and writes: *Would you like to know about Ultimate Love?* And before she has time to talk herself out of it, she folds it and hands it to him.

In the very next second she realizes what she has done. *Why?* Why has she written *those words?* She starts to snatch the note away, but it's too late. Cade has already unfolded it.

She can't watch, so she turns around and faces the front of the classroom. Could she tell you where she was in space and time? Could she say that there were any other human beings in the entire room aside from herself and Cade?

No, we can say with certainty. It was just Soleil and Cade and a note about Ultimate Love. And if anyone ever wished they could hitch a ride to California in an old beater, her name would be Soleil.

Cade Curtis

Say what?

Ultimate Love?

Fortunately Soleil has her back to him. He looks around to see if anyone else in the classroom has noticed the transaction. He glances at Martin, who is digging into his backpack for something. For sure, if Martin had seen it happen, he wouldn't be digging into his backpack.

In fact, it seems like all the other kids are in their own worlds too, as if he (Cade Curtis) and she (Soleil Broussard) are the only two people in the room. He quickly stuffs the note into his back pocket.

From the front of the classroom, Mrs. Franco begins to expound upon the events of the coming weeks. They are nearing the end of the grading period, and Cade tries to catch a few of the statements coming out of her mouth, fragments of speech about getting enough sleep and not wasting one's time playing Xbox. Mrs. Franco seems to hate Xbox. "They turn smart people into idiots," she claims. Cade wouldn't know. He doesn't really play Xbox. He is, however, great at pinball. Turns out, Walker's Art and Antiques—thanks to his dad—has become a repository for antique pinball machines, and Cade is extremely adept at playing them, especially one called the Phoenix, a circa 1978 vintage edition, made by Williams Electronics.

Martin too. The two of them have played untold games of post-school pinball on it. If they ever sell the Phoenix, Cade and Martin will probably have to hold a funeral.

Cade's thoughts are interrupted by Mrs. Franco. "Stand up, people," she says. "Let's have a seventh-inning stretch." Which was something Mrs. Franco believed in. "Too much sitting is almost as bad for your brains as Xbox," she says.

Cade pushes himself out of his desk. Should he say something to Soleil? What is he supposed to say? Maybe the note is a joke? Then again, Soleil has never seemed like the joking kind. But how would he know?

So many questions make him feel off-balance, and he has to grab his desk to right himself.

Mrs. Franco's mouth keeps moving. He sort of comprehends that she is saying something about the personal essay they are supposed to write. He should make note, he thinks, except there is no registering exactly what should be noted . . . except *the note*, which he is noting like crazy.

Just in time, the bell rings. Without waiting for Soleil to turn around, he scoops his books up into his arms and hurries through the door of the classroom.

Ultimate Love?

He's not naive. Even though he's not associated with any organized religion, he is fairly certain that the term *Ultimate Love* has something to do with Jesus.

Until minutes ago, Cade didn't think that Soleil even knew he existed. And yet she has handed him a note that is now pressing into his back pocket, as warm as toast.

Would you like to know about Ultimate Love?

And just like that, he swings from being somewhat *puzzled* to madly *confused*. The scratch just underneath his eyebrow suddenly feels like it's ablaze. In fact, his whole body feels ablaze, like if someone lit a match, he'd burst into flames.

The Six Steps

Cade and Paul and Mrs. Walker didn't spend Sunday mornings in church, but that didn't mean they didn't spend them in a consecrated place. In fact, on those Sundays when the weather permitted, Mrs. Walker packed a picnic lunch and they piled into her ancient Oldsmobile, which Paul managed to keep running—*on a wing and a prayer*, he liked to say—and they all drove to whatever cemetery was next on their list of possible "angel sanctuaries," the term Mrs. Walker applied to them.

Paul has become something of an expert in finding small, abandoned graveyards, often with only a handful of plots, by using Google Earth. He can even spot an angel this way. But in order to clearly see them, it helps to visit in the daytime.

SIDE NOTE: Houston is one of the most diverse cities in the world. But when it comes to interring human remains, the cemeteries have been segregated since before Texas was even a state. So it would be weird for them to be seen prowling around in a traditionally Hispanic or African American cemetery, or any other cemetery that wasn't for dead white folks. The exceptions are the small, off-the-beaten-path cemeteries that lie largely forgotten, slouching beneath ancient trees and hidden from the road, like the one that held the weeping angel. So Cade and Paul and Mrs. Walker, in all their whiteness, don't need to worry about being out of place in those. No one was sure what color skin the beloved wife, mother, daughter wore in her lifetime, or what race her graveyard neighbors were either. What's certain is that her bones were the same color as every bone ever interred, before or since.

Some have said that grave robbing is the second-oldest profession, having begun pretty much as soon as humans started burying their dead. And for many, there's no dishonor in doing so. Take for example Howard Carter and Lord Carnarvon, the Brits who unsealed King Tutankhamun's tomb in Egypt. They were hailed as great explorers, but in reality, what they did was lift a myriad of objects, treasures that had been kept with the boy king's mummified body for more than three thousand years. Most of them have been safely returned to Luxor, but not before being exhibited in museums around the world.

Mrs. Walker had loved Hans like crazy, and she was fairly certain that when they met back up in the Great Beyond, he wouldn't care one whit about her decision to sell his marble angel. "In fact," she said, "I think he'd be proud of me for being so resourceful." After all, hadn't she saved the family company, the same company that had been in constant business through two world wars, a couple of smaller wars that were no less damaging, the Great Depression, and any number of calamities and incidences, none of which were within the family's direct control? Why, yes, she had.

"Besides," she said as they strolled through the hallowed grounds, "it's got to get old, staring at the exact same spot," as if she felt sorry for the angels, stuck as they were for time eternal in one never-changing place. Then she would mumble something about re-homing, which always made Cade think of homing pigeons, and that made him wonder if the angels might return someday.

As if she were reading his thoughts, Mrs. Walker said, "It could happen."

It seems that Sunday mornings are popular times to visit the resting places of loved ones, even off the grid, near abandoned ones, so our angel hunters could explore the various gravesites and appear to be just another bereaved family, come to pay their respects.

The threesome had a six-step operation:

STEP 1: Casually stroll through the rows of graves until they found one with an angel. Once located, figure out what the angel was made of. If it was concrete, then there was no reason to take it, because in all likelihood it was simply an angel that had been poured into a mold, and could be bought on eBay. Look instead for angels that were carved out of marble or granite, or even limestone. Those were the ones that mattered and were more likely to be one of a kind, or at least a limited edition.

STEP 2: Measure. Be sure that the angel was not more than about four feet tall. Otherwise, it would be too heavy for two people—Paul and Cade—to lift. A four-foot-tall marble angel weighed about two hundred pounds, maybe a bit more, depending upon its girth. Any bigger, and loading it into the back of the pickup would be a struggle. (As unlikely as it seems, before Cade grew big enough to assist Paul, it was Mrs. Walker herself who had helped with the lifting. Years of shoving furniture around the shop had made her stronger than she appeared.)

STEP 3: Take note of the dates carved into the head-stone. If the deceased had been there for more than twenty or thirty years, it was highly unlikely that any-one in the family had visited the grave recently. This meant that once Paul and Cade liberated the angel, it would probably take a while before anyone noticed that it was missing. Along these lines, look for flowers or other trinkets that might have been left at the feet of the angel. If there were none, that was as good as a go.

STEP 4: The hard step. Return to make the steal. Wait for night, usually in the hours between midnight and dawn, when Houston's reliable fog rolled in. The older the angel, the easier it was to steal. Usually all Paul had to do was tap around the base of it with a chisel to get it to let go of its pedestal. Old grout was much softer than new grout. A few taps, and it turned to powder. The newer ones were more difficult because they were often bolted in place. The goal was always to get it into the back of the truck, where they had an old mattress for padding, without chipping it.

STEP 5: Call the Cowboy.

Once the first five steps were completed, the angel flew away to his or her new home, preferably someplace far from Houston.

STEP 6: Don't forget that an angel must only be taken after every other option was exhausted, and it was clear that *they* needed their services more than the dead.

CARDINAL RULE: Never take a baby angel, even though they're small and easy to carry.

Zorra

Houston is the fourth-largest city in the United States. Settled in 1837, over the years the city has gobbled up most of the wild spaces. Before that, however, before the city grew so large, when magnolia forests grew so thick the air teemed with the scent of their enormous flowers, there were ocelots. And passenger pigeons. And even bears. There were ivory-billed woodpeckers and red wolves and panthers and buffalo.

No longer.

However, if you rambled along the Buffalo Bayou, coursing through the very heart of the city, you'd notice that there are patches of wildness, thick brushy areas along its banks that are too dense to wander through. Most people avoid these wild, wet acres, filled with stinging vines and poisonous snakes.

Or so it would seem. But make no mistake, there are secret coves inside this wild. In fact, there is one such cover that has been cleared only enough to set a row of makeshift wooden cages along the banks, with only small wire windows in the doors, all painted green and brown so they are impossible to see. And one of those cages holds a small, starving ocelot. She is worth upward of twenty thousand dollars, maybe more to the right person. There are those who would pay to have a pet as exotic as an ocelot; pay a lot. They might pay just as much for her beautiful spotted coat. Either way, she's the most valuable creature the Caretaker's caught.

But over the past few days, the rain has kept him from feeding her. The bayou, normally so serene and quiet, is swollen and hard to navigate. Access has been difficult. Zorra is sleeping the sleep of the hungry.

If she could see the bayou through the wires of the door, she might notice the wisps of fog hovering over the water. They come and go, rise up and down above the bayou's surface, keep watch.

Zorra, motionless in her awful pen. She waits until at last the morning arrives with a clear blue sky, through the snuffling of the creatures nearby, waits for the now-familiar screech of the awful bird, waits like a statue, so still, until at last the air becomes as motionless as she does. Finally she stands on her shaking legs, stretches her sore body. She lifts her nose to the quiet air.

She smells him first. He reeks of something burnt. Then she hears him, the high-pitched sound he makes, like a bird, but not any bird she knows. There are no footsteps, only the soft sound of oars in the water. The river has risen so high the Caretaker can only get into this cove by boat.

Zorra pushes herself as hard as she can toward the back of the cage. As he opens the door, the blast of light that streams in momentarily blinds her. She blinks, and wraps her tail tight around her body. Her fur is on end. From the back of her swollen throat, she sends out a low, warning growl.

The Caretaker, his head even with the door, blows in her face and jabs at her sides with the wooden paddle, pressing into her ribs so that she can't bolt through the door. She swats at the oar, but he only laughs and presses the paddle harder. She cries out. But the Caretaker just blows in her face again. She recoils from his burnt breath and flattens her ears.

Then he quickly reaches into the cage and pulls out

the metal bowl and the paddle and locks the door. In a moment, he reopens it and sets the bowl back in her pen, filled at last with the rancid food.

Food.

Zorra's body trembles from the hunger that gnaws at her. She resists the urge to pounce on it. Instead, she waits until the Caretaker locks the door again. Waits until she can't smell his smoky breath or hear his bird-like whistle. Waits until at last she can't wait anymore.

Food.

It isn't warm. It isn't solid. There are no bones or skin to chew on. It isn't the true food of an ocelot, even though it takes away the horrible ache of hunger.

And just outside her cage, rising atop the water, the foggy spirits call her name, remind her who she is: *Zorra, Zorra. Zorra.* And once again, the rain begins to fall.

Buffalo Bayou

HOUSTON

A promise here. A promise there. The bayou has heard
them all.

> Girl: *Promise you'll drop him off.*
>
> Boy: *I will.*
>
> Girl: *They won't ask questions. It's the law;*
>   *they won't ask.*
>
> Boy: *I'll drop him off.*
>
> Girl: *If they ask his name . . .*
>
> Boy: *Moses. I'll tell them Baby Moses.*
>
> Girl: *It's the law.*
>
> Boy: *I promise.*

One promise: broken.
One baby: kept.

James Morgan

History turns on battles lost and battles won. Mexico lost the war, lost Texas at San Jacinto, in a battle that lasted all of twenty minutes. Santa Anna returned to Mexico in disgrace. Even the Texans could hardly believe that their ragtag army, under the leadership of Sam Houston, had beaten back the highly trained troops of the Mexican general, especially after the devastation at the Alamo.

Mexico lost and Texas became its own country, and thanks to that twenty minutes on the battlefield, only twenty minutes of warfare, the "peculiar institution" was granted a reprieve. No more interference from Mexico, where slavery was declared illegal. Now that Texas was free of Mexico and its emancipation law, thousands of

Negro slaves could be imported into the new republic.

In 1836, Texas had an estimated slave population of five thousand. The Texas Constitution legalized and preserved slavery. And before it joined the United States in 1846, ten years later, the Republic was home to at least thirty thousand enslaved people.

In 1845, there was one James Morgan, plantation owner, veteran of the Texian Army, friend of the Captain, and liege of a brand-new home in the brand-new town of Houston, and also several hundred acres near the mouth of the Brazos River. He needed his slaves.

"Cane doesn't chop itself," said Morgan. "Cotton doesn't git itself to the gin all by its lonesome." He spat on the ground and rubbed his boot heel in it. He'd been robbed! The girls, Mary Ann and Juba, had been promised to him, willed to his wife, but they had hied away before the Captain's body was even cold.

Never mind that they were taken by their mother. They weren't hers to take, and Morgan had the papers to prove it. He stood at the foot of the Captain's grave and made a promise. "Achsah," he said under his breath. "You won't get away with this. If I have to travel a thousand miles, I'll find you. Those girls are mine."

And he set a slave hunter on her trail, one who had a reputation for finding runaways.

Juba and Mary Ann. Five and three years old. His until they turned twenty-one.

His.

Achsah had her papers. She could have been a free woman. But she was a criminal now. For stealing her very own daughters.

Morgan kicked the loose dirt on his old friend's freshly dug grave. "I'll find her," he promised. "Make no bones about it."

Soleil Broussard

When Soleil's ancestors walked through the hip-deep water that poured over the banks of the Mississippi, her great-great uncle Armand held the accordion over his head until he couldn't anymore. He then strapped it to a mule. But the water kept on rising.

Listen, Soleil, the accordion holds that mule's bray.

The rain keeps falling. Soleil stands in the middle of her room and sways from side to side. She takes a step to the left and back. She twirls and twirls and twirls.

> "Jolie blonde, tu croyais il y avait just toi,
> Il y a pas just toi dans le pays pour moi
>   aimer.

Je peux trouver just une autre jolie blonde,
Bon Dieu sait, moi, j'ai un tas."

Soleil closes her eyes, and she can imagine her great-great uncles and aunts, her great-great grand-père and grand-mère. And all that water. Water sliding over the back of the mule, water grabbing their ankles and toes. She hears the persistent rain falling on the roof.

Water, she wonders, does it make you a little crazy?

Does Cade think she's crazy? Because she feels just a wee bit crazy right now. She had started to run after him right after class, but he had slipped away so fast she couldn't find him. Then she looked for him after school. Again, no luck.

She would send him a text if she had his number. She doesn't. She would fire off an e-mail, too. But does she have his address? Nope. She doesn't even know where he lives, and even if she did, wouldn't it be crazy to just show up on his doorstep?

"And where on the planet are the Byrds?!" she asks nobody.

Soleil flops onto her bed, belly-first. Lying there, her face in her pillow, she fully understands why people tear their hair out: because the world keeps going and there is absolutely nothing you can do to go back and fix it.

Cade Curtis

Ultimate Love. Walker's Art and Antiques Store always had on hand a variety of paintings of Jesus. Martin called them all "white Jesus," because they mostly were. Cade has seen plenty of statues of Jesus too. Cemeteries, especially Catholic cemeteries, tend to host them.

They all look the same. Long hair, head tilted, palms facing up. Serene. So serene. Cade has often wondered whether Jesus really looked like that. He seriously doubted it. Especially the serene part.

He and Paul have never stolen a statue of Jesus. It's bad enough, he thinks, that they steal angels, let alone the son of God.

Soleil Broussard

So, thanks to a long night of sleeplessness, Soleil came up with a plan. Cade was already seated when she arrived at their classroom, and she waited a full minute before she walked through the door.

The plan, she said to herself. She had a plan. The lack of sleep was making her a little punchy. But also, she thought, it was making her a little brave. What did she have to lose?

She turned around and before she could change her mind, she whispered, "Meet me after school at the flagpole." Then, without letting him answer, she turned her back to him.

That seemed like a thousand years ago. At last, the final bell rings, and she heads to the courtyard.

For the first time in several days, there's a weak sun shining through the clouds, and the rain has paused. It feels like a typical, warm Houston fall afternoon. It's also typically muggy. As soon as she walks out of the air-conditioned building, she feels a thin layer of sweat condense on her arms.

She paces around the flagpole and listens as the chain flaps against the metal. She looks up. There is the American flag, and right underneath it, the Lone Star flag of Texas, both of them flagging in the heat. She half smiles at her own pun.

Other kids race past her, getting on buses or walking out to the parking lot. Some of them wave. "Hey, Soleil," they say. She's so nervous all she can do is nod back.

The newly present sun beats down on her head; she reaches behind and wraps her hair in her hand and twists it away from her neck, an action that normally makes her feel a bit cooler, but not today. Where is he? She leans back against the flagpole and resists the temptation to slide down and just sit there, a human puddle at its base.

She closes her eyes and starts to pray, but she doesn't get past "O Lord," before she feels a tapping on her shoulder. There he is.

For a moment she can't say anything, like she is paralyzed, and she can feel embarrassment blazing across her cheeks. But then . . . "Here," she says, handing him the flyer that Lenny made.

He looks at it. Frowns. Turns the paper over to the blank side and then back to the printed side. While she's watching, she notices a thin scratch just underneath his eyebrow. She resists the temptation to reach up and rub it, when—

"A church party?"

"Yeah," she says, followed by, "It's fun?" She realizes she has said that last part with a rise in her voice, like a question, as if she's trying to convince herself as much as Cade. And she isn't entirely sure that *fun* is the right word for it.

So, of course, she blurts out, "Pizza!"

Cade's face turns from curious to confused. Quickly she adds, "Yes! There'll be pizza and stuff." And with that, really, what can she do but stand there, sweat pouring down her back and resting in a pond at the bottom of her spine?

She wants to tell him everything she knows about the Church on the Bayou, about how it's been in Houston for more than a century, since almost the start of Houston itself, about how it's not like most churches, that there used to be a family of Byrds, who have gone to California, taking Tyler with them, and there is a handbell choir too, and how there will be dancing, a disco ball, room to spare.

And how she knows that she will fit just beneath his chin. Especially that.

But her mouth is suddenly full of cotton, like she might strangle.

So instead, there is a long second of silence. Maybe the longest, most silent second ever recorded on terra firma. Soleil holds her breath and sweats some more. Finally she watches as he reaches into his back pocket, pulls out her first note to him, and wraps the flyer around it, kind of like a burrito. "I'll think about it," he says.

Then he rocks forward on his toes, almost as if he is leaning in to whisper something. She leans forward too, but then he quickly rocks back on his heels. And before she can say anything else, he turns around and walks away.

Soleil feels her cheeks blazing.

Pizza?!

Pizza?

Would Cade even consider coming on Sunday? Why would he? *Pizza?* She tugs on the tiny gold cross.

"Dear Lord," she prays, but she has no idea what to

put in the middle, and she is a long way from "Amen."

The fastest heart in the world is that of a blue-throated hummingbird, whose heart rate has been measured at more than twelve hundred beats per minute.

Right then, Soleil's heart is a hummingbird.

Pizza

LITTLE-KNOWN FACT: Over the years Cade and Paul have learned to perfect what Mrs. Walker calls "the Art of Pizza."

Once a week, usually on Fridays, but not always, they stand side by side in Mrs. Walker's kitchen and create a weekly *master pizza*. From time to time they blow it, like the night Paul insisted on using kale— "Hey, it tasted good in chili."

But more often than not, their pizzas are delicious. And in the world of Mrs. Walker, Paul, and Cade—and also Martin—you could call them famous.

Achsah

Achsah was born a slave, birthed on a mat woven from reeds in a tiny cabin next to a field, somewhere along the Mississippi River, near Alexandria, Louisiana. Been a slave her entire eighteen years.

When she left that morning that the Captain died, her two young daughters right beside her, she made sure to run to the river. Even though she knew that there were snakes and alligators hidden in its slow-moving currents, she had to take that risk. In one hand she held the iron kettle, packed with their few provisions. With the other she held on to Juba, who in turn held on to Mary Ann. Unlike the Mississippi that she had grown up on, this river was narrow, and according to the Captain, not that deep. That was small consolation to

Achsah, who couldn't swim, nor could her girls.

Thankfully the banks were largely hidden by thick forest and undergrowth. A person could slip into that brush and disappear, which was what Achsah did. But she knew that no matter how thick the brush, a good dog would be able to track her, and she was sure that as soon as Morgan discovered her gone, he would set a whole pack after them.

She had seen what dogs could do to a body, and she couldn't let that happen to her girls. She pulled them down to the water's edge, where they stepped into the muddy river. It tugged at the hems of their dresses, dragged at them. Still, they waded in, until the water came to Juba's waist and Mary Ann's chest. Fear ran across her younger daughter's face, and Achsah realized her mistake. She needed to move Mary Ann to the middle so that Juba, who was a head taller than her little sister, could help keep her above the surface.

"There," she whispered. The fear on Mary Ann's face eased a tiny bit. "Be brave," she said to both of them. And while she pulled them forward, Achsah prayed that there were no sinkholes, no snakes, no quicksand beneath their feet.

"Snakes aren't as mean as the dogs," she told her girls. "They're scared of us. Not like the dogs, who ain't."

And then she added, "Mother River, help us," as she tugged on Mary Ann's hand, all the while holding the kettle up like she might hold a lantern.

They pushed through the shallow water, the sun creeping up too fast, and they stayed as near to the shore as they could, to take advantage of the vines that swung down from the overhanging branches of the willow trees like a curtain. But not so close that a hound could detect their presence. Still, Achsah knew that water wasn't a deterrent for a bloodhound. It might confuse it, but not for long.

As much as she longed for the morning to stop coming at them, the sun crept higher. With the gathering light, Achsah knew they needed to get out of the water and into the woods. Otherwise someone might spot them from the other bank. Ever since Houston had been established, more and more boats were arriving, bringing their wares in and trading them for goods to ship out. In only a few short years, the wharves of the new city had teemed with barges loaded down with goods, and steamboats full of new arrivals. And now, with talk of Texas joining the Union, there were more arrivals all the time.

Some of the boats, she knew, carried passengers like her, Negro slaves. Coming in to chop sugarcane and work the cotton fields, coming in to serve masters who would treasure them, night after night, and then trick them. Some might be arriving from the Forks of the Road Slave Market, just like she had. And for a second, she thought about that thin boy she had been chained to. The carving in her pocket bumped against her leg. Didn't even know his name. And then she realized it didn't matter. She had missed him anyways. All these six years later, she had missed him.

She trudged through the water. She couldn't think about him now. She had to find a place along the banks that would shelter them until dark. She looked over her shoulder at her two girls, their mouths clamped shut so as not to make a sound.

She wished she had prepared them better, but then again, she hadn't expected to be tricked. The Captain didn't tell her that he was giving guardianship of the girls to Mrs. Morgan until days before he died.

Besides, no amount of preparation could take away the silted water that tugged at their skirts and the thick mud that sucked at their feet. Achsah knew that. She also knew that she was a strong woman. *Big for my age,* she thought. And for once, she was glad of it.

The Marble Carver

He wasn't the first to carve a figure out of the rose-pink marble that dwelt just underneath the topsoil near the north shore of the Etowah River in Georgia. A thousand years earlier, maybe longer, there had been others who discerned how to take a slender thumb-size chunk of the glittery material and then use a rough stone to smooth and shape it into tiny animals and humans.

Each generation, there was an artisan, or two or four, who saw shapes inside the marble and, using the tools at hand, set them loose from the stone.

Anyone walking through those Georgia hills could stumble over a carved figure, dropped there by its owner and not found for centuries, until at last it's dug up by a rabbit or washed out by the rain, making its way to the surface again, making its way to the sun.

Marble loves the sun, loves the way it warms its surface and bounces light back into the sky. It might stay underground for a million years, sleeping there, until at last an earthquake pushes it up through the topsoil. Or, more likely, a digger comes along and uncovers it. Maybe that digger will use its nails or claws, or a shovel or a pick. Maybe a steam shovel. Maybe a drill. Doesn't matter. After so many thousands of years of being buried, the marble is happy to greet the sun again.

There was a long line of carvers—Etowah, Cherokee, Creek—who mined the marble of the Long Swamp Valley in Georgia. But then came the forced removal, those terrible years when the Creek and Cherokee, the Seminole, the Choctaw, the Chickasaw, all were driven out of their lands where they had lived for generations, raised their babies, built their homes, buried their dead.

Say it, *removal.* Such a soft word, no hard consonants to bump against your teeth. How can it even stand for thousands of people who were driven out, taking with them only what they could carry? They pulled their children behind them, among them a tall, thin boy whose fingers loved the cool touch of the stone. This boy of a Cherokee father and a Gullah mother. He saw himself in the veins of the marble, a shot of black streaming through the middle, a deep vein of brown running through a field of dusky pink. He understood what the marble had to offer, knew that once carved, if he polished it with a sand-filled cloth soaked with river water, it would soon begin to glow.

Then came the troops, sent by Martin Van Buren.

It was just before the harvest; the soldiers rounded up his family, his kin, his neighbors—forced them from their homes, made to leave in the middle of meals, food still on the table, the crops in fields, left the horses hitched to their plows. Forced everyone into stockades with little to eat, little for shelter, crammed together beneath the autumn skies, waiting and waiting and waiting, growing thinner, weaker, until they were lined up and driven onto the trail.

More troops. Never mind that it was soon winter, that the freezing air burned their lungs, that the frozen ground ate the soles off their feet and chewed their calves, then their knees and upward until there was nothing left but bones. Walking bones.

And those bones took one frozen step after another for hundreds of miles. From the Georgia marble fields west to Indian Territory. Many grew sick, too weak to move. Some died lying down, some died standing up, some died in the midst of taking a step.

Once in Indian Territory, the survivors would build and begin anew. But still, so much was lost, including somewhere along the way, maybe in the deep pine forest of southern Tennessee, a tall, thin boy whose parents died along the trail, one after the other, one day apart. With no one watching, no one paying attention, he faded into the trees, steps soft as a panther, heart pounding. But the forest offered little refuge. If he hadn't looked so much like his black Gullah mother, and more like his Cherokee father with his paler skin and straighter hair, he might have stayed there, in those trees.

Instead, he was nabbed in broad daylight by a band of marauders and carried first to Alexandria, then forced to march again, this time to Natchez, to the Forks of the Road Slave Market, chained to a girl his very own age, and every now and again, despite his raw, blistered feet and the hunger that gnawed at his insides, he'd managed to smile at her. He didn't care if she smiled back or not.

Achsah was her name. "Achsah," she told him. He never told her his. Instead, he gave her his only possession, the figure he'd carved from the rose-pink marble of his Georgian hills, a tiny figure of a woman, its mouth forming an O, as if it was surprised.

It was all he had.

Mother River Church of God's Blessings

If a church stays in one location for long enough, sooner or later it's likely to need a place for its departed brethren and sistren to rest in peace. So, not too long after the new chapel was constructed, the congregation at Mother River Church of God's Blessings set aside a couple of acres of land to provide graves for its members.

The Reverend Phillips consecrated it on Easter Sunday morning, Easter seeming like the perfect day to ask for God's blessing for land that would be the final sleeping places of his congregants. On that day, the church members gathered for services outdoors. The reverend had them all stand in a circle and hold hands; all the white folks, that is. The Negroes stood behind the circle, including Major Bay, their heads lowered.

Then the reverend called on the Lord to be generous with His tears so that the ground would not be too hard; and to shine His radiance on the green grass so that the ground would not be too soft. He asked Jesus to shower them all with love and peace. The whole thing took a little over two hours, by which time everyone was sick of holding hands.

At last the ladies of the church laid out an Easter dinner for everyone to enjoy. They set it on a long table that Major Bay had built just for the occasion, right between a pair of tall cypress trees. Ham, beans, corn pudding, rice cakes, boiled crabs, steamed fish, sweet muffins. Of course, the white parishioners ate first, followed by the Mexicans, and only when the last one went through the line were the Negroes allowed to eat. Still, it's said that on that one day at least, there was plenty for all.

Afterward, children chased one another through the new cemetery, which at the moment had nary a single grave. Babies napped amid a patchwork of quilts and blankets thrown right atop that consecrated ground. Men strolled in groups of two and three, taking note of the broad-leafed magnolia trees that ringed its borders and the gentle way it sloped upward to the edge of the river.

It must also be mentioned that right in the very

middle of the two acres, standing in a ray of sunlight, was a statue of a woman. She had traveled all the way from the foot hills of Georgia, wrapped in the back of a wagon in a heavy tarp and fastened with rope. She had remained in that tarp for a couple of years until finally she was set free and placed in the middle of the new cemetery.

It was fortunate that they had Major Bay to help install her atop the cement pedestal. Now, a statue carved of Georgia marble is too heavy for one man— even a man as large as Major Bay—to manage on his own. Nevertheless, it was Major Bay who directed her placement, and Major Bay who did the heaviest lifting.

Folks didn't really know what to make of her. She wasn't exactly an angel, although there was no denying her beauty. And her robe fell under her exposed breast in a way that caused some of the women to raise their eyebrows and some of the men to stare.

If you could take your eyes off the exposed breast, you might notice that unlike so many carvings that stood in graveyards, her face was turned up, not really toward the sky, but not at all toward the ground; more like over her shoulder. Something else . . . her hands . . . one of them, the left, was outstretched, palm up. But the other, the right, hung by her side in a curled fist.

Was she holding on to something other than a fistful of marble? It's more likely that the sculptor grew tired of carving fingers, which any carver will tell you are the hardest things about the human anatomy to get right. The left hand, outstretched, was so lovely, each finger in perfect proportion to the palm, the arm, the shoulder, that maybe the sculptor just felt he had already carved one perfect hand and didn't want to worry over another?

Another thing . . . if you stood in front of her for more than a moment, it might seem to you that she had something to tell you. But no one on that Easter afternoon stopped long enough to listen.

So when all the food was eaten, and the sun began her setting down over the river, Reverend Phillips asked for another prayer, and this time nobody had to form a circle or hold hands. Everyone together, big and small, in one big group, lowered their heads, and the reverend spoke in a quiet, low voice:

> "Oh Lord, let this beautiful place be a
> refuge for all who need it.
> Let us be worthy. Let us be brave. Let us
> be kind.
> Amen."

It was just the right prayer. And later that night, while Reverend Phillips held his wife, Celia, in his arms, she told him so. "It was perfect," she said. And she kissed him on his rough cheek.

The next day she employed a local woodworker to carve the prayer into the front doors of the church. And there it remained, year after year after year, Mother River running by.

Cade Curtis

Ultimate Love? Cade sits at his desk in the bachelor pad, facing a pile of homework. He wonders if he should be mad. Religion is something he's hardly even discussed with Martin, and only partly because he doesn't ever want the conversation to veer into angels, which might segue into life after death, and that seems dangerously close to the topic of cemeteries. Better to leave it alone, he thinks. Sometimes Martin talks about his Catholic church, and Cade has actually gone to mass once or twice when he's spent the night at Martin's house, but overall, religion isn't their subject of discussion.

The bigger reason is: "Evie belonged to a church," Paul told him. "It didn't work out well." So Paul has hardly ever brought it up, at least not in any philosophical way.

And now . . . here was this invitation, complete with pizza, and more important, complete with Soleil.

Since the moment she landed in the desk in front of him in American literature on the first day of school, he's become increasingly aware of her. In fact, it wasn't long before he felt like she had cast a spell on him. He even started drumming his fingers on his desk, something he'd never done before, and doesn't do in any of his other classes.

He knows he wants more of her than just fifty minutes in class, more than just a drive-by at the flagpole. As much as anything, he wants to know about the tattoo on her wrist. In the history of Soleil, why a honey bear jar?

But if she shares her history with him, won't she expect him to do the same? And then, what about the angels? What would she do if she found out that he was a thief? What then? Can he take a chance? Should he?

Cade looks at the purple flyer smoothed out on his desk. Sunday night at seven. He notices that it doesn't actually say anything at all about Jesus or Ultimate Love or prayers or faith or any of the other words that he has heard over and over. It's just a straightforward invitation to *join in fellowship,* followed by, *there is room to spare.*

He rubs the scratch just beneath his eyebrow. It's

healing, but it reminds him. Something good. He needs to do something good. It also seems to him that Soleil, with her open-ended name, has taken a chance too. On him.

Yes, he thinks. He can say yes.

Zorra

Zorra needs to find a way to get out of the awful wooden enclosure. She licks her sore paws with her rough tongue. And then she cocks her ears. There is a new sound outside her pen. Actually it's an absence of sound. The rain, so constant over the past few days, has stopped.

And there is something else. The river.

It's rising! If the tiny window of her cage door were larger, she could see it, churning up the banks beneath her enclosure. The screech of the unknown bird startles her, and Zorra spins in a tight circle; her tail whacks against the side, and when it does, the whole pen shifts. She backs into the corner, and it shifts again, as if someone was pushing at it, bumping against it.

The sound of the water draws closer and closer.

The current rolls, faster and faster. All those days of constant rain, all that water. It has to go somewhere.

Zorra, hold on. The bayou is coming for you.

And just like that, the rain returns.

Mother River Church of God's Blessings

HOUSTON, REPUBLIC OF TEXAS

1845

The vegetation in Houston grows quickly. Anyone who has ever been the caretaker of a lawn there knows that. And nobody knew it better than Major Bay. The Reverend Phillips had put him in charge of maintaining the grounds for Mother River Church. He was responsible for keeping the crabgrass at heel and for trimming the gardenia bushes next to the front steps. He cared for the mules and greased the wheels on the wagon, repaired a broken pane, and mopped the wooden aisles of the church every fortnight. He was also the person who dug a grave whenever one of the members of the congregation passed on, and then covered it back up, smoothing the dirt into a perfect oblong mound. He took care with each grave, treated it with respect.

He buried the white folks in the main part of the cemetery. Their graves would be marked with headstones, their names carved into solid granite. There was a special area for the few Mexicans who attended the church. They too had headstones. And lastly he buried the slaves nearer the river, marked their resting places with only small wooden crosses, no names, no attributes.

Major Bay had no choice in the matter. He had ridden in the back of Reverend Phillips's wagon all the way from Georgia to Texas, chains around his wrists.

Had he fallen off that wagon, who knows what might have happened? He might have been dragged by the two mules that pulled the cart, pulled underneath the four carved wagon wheels. On the other hand, he might have yanked the chain free and run away. Who can say?

What is certain is that Major Bay kept the grounds of the little chapel, with its lovely yard, surrounded by an ancient grove of magnolia and hickory trees, nestled right up on the shores of the Mother River, neat and tidy.

The exception was the old brush arbor, no longer in use. He let the wild roses and the morning glories and honeysuckle vines climb up over its sides, covering the arbor in thick greenery, bound by the thorns of the roses and the prickly nettles of dewberry bushes. Underneath the once open arch, where Reverend Phillips had begun his ministry, Major Bay encouraged a wild stand of yaupons to twine their branches together in a tight weave of wood and leaves. In the spring, their tiny berries gleamed in the blazing sun, and the cedar waxwings, on their way from Mexico, would flock onto their branches and strip the berries in a bustling rush of hectic chirping, then fly off again.

Unless you happened to amble through the churchyard at the exact moment when the waxwings flew in and then flew out again, you probably wouldn't even realize that the old brush arbor was there, or that it ever had been. All you would see was a thick stand of bushes and vines, nestled up against the banks of the bayou. Nothing more.

Soleil Broussard

To say that Soleil is distracted would be an understatement. No one has heard from the Byrd family. Plus, she has invited a boy she barely knows to come to a party where there will be a disco ball.

A boy who stops her dead in her tracks, so that the only word she seems able to say in his presence is *pizza*.

For crying out loud. What is wrong with her? She reaches behind her head with both hands and twists her hair into a knot, then lets it tumble back down. Then she does it again. Twist. Release. Twist. Release.

"Lay-Lay! Stop it!" Mama reaches for her arm, tugs on it. "You're going to pull all your hair out—literally!" Soleil lets her hair go again, but then she doesn't know what to do with her hands. She rubs the tattoo on her wrist.

"Find something to do," says Mama. "Walk the dog or something." Considering that they don't have a dog, that should be funny, and normally, Soleil would have laughed, but right then, it just makes her more frustrated than ever. Even if they had a dog, it's raining again, and walking a dog in the rain doesn't seem funny at all.

With no Tyler to entertain, and no dog to walk, she grabs her backpack and heads to her room. Even though it is a Friday night, she might as well do some homework. Usually she and Channing and Grapes might have gotten together and gone to a movie or something, but Grapes had family coming in to visit for the weekend, and Channing was down with serious cramps, something Soleil didn't envy.

"At least I'm not dealing with that right now," she says to absolutely nobody, which gives her only a small amount of comfort. She plops down at her desk and opens her laptop. The familiar chiming of the computer as she wakes it up actually gives her a little cheer.

As if Lenny has been reading her thoughts, she opens her e-mail and finds a message:

To: Campers

From: lenny@cotb.org

Subject: Room to spare?

    Hello. I'm sure that some of you are wondering who to bring with you on Sunday night. You might be feeling a little shy about inviting them. No worries. But remember, everyone is welcome, regardless of their faith or even their non-faith. There's no place for judgment here.

    We have a lot to share. We have room to spare.

    Yours in fellowship (and rhyme),

    Lenny

    Let us not lose heart in doing good, for in due time we will reap if we do not grow weary.—Galatians 6:9

After reading Lenny's e-mail, Soleil feels a little better, which of course makes her think about . . .

Cade.

She reaches up to her throat and tugs on the tiny gold cross. "All the ways of the Lord are loving and faithful." The words of King David echo in her ears. The little cross is warm between her fingertips.

And then she looks at the honey bear jar on her wrist. She was surprised that her parents didn't object. She had saved up her babysitting money, and after much discussion, which included not only the perils and pain of tattoos, as well as the infinity of them, her dad had taken her to a place called Tattoo-Lize, where she watched with both terror and amazement as the artist engraved the soft skin of her wrist with the image of a honey bear.

She wanted to whimper at the burn of it, but instead, she chewed on the inside of her mouth and breathed hard until it was finished. The soreness of it has almost vanished, just a small tenderness, really.

It makes her think about Tyler and the miracle of the honey bear jar. And she can't help but think that there is some kind of miracle about Cade, too. But what that is, she hasn't a clue.

Buffalo Bayou

HOUSTON

She's not greedy, the bayou, but she has a hankering for coins. She collects them from every realm. Pass your plate and drop one in, pray for the fish and oysters.

Ask her in your sweetest voice, she is reluctant to hand over even one.

Pennies, dimes, coppers, silver pesos, gold dollars with the face of Sacajawea on one side, silver dollars with the face of Lady Liberty. She loves how they spin and roll in her wavy current until at last they settle into the silt, and how they throw off flickers of light when the sun hits them just so.

The bayou is particularly fond of the coins that come with wishes. She isn't wild about granting wishes, but she understands their yearnings. After all, the tug of a wish is not so different from the pull of gravity, its longing for redemption.

Above all, she appreciates the rare buffalo nickel. There might be a thousand of them, buried in her bed. Maybe more.

She's not telling.

Achsah

The Republic of Texas had little in the way of silver and gold. It never minted any coins. It did issue a paper bill called "star money," for the small star printed on its face, but it never held much value, could hardly be redeemed.

In Achsah's pocket, there were no coins, no pesos, no dollars, no star money. The only thing she carried was a marble figurine that fit in the palm of her hand, given to her by the boy she walked beside from Alexandria to Natchez. How many times had she run her fingers over it, held it tightly until, warmed by her hand, it felt almost alive, as if the small O for its mouth was breathing in and out? It was her very own secret. She had never shown it to anyone, not a single soul.

She knew it would not buy passage on a boat from

Houston to Galveston and then on to Mexico. She wasn't sure she could part with it anyways.

The papers, the ones that claimed her free to go, signed by the Captain himself, she had stuffed inside her blouse, and she hoped they were staying dry enough to keep from being ruined by her own sweat. She'd surely need them for passage out of Galveston.

Achsah's stomach ached from emptiness. She had given most of the food to the girls, taking only a few bites for herself.

All night they had trudged along this shoreline, had grasped the low-hanging vines to steady them in the slow-moving current that pushed against them, while they walked in the muddy water. In all those hours, they had not encountered any snakes or alligators. The same wasn't true of the mosquitoes. Every inch of their exposed skin was covered in bumps. All three of their faces were swollen from a thousand bites, and the thick, motionless air rang with the insects' poisonous high-pitched songs.

Finding the Lady was her only chance. If she and her daughters could get to the Lady, they might make it.

Achsah knew exactly where she was. Not far at all, and closing in—she was sure of it—were dogs and a slave hunter and her own weary self, her legs weak from walking in water and mud. There were also two little girls, tired and scared. Mary Ann. Juba.

They were hers and nobody else's. Like the figurine. So many times she had gripped it, gripped it hard. Times when she had to bite her lip to keep from shouting, times when she had to smile to keep from crying. She had gripped it tight, just as she had when she gave birth three times, refusing to scream, swallowing her big fear, bearing down on the pain that tore through her body.

She had waited for this, for the Captain to keep his promise, and nobody, no one, was going to take her girls away from her.

Just look at them.

Juba, quick on her feet, quick to pick up all the things that Achsah had taught her, like keeping her head bowed when the Captain was in the room, like how to boil a kettle of tea, like how to hem a skirt and how to split kindling for the kitchen fire. Juba had been born on a winter's morning, just as the sun showed itself above the clouds. And just like the sun, she was round faced and steady. Quiet, too, like the moon. Achsah could rely upon her older daughter.

Mary Ann, still small, just outgrowing her baby ways, even though she was old for that, three after all.

She was more restless than her big sister. All the time, she babbled and chattered. Little singer. Little bird. Not so serious-minded as Juba.

They were *her* girls. Hers. Even the bayou could tell her that.

As the trio pushed through that quiet, dark water, the stars in the deep sky showed themselves between the branches of the thick wooded cove, the fog haints rose into the air and whispered to her, *Achsah, take your babies and run.*

The Marble Carver

Give us Georgia after the long march, after the thin boy and his people were forced out of their mountains and all they knew, when the marble lay there untouched, quiet, just as it had when it formed on the bottom of the ancient sea floor, pressed down by water and ice, pressed first into limestone and then into marble. Metamorphic. Silent. Rising up through the receding waters until it sat just beneath the Georgia dirt, waiting. Waiting for a new carver.

Then give us Etienne Bel James. He arrived in New Orleans from Nova Scotia. One day while working in a blacksmith shop, over the pounding of metal on metal, he overheard mention of a vast field of marble in the mountains of Georgia, and as soon as he could, he managed to make his way there. It couldn't be said that he was a particularly gifted artist, but he had a good eye, and it wasn't long before he had a thriving trade, engraving headstones and carving statuary.

It also wasn't long before he realized that he needed a helper. So Etienne decided to make his way to the slave market at Forks of the Road, near Natchez. It was a long week of travel astride a horse.

He had never before thought of himself as a slaveholder, but he needed someone who could help lift the heavy marble and spend the long hours polishing and sanding until the marble turned translucent and soft, as if it were lit from within. A slave would be cheaper than a hired hand.

Luck was with him that day, on the banks of the Mississippi. A new coffle had arrived from Alexandria. Right away, he noticed a tall, lanky boy. Despite his gangly frame, the boy stood with his shoulders back, his face forward. It made no difference to Etienne that he was not yet fully grown.

So Etienne haggled with the slave agent, and for forty-five dollars he was handed one end of a chain, the other being a collar around the boy's neck. A fair price, he thought.

Etienne spoke French, but the boy did not. When he

asked about his name, the boy didn't answer. In fact, the boy would never tell him his true name anyway. Everyone who had ever known it was gone to him. Either died along the trail, or resettled to Indian Territory. But Etienne needed to call him something. So he renamed him: Luc. A simple name. After the gospel.

And as was the custom with slaveholders, he bestowed his own last name on him: Bel James. He had a bill of sale, and the last name ensured it. Then he reached down and pulled the boy up behind the saddle on the back of the horse, and together they set off.

It was slow going but steady. A week later, dusty and saddle-sore, they arrived back at Etienne's homestead, with his small cabin and his workshop, and when the boy—now Luc—realized that he was back in the marble mountains where he had grown up, he started shaking. For a moment he thought he was being tricked, that maybe he was going to be forced to start all over, to return to the trail again, to ice and snow and horses that dropped dead while harnessed to their carts.

The shaking overwhelmed him, and he felt the horse underneath him begin to shake too. Neither of them seemed able to stop until Etienne grabbed him and pulled him down. The boy slumped onto the ground.

Etienne threw a blanket over him and left him there, chained to a tree. For three days, the boy slept like that, shivering, until at last he finally sat up.

The landscape was so familiar that he cocked his ears and listened for the voices of his mother and his father and his sisters and brother. Their absence was so large that he felt as if the hole of their not-being might pull him down and smother him. He turned his face toward the whisper of the pine needles, but there was still nothing, not his family, his friends, no one he knew. Only Etienne, the man who had paid for him at the slave market at Forks of the Road. He was the only one who seemed to know that the boy was real.

And though Etienne knew he was taking a chance, he unlocked the collar and tossed it aside. The boy might run away, and he wouldn't blame him if he did. But the chain would likely not have stopped him anyways. Instead, he showed the boy, now Luc, the small room beside the workshop where a clean pallet of straw was set out for him to sleep on, and a small stove with a supply of wood stood ready to keep him warm.

Luc realized he could leave, run. This was where he had grown up, after all. He knew where to find the shallow caves of the panthers, and the deep dens of the black bear, all tucked away; but he also knew that his freedom would be short. If he weren't attacked by a panther or bear, he'd likely be caught again. Maybe he'd be returned to Etienne, maybe he'd be sold to some other owner, someone who might just call him *boy* and beat him until there was little skin left on his back. He'd seen the scars of former runaways as he walked in the coffle to Natchez. Men, women, even children, their backs crisscrossed like maps of rivers, rivers that ran with their very own blood.

No, he wouldn't leave now. And besides, once in a while, sometimes, when the moon bounced between the branches of the night trees, he could close his eyes and hear his true name, whispered amid the clattering of the pine needles. Mountains, it seems, have long memories, and these Georgia mountains remembered this boy.

And so that's the way it was. Etienne taught Luc everything he knew about carving marble. He showed him the techniques and artistry that he had been taught in France before he moved to Nova Scotia. And in return Luc showed him what he knew, what had been passed down. And as the years passed, the boy became the truer artist, even though he never, not once, carved his true name into his work, and as far as anyone knows, only the mountains remember it.

Give us a tall, thin boy who carved figures out of the Cherokee and Etowah marble. Some the size of a thumb, others the size of a person. Tie one to a cart bound for Texas.

Give us the Lady.

Zorra

It was a thief who stole Zorra from her thicket in the Laguna Atascosa with its cottonwoods, stole her away from the coyote and its evening lullaby, shot her with a dart that made her sleep and sleep and sleep, and shoved her into a wooden pen that was built for a different animal, not an animal with wide paws for climbing and sturdy legs for pouncing and a spotted coat that changed shades with every stride.

Not for Zorra. *Leopardus pardalis.* Honored cat of the Moche people of Peru. Citizen of the valley, where the Rio Grande sliced her habitat in two.

And now that pen is tilting, leaning on its wooden legs that stand in the rising water of the bayou. The water pushes, pulls, pushes, pulls. It makes a swirling eddy as it bumps against the banks and eats away at the mud that holds the pen.

Zorra curls into a tight ball, every muscle tensed. And every once in a while, something in the water— maybe a log, maybe a tire, maybe a capsized boat— bumps against the legs and shakes her pen.

The haints of the water churn too. *Zorra*, they call. *Zorra. The bayou is coming for you.*

And Zorra, wild with worry, spins in her tiny cage, overturns the empty metal bowl, cries into the foggy night, her voice raspy, and then she feels a huge and solid bump. The wooden legs beneath her cage, rotted from standing in water for such a long time, buckle, and the pen, unmoored, sways in the air for a full five seconds, then crashes into the bayou.

Zorra, cry the water sprites.

Hold on, they call.

But Zorra doesn't hear them. It seems that terror has made her deaf. And so does the water that rushes into her cage.

Buffalo Bayou

HOUSTON

Let it be said that the bayou, she of many names, could also be called a collector. Scour her muddy shelves and you will find:

- wedding rings—both tossed and lost
- guns and bullets and spent shell casings
- watches with Mickey Mouse and Road Runner faces
- bracelets and earrings and cuff links and Cross pens
- measuring spoons and silver forks

Look again, and there will be:

- transistor radios
- Game Boys

- more guns, and many more
- Princess phones
- cell phones
- boom boxes

She gets a kick out of all these things, each one a gift. But once in a while she gets the urge to purge and so gives something up. Take the wheel, for example. It's tall, fifty-six inches in diameter, with spokes that are twenty-two inches in length. The hub was hand carved, not turned on a lathe. It's a beauty of a wheel, made by a master wheelwright, circa 1840.

All these rains have churned up the mud on the bottom, where she's kept it for more than a century, almost two. Enough, she's decided. So she has tossed it onto the banks, where no one who finds it will know its true story. Not a single person alive today will recall that this wheel once had three matching partners that rolled underneath a wagon all the way from Georgia to Texas with a carved marble statue in its bed, wrapped in a tarp and fastened with sturdy rope. No one will remember that.

But the bayou does. She never forgets.

James Morgan

Born and bred in Tennessee, the son of a mercantile grocer, James Morgan who learned his trade so well that in the year of 1829, when he was only twenty-one, his father gave him a large amount of cash and enough supplies to establish a business in Austin's Colony in the Mexican territory of Texas. He didn't travel alone. He brought his brand-new wife, his infant son, and five wagons loaded down with supplies, with two slaves to drive each wagon.

When Texas became a republic, he was given a headright grant—that is, a grant given to heads of families who weren't African or Indian. It was a "first class" headright of one league and one labor: 4,605.5 acres.

His headright bumped against the Brazos de Dios,

just upriver from the Gulf of Mexico, where he could easily ship goods in and out of Galveston, the largest city in Texas. The land was prime for cotton and sugar, so that was what he grew.

Soon he started a cattle herd with a handful of longhorn cows driven north from the Rio Grande. Sturdy creatures, with horns that spanned five feet or more.

And he raised slaves, too. From Cuba and Barbados and the southern states, he imported them and then bred them like any other livestock—horses, cattle, hogs. They said that James Morgan had an eye for the Negroes, knew which of the men could withstand the brutal heat, and which of the women could work for hours under the Texas sun, who could boil the laundry and hang it out, keep the kitchen garden, nurse his babies. His babies.

It was also said that he was good with children, that his mellifluous voice carried over the water of the Brazos and sang the seagulls to sleep, that he had a thousand stories to tell, especially stories about his heroism in the fight against Mexico. White, black, brown, he liked children, some better than others. He regaled them with stories about his exploits, about how many Mexicans he had shot and killed.

He had served in the Texian Army, right beside

Sam Houston at the Battle of San Jacinto, the battle that finally defeated Santa Anna. Texas was no longer part of Mexico. No longer did it answer to the half-African, half-Mexican president of Mexico, Vicente R. Guerrero, or any of the leaders who followed. Mexico could go ahead and set her slaves free. But not Texas. Texas could keep hers. And James Morgan did. He kept every one.

But there were two who he had been promised, the daughters of Achsah. Mary Ann. Juba. There was enough of the Captain in them that their skin was paler than their mother's; their hair was paler too, and not as curly. They would bring a high price as lady's maids; they could serve in the household of any well-heeled family. A genteel wife would be happy to show them off. A genteel man would appreciate them for their pale, their tender skin.

Mary Ann. Juba. He had no intention of selling them. But he had been robbed. Achsah had taken them, and so far the hunter with his dogs had not tracked them down. So far.

Achsah

Mexico. Achsah needed to make her way to Mexico. Mexico meant freedom. It had been two nights of slogging through the muddy water, and two days of trying to sleep in the arms of trees and underneath the brushy vines. Two of each since the Captain died. Surely they should be getting close by now, but the bayou seemed endless, especially as they were traveling by night, when it was impossible to judge the distance.

If she had been able to walk alone on the road from the Captain's house—south of the city, near Harrisburg—to the church, it might have taken a full day, and part of a night; maybe a bit more. But she wasn't on the dry road. She was trudging along the banks of the river, with all its twists and turns, with her small daughters in tow. As well, whenever the banks got too steep, she had to walk in the water itself. She was going north, against the current.

The instructions sent by Major Bay had said to look for a set of wooden steps embedded into the banks. They were used for taking congregants down to the water for baptisms. She had been looking for them, willing them to appear, but so far there were no steps— only the water and the night, and the exhaustion sunk all the way to her bones.

To make matters worse, she thought she heard the far-off bay of a hound. She couldn't be sure, it was so faint. Maybe, she thought, it was something else—the cry of a fox, or the wail of a coyote. She tipped her ear in the direction it seemed to come from, but there was nothing. On this Earth, there was no other sound like that of a bloodhound, at once urgent and sad. As well, she knew that Morgan had probably put a bounty on her head by now, so it was not only the tracker, but anyone who needed some cash who was likely on her trail.

With the rising sun, they were forced to stop. She managed to help the girls climb into the branches of a sturdy magnolia tree, one laden with blossoms. They'd have to wait out the day there.

Achsah hoped the fragrance of the flowers would make a mask, throw off their scent. Her girls were so weary they could hardly move. Their faces, and the tops of their hands, every place where their skin was exposed, were swollen from the sting of mosquitoes.

She gave them the last of the provisions from the kettle and bade them to wrap their arms around the tree's trunk. And the tree, as if it understood its holy task, held on to them, as if its branches were arms, were cradles. Achsah silently thanked the gentle tree, then straddled the lower branch, leaned against the trunk, and closed her eyes.

She was too tired to sleep, but not too tired to dream. With the palm of her hand, she felt the tiny figurine in her skirt pocket. Somewhere, she knew, there was a thin boy who knew her name. She wondered if he missed her the same.

Probably not. But the dream of him felt so soft that she took a deep breath and let herself drift off to sleep. And the wispy haints of the river gathered in a group and made a thick circle of fog, fog so deep no hound, no tracker, no bounty hunter could find them, not then anyway, that's how thick their circle was.

Achsah, they whispered. *Find the Lady.*

Juba and Mary Ann

HOUSTON, REPUBLIC OF TEXAS
1845

Juba felt the heat in her little sister. Despite the cool morning air, Mary Ann's hand was like a warm biscuit straight out of the pan. And something else: Mary Ann was quiet. Too quiet.

Mary Ann. She leaned against the trunk of the friendly tree, all of her so very, very sleepy. All of her singing, with no sound at all: *you shall wear de starry crown, oh Lord. . . .*

Mrs. Walker

Who can put a value on an angel? Is one worth more than another? It depends on the realms in which they reside. As it turns out, hand carved angels here on planet Earth can fetch a handsome sum. The sale of Hans's angel, made of the finest Carrara marble, marble that came from the same quarry as Michelangelo's famous *Pieta*, set Mrs. Walker up for quite a while. It gave her enough to weather the downturn in oil prices and gave her the capital she was able to operate on for a good long time when Paul and Cade showed up a few years later, as well as keep Cade in sneakers, which he seemed to outgrow, faster than a speeding train.

It's funny about love, isn't it? She didn't think that she could ever love anyone more fully or wholeheartedly than Hans. And for a long time after he died, she figured that love was done with her, at least in the earthly sense. The idea that it would show up in any other form seemed as remote to her as Cuba.

And then, there they were, Paul and Cade. They were the last two people she expected to find on her doorstep.

Having them in her life made her feel enormously lucky, not to mention a little sorry for the families who chose not to keep them, a fact she could never understand. Watching both of them grow up, well, she saw that as a rare gift. She would do anything for them. It was especially important to her to keep the store running so that when she left, it would be there for Paul.

Yes, she planned to leave it to him, with the caveat that he would not have to keep it if he didn't want to.

And that was the thing. The day when she would do that leaving was coming. She had known it for a while now, could tell that each day was bringing her closer to reuniting with Hans. She wasn't sorry, or even sad to be leaving. She had been here a very long time, after all, longer than most.

But she wanted to be sure that Paul would have enough for him and Cade to settle the estate and to get by for a little while. Maybe they would both go to college. Or travel. Or start some other business. Whatever it was they wanted, she wanted for them. And she knew that the property all by itself, once sold, would be enough to give them a good start.

And while angels weren't the hot commodity they had been twenty years earlier, they were still highly prized.

If the well-heeled didn't have an angel in their garden, particularly one carved of granite or marble, well, they were missing out. Mrs. Walker knew that. The man from Galveston who wore the Tony Lama ostrich-skin boots knew that too. Whenever she needed a few extra bucks, all she had to do was call. And since he was what would be known as "off the grid of legitimacy," he never divulged his real name, so Trudy Walker just called him the Cowboy, and let it go at that.

And as it turned out, the Cowboy was happy to see the weeping angel. "I have a client in Dublin who will love her," he said. But as they bundled her up in packing quilts, Mrs. Walker couldn't help but think that Dublin was a long way for an angel from Texas to fly.

Zorra

For a long fifteen seconds, maybe more, the bayou pulled Zorra's toppled cage down, down, down into the circling eddy. Once, twice, three times around. She held her breath. She was a strong swimmer, but inside the cage, she had nowhere to go, no way to get out. She kicked her legs against the current, pawed at the walls, twisted and twisted against the murderous water.

And just when she thought her lungs would burst, like that, the bayou let her go. With a strong push it heaved the wooden cage to the surface, where it bobbed like a boat. Zorra couldn't get her bearings. Inside the cage, the water came to her belly, it pressed her head against the top of the enclosure so that she was mostly submerged.

The cage-boat bounced against debris that flowed from upstream, pushed her downstream, away from the hidden cove, floated several more yards, then drifted into a raft of broken tree limbs and lumber and a pair of lawn chairs, their aluminum frames twisted and bent.

Zorra pressed herself to the back of the cage, making the small opening of the pen face upward, so all she could see from inside her watery craft were the gray sky and clouds, and the underneath of a concrete-and-steel structure, that, had she been a denizen of the city, she would have called a bridge.

Thousands of cars, with thousands of passengers, drive over those bridges every day and every night, but did anyone notice Zorra, caught in her awful boat? With only a metal bowl for company. We can say that thousands missed her.

But the bayou didn't. The bayou loves ocelots. Once they had been as familiar along her waterway as the alligators, roaming the magnolia forests along her muddy banks. She didn't want to lose another, so as soon as she could, she pushed the tiny craft against the opposite shore, lodged it against the trunk of a century-old hickory tree, its leaves turning red in the cooling fall air. And just beside it, the bridge, one that housed a few thousand bats, Mexican free-tails.

Zorra, exhausted, feels the water drain from her leaky cage, and shivering, she sinks onto its rotten wooden floor. Every inch of her aches. Every muscle screams. Her coat is covered in mud and the residue that has settled in the bayou over decades and longer—oil and kerosene and sewage—all the stuff that churns up after a heavy rain. She is alive, but not very.

She lowers her head onto her front paws, but for some reason, just before she falls asleep, she looks up through the cage-door window, through the tree's leaves, and there, just beside the noisy bridge, is a face she knows—the friendly moon.

She listens as hard as she can, but there is no coyote's song in her ears. Nothing warm or soft. Not even the crickets pipe up. And no one in those thousands of cars spots her, trapped in a water-soaked cage, watching the moon float by. No one.

Cade Curtis

HOUSTON, TEXAS

A HISTORY

In the Old Testament, there is the story of Moses, how his mother, Jochebed—a slave—wrapped him in a blanket when he was a baby and tucked him into a basket woven of reeds. Then she set him atop the water of the Nile and quickly turned away. It was the only thing she could do to save her newborn son from the wrath of the Pharaoh. And while we can't know how much her heart broke that day, we do know that the current on the river carried the baby Moses straight into the arms of the Pharaoh's daughter. Bithiah, that was her name; she loved him as hard as any mother could.

In the great state of Texas, there is a law named for baby Moses. Read the pamphlet, and it'll tell you that if you can't keep your baby, you can surrender him or her, no questions asked. Take that baby to a hospital or a fire station or a twenty-four-hour emergency medical clinic.

You do not have to give a reason. You do not have to give your name. There is no penalty. There is no judgment.

It's a decent law. It saves babies from being abandoned in dumpsters, or being left on the sides of roads, or falling victim to abuse. It saves mothers, too. Mothers who can't support their babies. Mothers who might be addicted or sick. Mothers from abusive homes . . .

In the history of Cade, there was a promise. Paul promised Evie that he would take their baby to a hospital or a fire station or a twenty-four-hour emergency medical clinic and leave him there.

It was an option.

"She loved you so much," Paul told Cade. "She *had* to let you go.

"But I loved you so much too," he added. And he pulled Cade into one of his famous dad hugs. "I *couldn't* let you go."

But Cade also knows that he is not Evie's only child. There are others, and unlike him, Evie couldn't let them go.

Evie Nelson

It was all because of a good-bye–not-given, the one Evie meant for Paul, that she found herself in Walker's Art and Antique Store.

How could she have known that Paul had broken his promise? How could she?

Then again, how could anyone know that there isn't a day goes by when she doesn't think about her boy, when she doesn't whisper, "Cade."

Yes, she knows his name. And every single day she hides the tears that she can't keep from falling.

Achsah

Achsah didn't have time to cry. She only needed to find the Lady and make her way to Mexico. And she had to do it soon. Maybe she was imagining it, but she now felt certain that she heard the dogs. A bloodhound's bay can carry for miles. She and the girls had time, but it was shorter by the hour. Moreover, the kettle she had filled with potatoes and dried meat and biscuits was empty, and she knew that her little ones' stomachs were empty too. For herself, she had not eaten but a few bites of biscuit since the morning the Captain had died and given her daughters to James Morgan. Where was the justice in that?

No, Achsah would not find justice in Texas.

She had heard about los cimarrones and how they

settled in a region called Costa Chica, somewhere near Acapulco in southwestern Mexico. She and her girls would be free there.

It was dark, a blue-gray kind of dark that happens just as the sun creeps below the horizon, when the world becomes as still as stone, so still the crickets had stopped chirping, and the only sounds were the merciless mosquitoes, which rose out of the low-lying marsh grass in clouds. Achsah brushed them away as much as she could. She knew her girls were suffering too. Neither of them complained, neither of them cried out. Though she was grateful, their stoic silence felt just as painful as the welts that covered their faces.

She tugged on the hems of her daughters' skirts. Under the cover of the darkness, she held her arms open as the girls lowered themselves out of the sturdy magnolia and into the thick underbrush that surrounded them. "Hurry," she whispered. She knew that soon, Morgan's tracker would have his dogs out again. Their bites would be far worse than the stings of the relentless mosquitoes.

And she also knew that by now, the entire town of Houston would be informed of her escape. She was counting on that.

What she wasn't counting on was the heat in Mary Ann's hand, burning against the skin of her own.

Mother River Church of God's Blessings

The Reverend Phillips knelt in the corner of a pew next to a window inside the church building. Anyone passing by would simply see a man of the Book engaged in prayer, his face lit by a kerosene lantern. They would probably not notice that every few minutes, despite the morning's darkness, he looked out the open window in the direction of the river. It was already hot, despite the early hour, and he could feel a thin bead of sweat trickle down his sides underneath his black woolen coat.

The coat was one of the only things he disliked about being a minister, and if it hadn't been for Celia, who admonished him to wear it for the authority it bestowed upon him, he might have flung it off and gone about in his white cotton shirt. But he understood her reasoning. Plus, he had to admit, a hot coat was a small discomfort considering the many blessings that went with his profession, even though some blessings were greater than others.

He paused in his prayer and looked out the window again. News traveled quickly through the slave community. Thanks to Major Bay, Reverend Phillips had been privy to the escape almost as soon as it had happened, and he had been waiting. He also knew that Morgan had not discovered the death of the Captain until the following day, giving Achsah a lead. Nevertheless, two full days and two full nights was a long time to evade the dogs, not to mention the trackers who would surely be on her trail. Also, she was traveling with children. That would make her run more complicated. A woman with two little girls could not have gotten very far very fast.

He wiped the sweat off his forehead with the back of his hand, but it gave him little relief. According to Major Bay, no one had seen her yet, which meant that she was probably nearby, maybe right under their noses.

Someone would eventually smoke them out. Or she'd give up out of hunger and thirst. He'd seen it happen more than once. For every successful escape, there were ten that weren't. If she was going to get out, she needed to make a move. Soon.

He'd seen the printed posters that Morgan had distributed around town. There was a substantial reward for the return of the little girls. As well, the sheriff had posted notices for the mother, whose name was Achsah. If she were captured, she'd be treated as a criminal.

James Morgan was present when the constitution for the new republic was written. Its intent was clear: stealing a slave was considered an act of piracy.

No matter that she was the girls' mother. No matter that she was a free woman, freed by the father of her children. No matter. In the eyes of the law, those girls were stolen property. Piracy was a hanging offense. Reverend Phillips closed his eyes, but quickly opened them. The image of a woman dangling at the end of a rope sent a shiver down his back despite his heavy coat.

He knew that Morgan could afford to pay a handsome sum for their return, which meant that every man with a dog and a gun was likely on their trail. Three days and no sign yet. It couldn't be much longer. As if the sun agreed, it crept over the edge of the bayou and sent a long stream of light right into the church window, momentarily blinding him.

Dear God! He clasped his hands together and pressed them against his forehead. "Hurry," he prayed. "Hurry!"

Buffalo Bayou

HOUSTON

Pirates. She's seen them travel on steamboats, paddles churning up her brackish water. They cheated at poker and blackjack. They smuggled an array of goods into the brand-new city. Silk for the fine ladies. Tobacco for the soldiers. Slave labor for the sugar barons.

In they came, pirates, from New Orleans, from Barbados and the China Sea, past the Keys in Florida and across the Gulf of Mexico, they sailed in through the port of Galveston and traveled upstream. A new life. In a new place. In a new country.

Keep your eyes open. They come and go. They sail upon the old channels of this wandering bayou, they hide along her wild, wild banks.

Zorra

Exhausted from her trip downstream, Zorra slept through the night and most of the day, and now evening is approaching. But there is no food, nor any water in her metal bowl. She paws at it until it flips over, making a ringing noise in her ears.

She looks up, back out at the sky through the wires of the small window, which is all she can see. And then, miracle of miracles, a bright green lizard, an anole, slips through the wires. Zorra watches as it pauses just inside her cage and looks around. Quicker than light, she strikes it with her paw and pops it into her mouth.

It is spicy and warm and delicious.

It isn't enough, but it will do for now. She rolls onto her back and stares through the wires of the opening.

As she watches, a pair of nighthawks swoop into view and fly in a circle, as if they are dancing in the air, wings spread wide.

Zorra, sing the spirits of the bayou.

Zorra, they call.

Zorra. Don't forget who you are.

j

Cade walks on the edge of the concrete trail that runs along the bayou. He has followed it before, sometimes with Martin, more times with Paul, but usually by himself.

The bridge that spans the bayou to the other side harbors a colony of bats, thousands of them. At dusk they'll pour out from under it, weaving and spinning, tiny Mexican free-tails. From this distance they'll look like small puffs of smoke just above the water's surface.

It has finally stopped raining long enough to venture out, and for a second he wishes Paul was there with him. Then again, Cade needs some time to think, so it is just as well that his dad has stayed home to watch the baseball game.

Paul was a star player for his high school team. Apparently there had even been some pro scouts who had been keeping their eyes on him. Paul's life would have been markedly different if Cade had never been born.

(And also, as Martin has said more than once, "if your grandparents hadn't been such *asshats*.")

Who knew? His dad might have gone on to college, and then maybe to play professional baseball, and instead of posters of Nolan Ryan on their walls, there might be posters of Paul Curtis.

Whenever Cade tries to bring up Paul's missed opportunity in baseball, Paul cuts him off. "Don't worry about it, Li'l Dude," he says. "I wrote my own history. I'm cool with it." And then he wraps Cade in a big bear hug. One thing about Paul, he is a major hugger.

"And besides," Paul says. "You're the best thing about me. Ballplayers flame out early. You and me, we're good for life." And Cade knows his dad means that, and he also knows how painful that must feel, considering that Paul's dad never said it to him.

Asshats. Martin was right. Same for his mother, Evie.

The Astros were having a great season, and even though he and Paul didn't live very far from the stadium,

Paul prefers watching the games on television. He likes being able to see the instant replays.

Now Cade stands there on the edge of the bayou alone, the daylight fading. As he watches the water rumble past, he sees a bundled-up bag of trash go by— it has the familiar logo of Whataburger on its side. God, he hates people who throw trash into the water. He'd grab it if he could, but it's out of his reach, so all he can do is watch as it floats downstream and finally disappears underneath the bridge.

"Jerks," he says out loud. But then he pauses. *Jerks. Asshats. Jerks. Asshats.* And he has to ask himself: Who is he to call anyone a name? The question eats at him.

He gathers a handful of rocks, and one by one, he pulls his arm back and lets fly. Each rock skips across the water—once, twice, three times—before it sinks out of view. Even though Cade is not the baseball player that his dad must have been—in fact, he has no interest in playing at all—he doesn't have a bad arm.

The water is running higher and faster than usual.

From where he stands on the trail, he can look across the bayou and see Houston's brilliant steel-and-glass skyline. Downtown's cluster of skyscrapers is only a couple of miles away. He could walk there if he crossed the bridge and kept going. It wouldn't take long.

Standing there, the rays of the sinking sun dodging between them, the buildings appear shinier than ever. Nearby, he knows, is the Church on the Bayou. He's seen it before, but only from the street.

The words, *Ultimate Love*, swim through his brain. They bump up against another word, *Soleil*. Together, they all circle around each other, like fish in a pool. He pats the pocket of his jeans. The note is there, tucked inside the purple flyer.

"Whatever you do," says Paul, "be careful around girls." Then he pauses, raises his right eyebrow, and adds, "Especially in the biblical sense." The first time Paul said that, Cade had no idea what "the biblical sense" meant. So Paul explained it to him, along with a whole lecture about using protection, followed by the overwhelming merits of abstaining altogether.

Even though Paul was semi-joking, he was also dead serious. Of course, he didn't really need to worry, since Cade's experience with girls was minimal. He had gone out in groups before, where girls were present, but those encounters were nothing more than study sessions at a coffee bar, or a meet-up for the school dance. He'd only been kissed a couple of times, and one of those times was in kindergarten, when Marsha Esposito came dashing toward him on the playground and out of nowhere planted a huge kiss right on his mouth.

The second kiss was almost as much a surprise as the first, when in eighth grade, Libby Franks zoomed by his locker, paused long enough to say "Hey," or something similar to that, and gave him a smack on the cheek, and forever after that, even now, hardly acknowledged his existence. In fact, he'd be lying if he said he didn't wonder if he'd always be the recipient of drive-by kisses, since that was his experience so far.

But now here he is, in a position that can only be considered enormously ironic, being asked to go to a church party by a girl who wears a gold cross on a nearly invisible chain around her neck. It all seems fairly biblical to him, especially considering the fact that aside from going with Martin to All Saints Catholic Church a couple of times, the closest he had come to any sort of regular attendance of holy territory was prowling around in old graveyards, searching for statuary that could be loosened from its moorings and lifted into the back of his father's pickup truck.

As he stands here, watching the bayou rumble by, another question zooms up behind it. Would Soleil have invited him if she knew he was a thief? Of course, he knows the answer, and the knowing of that presses into him, as if he is caught in a swinging door, not able to exit on either side without getting slammed.

With that, he hauls off and throws the last rock so hard it lands on the opposite side of the bayou, right at the foot of the bat bridge. If he had stood there for even a split second longer and waited for it to land, he might have noticed a loud *thunk*.

But he has already turned away. Even if he had heard it, he wouldn't have seen what the rock hit, camouflaged as it is behind a thick stand of vines, snugged up in the twisted roots of an old hickory, invisible to the eye, invisible to everyone but the pair of nighthawks swooping atop the thermals that spin in the air above it.

Zorra

An ocelot needs more than the bayou can give.

She paws at the empty bowl, sniffs at it. The only thing in it now is a tiny glimmer, sent by the waning moon. Nothing she can eat or drink.

Oh, Zorra, the bayou has carried you far from the hidden cove, away from the smoky breath of the Caretaker. She saved you from his hard wooden paddle. The bayou summoned her foggy haints to sing you a lullaby. But one thing she can't manage, no matter how hard she tries, is to unlock the door to your cage.

There is only so much the bayou can do.

Soleil Broussard

What kind of person uses Jesus to get a date? Soleil feels only slightly less than horrible. But she is also feeling a little hopeful, too.

At once, there are steps in her feet that she needs to take, three-quarter waltz kind of steps. She scrolls through her playlist. Ed Sheeran's voice fills her room. *"People fall in love in mysterious ways."*

It's not so different from what her mom says: *Some things are beyond knowing.*

What isn't beyond knowing is that more than anything, Soleil wants Cade to be in her life, wants him to come to the gathering on Sunday night, and she genuinely hopes that Jesus won't mind that she's used His love like this, even if it wasn't intentional.

Mother River Church of God's Blessings

HOUSTON, REPUBLIC OF TEXAS
1845

Celia Phillips sat at the piano in the front of the church. The pews were empty and the morning sunlight streamed through the open windows. She was thumbing through the sheets of music in front of her when she noticed that someone had stepped inside.

She paid no mind. The doors of the chapel were always open, and it wasn't unusual for a person to wander in. The Houston heat was relentless, and sometimes a body just needed a place to cool off, and sometimes a body just wanted to sit back and listen to Miss Celia practice. That was fine by her. She loved her piano. It had been in her family for years, and when she and the reverend told her kinfolk about the new chapel, they had it shipped to her, as a personal gift, they said, "to the glory of God."

It had arrived soon after the chapel was built. It was placed right up front, next to the altar, where Miss Celia played it with verve. Whenever she hit the keys, the ringing sound of her piano could be heard all the way down Main Street, even as far over as the Hotel de Chene, with its wide front porch that overlooked the bayou.

Passengers on boats going upstream and down could hear it too. Even when Miss Celia played a quieter hymn, the notes on that piano soared. She was a fine player, too, having come from a musical family.

So there she was, deep into the notes of "Lead, Kindly Light," when she suddenly heard a man's deep, resonant voice, singing the lovely verses:

Lead, kindly light, amid th' encircling gloom
Lead Thou me on!
The night is dark, and I am far from home
Lead Thou me on!
Keep Thou my feet; I do not ask to see
The distant scene; one step enough for me.

So long Thy pow'r has blest me, sure it still
Will lead me on,

O'er moor and fen, o'er crag and torrent, till
The night is gone.
And with the morn those angel faces smile
Which I have loved long since, and lost awhile.

The voice was so warm and mellifluous that she continued to follow the sheet music in front of her, playing each line with a delicate touch so as to allow the words of the hymn to float above the sound of the piano. It wasn't until the song ended that she looked up, straight into the eyes of James Morgan. She hoped her surprise hadn't shown on her face, but she felt the fine hairs on her arms lift up, and she found herself quickly looking back at the sheet music, flipping through the pages as if to organize them.

"Mrs. Phillips," Morgan said, placing a hand on her own, so as to make her stop shuffling the music. She froze and he moved his hand. Then he gave her a slight bow.

"You play quite well," he said. The voice she had so enjoyed while playing the song now burned in her ears. She resisted the impulse to cup her hands over them. James Morgan was not a member of the Mother River Church, but she certainly knew who he was. She scooted over on her bench, to put as much distance as she could between herself and her visitor.

"I came to speak to your husband. Where might I find him?" Morgan asked.

The reverend had told her that he and Major Bay had some business to take care of in Frost Town, a few miles upstream. She knew that they might not return for several hours. Should she say this to James Morgan? Morgan was a highly respected businessman in these parts. Even though he lived farther north, on a plantation near the Brazos River, he spent enough time in Houston to be a commanding presence. He and his wife even had a home nearby, where they often feted the more well-to-do citizens of the new city.

She cleared her throat. "The reverend should return any time now," she said, trying to be as calm as possible. "Would you care to wait?"

He reached for her hand again, lifted it in front of her, and ran his thumb over her knuckles. She tried to pull it away from him, but he held on, drawing her nearer to him.

And then, in a voice that was even silkier than the one he had so recently raised to sing of moor and fen, he smiled in a way that showed a full set of teeth and said, "Word is that your husband has been preaching a dangerous gospel, Mrs. Phillips."

She tugged her hand again, and he clenched it even tighter. "I don't know what you mean," she said.

"You do know that there are runaways. . . ." He relaxed his grip. "A woman and two girls."

Morgan continued to smile. "Those girls belong to my wife."

At that, Miss Celia stood up and looked directly at his face. "I'm sorry for your loss, sir. I don't know what we'd do if Major Bay ran away." With her loose hand, she crossed her heart, an effort to show her earnestness. She hoped her statement would reassure him.

It must have because he paused, but then he said, "Just be sure to let your husband know that we're going to find them." With that, he let her hand drop, but he said it again, "We'll find them."

Miss Celia tucked her freed hand behind her waist, as if to hide it from Morgan. She resisted the urge to shake it, to throw off the awful feel of his fingers.

What else should she say? They had been so very careful, she and the reverend and Major Bay. She glanced down at the words on the sheet music.

> And with the morn those angel faces smile
> Which I have loved long since, and lost
> awhile.

"Why, Mr. Morgan," she said at last, her hand still behind her, "God bless you, sir."

He stepped back and then turned on his heel, but not before looking over his shoulder at her and smiling again. "Good day, Mrs. Phillips."

She remained standing as she watched him walk out through the carved doors. For several long minutes she waited, fearful that he might walk back in. She let out a long, deep breath, one she hadn't even realized she'd been holding. Then she sat back down at her bench, laid her hands back on the keys, and played, softly at first, then more forcefully, the notes rushing into the air of the friendly chapel and slipping out the windows. Finally she leaned into the piano, as if Jesus Himself was watching her. She played until at last she could no longer feel the imprint of James Morgan's thumb pressing on her knuckles. She closed the cover down over the keyboard, wiped it with her fingertips, then pressed her palms together and prayed, "Lord, where? Where are those angel faces?" And with her whole heart she begged Him to show His ever-loving mercy.

Achsah

Achsah looked into her baby girls' faces and saw
something in Mary Ann's that made her swallow, hard.
Fever. The night was warm, still holding on to the day's
heat. All three of them were coated in a light sheen of
sweat. But she could tell by the glassiness in her daughter's eyes that there was something else.

She gripped Mary Ann's hand. "Not far now, baby,"
she said. Mary Ann nodded, her chin drooping farther
down with each nod. In her hand, Achsah couldn't help
but feel her daughter shiver, as if something had run
up her back. Achsah knew that childhood fevers came
and went. Both of her girls had suffered through coughs
and sore throats and rashes. She tried to convince herself that Mary Ann just had the ague from walking in

the night air, nothing more. Just that, a nighttime chill, likely stirred up by one of the river haints. She tried to convince herself that that was all it was. Nothing more.

But she had watched the yellow jack take the Captain. It had started like this, the fever, the glassy eyes. The shakes.

"Mama," Mary Ann whispered. Achsah turned toward her, just in time to catch her before she slumped onto the ground, pulling Juba with her. Brave Juba. Another child might have cried out, but she clamped her teeth shut and held on to her mother and sister like their lives depended on her. Achsah resisted her own urge to cry out for help. She knew they couldn't be far from their destination, from the steps, from the Lady who would guide them to freedom. Not far at all.

But now her daughter needed help. Urgency pounded in her chest. But indecision climbed over her like a creeping vine. If she turned herself in, Mary Ann could get medical treatment.

But, Achsah knew, that would mean being under the control of James Morgan. Memories of her life with the Captain, of being trapped in his cabin aboard his boat, of being kept in his bed since she was twelve rushed through her.

"You're my treasure," the Captain had told her.

She clung to her girls.

No. She could not let them go to James Morgan. Never. She'd rather take her chances with the bayou.

She knelt there for a moment, her arms around them both. She was so very tired. Every bone, every muscle, every inch of her screamed for rest.

In that moment, all she wanted to do was lie down along the shoreline and sink into the water, let it take her away, past the town of Harrisburg, past the wharves of Brazoria, past the port of Galveston and into the blue, blue Gulf of Mexico.

She felt Mary Ann shudder, felt Juba's small arms around her shoulders. Her babies. Her babies. She held them as tight as she could. She remembered her own mama, holding on to her. Happiness. She remembered the master, pulling them apart, ripping her away . . . away . . . away . . .

And then, as if they knew they had been summoned, the haints spoke.

Achsah.

She closed her eyes.

Achsah, they said.

The Lady is waiting.

Hurry.

It was what she needed to hear.

So she put her hands under Mary Ann's arms and pulled her up. Then she lifted her so that her girl's head rested on her shoulder. She breathed in the smell of her, her little-girl smell. She looked down at Juba, her hair all matted and messy, so sweet in her messiness, and told her, in a voice so low it sounded like part of the breeze, "Put the kettle in the river and shove it as hard as you can," which Juba did. And from their place on the bank, they watched it float out into the current like a tiny round boat, watched it sail downstream. But only briefly, because they couldn't hesitate one more minute. Achsah knew: what they had to do was run.

Mrs. Walker

Mrs. Walker and her boys—that's how she referred to Paul and Cade, as "her boys"—didn't spend a lot of time watching television. Running the antiques store took up a lot of long hours, and after it closed in the evenings, there was always something else to do. While Paul closed up the shop, she'd mosey up to her apartment above the store, where she prepared dinner for the three of them. Maybe did a load of laundry. You get the picture.

In the meantime, Cade and Martin typically spent at least an hour playing pinball together before Martin headed to his own home.

"Pinball. Makes for good eye-hand coordination," said Paul.

And then, around eight or so, after dinner anyways, Cade and Paul would make their way to their tiny apartment for the evening, and Mrs. Walker, left alone for the night, would usually read until she was sleepy, at which time, she'd tell the photo of Hans that she still loved him, turn off the lamp, and curl up for the evening.

Paul called their whole layout (which included the store, Mrs. Walker's flat, and the bachelor pad above the garage—where the old Packard still sat) the Compound. That's kind of the way it was, actually, with the store as the central, beating heart of it all.

At any rate, there was little time for television, but one night, after years of refusing to watch it, Mrs. Walker turned on the Houston Public Broadcasting station and accidentally hit *Antiques Roadshow.*

She had never wanted to watch it before because it was too much like being at work, but for some reason that night, she felt herself drawn in. And after a few weeks, she became a regular. She even watched the reruns over the summer months, when the regular season ended.

So each Monday night, she tuned in to see what treasures would show up and what the appraisal amounts would be. You'd think that someone who spent all day, every day, dealing in antiques would hate watching a show about antiques on television, but in fact, Mrs. Walker was enamored. Every Tuesday she recounted the previous night's episode to Paul, regaling him with any new facts that she had learned, or even relearned.

Paul didn't think anyone could know more about antiques than Trudy Walker. "You'd be amazed how many things I've forgotten over the years," she said.

One Monday night she invited the boys to watch it for themselves, and pretty soon, they all three became Monday night, dedicated watchers of *Antiques Roadshow*. Which is how they learned about a pair of sculptors whom they had never heard of—Etienne Bel James and his slave, Luc Bel James—from Pickens County, Georgia. The two had lived and worked in the early to mid-nineteenth century, specializing in—of course—cemetery statues.

"But," the appraiser mentioned, "they also did absolutely amazing carvings of the human figure, some of which were commissioned for wealthy landowners, who put them in their foyers or their gardens." Then the camera showed an exquisite carving of a woman. About four feet tall, she was carved out of pink Georgia marble, with rust-red veins that flowed in between the folds of her gown, a gown that rose just above her toes, as if a gentle breeze had barely lifted her hem.

The marble was so beautifully buffed that she seemed almost transparent, as if there was an interior lamp that beamed through the outer surface of it.

The woman who owned the statue said something about receiving it as a gift from her aunt, who had collected carvings made of Georgia marble. Apparently it had been in their family for well over a hundred years. "I just want to know a little more about it."

"What you have here is a very rare sculpture by Luc Bel James," declared the appraiser. "He was a slave, owned by a master carver, Etienne Bel James, who was born in France and immigrated to the United States in the 1820s. He purchased Luc around 1839 or so and turned him into an apprentice."

"My," said the owner.

The appraiser continued, "It's a fact that Luc never signed any of his statues. As you know, it was illegal for a slave to know how to read, so a signature would have been a dangerous thing to do. And we know as well that his master was the one who was getting paid for his services, not Luc. It wasn't until after the Civil War that records about Luc became available, and those were through the oral slave narratives that were recorded by the Works Progress Administration during the 1930s. By then, Luc was long gone."

Cade had only a fleeting knowledge of the Works Progress Administration, a wide-ranging government program that had put a lot of photographers and writers and artists to work during the Great Depression. He had studied it in his ninth-grade English class, when they had been required to read *The Grapes of Wrath*. He'd never heard of the slave narratives.

The appraiser went on. "In fact, we don't know what happened to Luc after Etienne died. We don't have much to go on, but one way we can tell that this is a Luc Bel James is by the closed fist." Then he pointed out that in almost every female figure that Luc Bel James had carved, he left one hand open, but he closed the other. "You see," he said, "it's almost as if the carving is holding something, isn't it?"

The woman nodded. Mrs. Walker nodded. Cade and Paul nodded.

"It was his trademark, so to speak," said the appraiser. Then he told the woman that nobody really knew how many Luc Bel James statues were out there. He suspected that some had been destroyed in the Civil War, and some were likely hidden in old gardens or forgotten cemeteries. He doubted that there were more than a handful, if that many, left out there in the world.

"So your statue is extremely rare," and he added, "extremely valuable."

"How much is it worth?" asked the woman.

Mrs. Walker, Paul, and Cade all leaned forward. The woman on the set moved forward.

"At least a half million dollars," the appraiser said. "Maybe more. In a good auction, it could go higher."

The woman gasped.

"Whew!" said Mrs. Walker.

And Paul followed that with, "If only we could find one of those, it would be the last one we'd ever have to steal." And Cade knew his father was only half joking, because since that night, every time they visited a cemetery, they double-checked to see if just by chance, a Luc Bel James statue might show up. Even though the odds were a million to one of ever finding one, they always looked to see if there were any statues with one hand open and the other curled into a fist, the trademark of a tall, thin boy, a black Cherokee, who was once chained to a girl named Achsah, big for her age, who walked next to him, mile after mile, from Alexandria to Natchez. He gave her a tiny carving, and the last time he saw her, she held it in her hand, her fingers curled around it, like she could never let it go.

Zorra

Oh, Zorra, remember the sun, remember how to love her when she soaks into your coal-black spots, the coal-black stripes that run from your nose and along your cheeks, the defining marks of *ocelot*.

It's so hard to remember what you love when you are trapped, hidden behind a stand of yaupons, berries blazing in the afternoon light.

All you can see is the blue sky above you, just a tiny patch of it. It's all the small window will allow.

Zorra. *La chica bella.*

Zorra. *Bambina.*

Zorra. *La* bayou, *te ama.*

But that is so hard to believe when memories of what you love are fading far too fast.

Buffalo Bayou

HOUSTON

She has her own calling—to run to the sea. As soon as she smells it, there's no stopping her. From her underground springs beneath the Addicks Prairie, the bayou bubbles up to the grassy surface. She wanders past the rice fields and through thick stands of pecan trees and weeping willows. Eventually she joins her sister, the White Oak, and together they saunter through the city, past the parks and high-rises and concrete roads, underneath a dozen bridges, more.

She welcomes her smaller branches, takes them into her arms, and soon they meet the tide, pulled by the moon, tugged by the sea, announcing the presence of the San Jacinto River, her bigger sister. They tumble together like fat, clumsy puppies and hurry to the port, where ships containing automobiles from Korea and wheat from Saskatchewan and tennis shoes from China and anything else the world might want, come and go, loading and unloading their cargo holds.

And all along the way, she says her grateful prayer to Gravity, the goddess of every drop of water in the whole wide world.

Juba and Mary Ann

Water was what Mary Ann needed, fresh water, not the brackish water of the river. She hung on to her mother's neck, her legs no longer able to hold her body up. Her mouth was dry as cotton, and her throat burned with each gulp of night air. Where was the starry crown, oh Lord?

Sleep kept grabbing at her eyes like a cat. She'd try to open them, and Sleep's paws would bat them shut again. So she closed those eyes and held on as tight as she could.

And meanwhile Juba grabbed on to her mother's skirt. If she were only a little bit bigger, she would have carried her little sister, she would have taken a turn, even though she was too small for that. She would have carried her mama, too.

If only she could have, she would have.

Cade Curtis

Atop the steps of the Church on the Bayou on a brisk October evening is not a place that Cade Curtis ever expected to find himself. And yet, here he is, at least thirty minutes early, hands in pockets, shirttail tucked in, waiting for Soleil, waiting to attend her church group party. He has only read the Bible in bits and pieces, and while he stands there, he realizes that he has yet another thing to keep from Soleil: that most of his reading about the Bible has come from comic-book versions.

One of the perks of growing up in an antiques store is that people often drop off boxes of books from old estates. A few years ago someone brought in a huge crate of comic books, and included in the stack was a series called Bible Heroes. They were all mixed up with

Archie, Betty & Veronica, the Hulk, and an eye-opening batch of manga comics all written in Japanese. With the latter especially, the words didn't matter so much.

He is sure that Soleil would not approve of manga comics, and though he can't say for certain, he doubts that she would be impressed by the fact that Cade's first readings of Jesus were in the same stack as *Superman* and the *Fabulous Furry Freak Brothers*, especially the latter.

Geez, he realizes, the number of things that he can never tell this girl is increasing by the minute.

Comic Book Jesus! He stuffs his hands farther down into his pockets.

The note! He curls his fingers over it, pulls it out. There is Soleil's neat, steady handwriting, so different from his own scribbly scrawl. *Would you like to know about Ultimate Love?* That single sentence still catches him by surprise. He folds it back up, rubs his fingers along the edges, stuffs it back into his pocket. Then he sinks down onto the top step. He looks out at the street. Maybe if he stares at it long enough, Soleil will automatically appear, even though it is still thirty minutes before the party is supposed to start.

Paul dropped him off early because he said he had some errands to run. He was puzzled when Cade told him he wanted to go to a church party, but he didn't object.

Cade pulls his shoulders up to his ears. The sun is on the way out, and there is a fall chill in the air. He hasn't thought to bring a jacket, and the damp concrete step he sits on makes him feel even colder.

He stands up and dusts off the seat of his jeans. The large doors of the church look friendly enough. There's something carved across the top of them, maybe a prayer, but in the shadow of the encroaching dusk, he can't read it clearly. To his surprise, when he pulls on the handle, he discovers that the doors are unlocked.

They open into a large, brightly lit hallway. On the left is a bank of closed doors that he assumes lead into the sanctuary. On the right is a tall wall that resembles a museum. It's covered with paintings and photographs and plaques, and an assortment of other ephemera. (Another perk of growing up in an antiques store—your vocabulary. Cade knows ephemera when he sees it.)

Cade can also see that the wall is like a history exhibit of the Church on the Bayou. There are dozens of old faded newsletters; drawings done by children; photos of the church in various stages of construction, circa 1936–37; photos of groups with titles like *Missionary*

Trip, Honduras, 1948, and *Dinner on the Ground, 1952.* There are newspaper clippings and old Sunday school bulletins.

Just above the bulletin board, he notices an oil painting of a different church, a small chapel that sits neatly beside a stream. He looks at the signature—*Magnolia Phillips, 1862.* The painting is faded and cracked, but having been raised in an antiques store, Cade can see the value of it in the lovely lines and the deft strokes of the artist. Even though he is familiar with some of the early local artists of Houston—only a few of which, like this one, were pre–Civil War—he has never heard of Magnolia Phillips. He makes a mental note to ask Mrs. Walker about her.

Anyone else looking at this wall of history might have just scanned it, smiling at the children's drawings, noting the age on the photos, skimming over the various newspaper clippings, and then stepped back to look at it in its entirety. But anyone who knows about ephemera knows to pay attention to details.

He checks his phone to see what time it is, just to realize that only a few minutes have passed. He continues studying the wall.

What Cade sees next makes him stop dead in his tracks. He reads it, then reads it again, then states, right out loud, "Oh. My. Fucking. God," and in the next moment, the singular girl he's been waiting for steps through the heavy wooden doors. Not even Comic Book Jesus could have planned that.

THE HOUSTON DAILY POST
December 8, 1945

"The Lost Lady"

Readers will remember it has been ten years since the devastating floods of 1935. Engineers estimate that the Buffalo Bayou rose over fifty feet above normal flood level. Longtime residents will recall the destruction that the bayou caused, destroying homes and businesses and churches. Seven of our precious citizens lost their lives, and it has taken many merciful acts of our Lord to rebuild this fair city.

One such loss was the hundred-year-old non-denominational church that sat near the banks in the old Germantown development in the Sixth Ward. The water knocked the chapel off its piers and beams, and only a few parts of it were discovered several miles downstream, as the mighty waters of the bayou tore it away. Only the front doors were salvageable.

Sadly the iconic statue of a woman that had graced

the church's yard for a century was pushed from her pedestal, and a decade since the flood of the century occurred, it has not been recovered. It's assumed that the statue is likely at the bottom of the bayou. "It's a shame," declared Mrs. Weisskopf, a former member of the congregation. "The statue was carved from pink Georgia marble and was quite beautiful."

She recalled that at one time the statue was somewhat controversial, since one breast was left uncovered by the artist, which was very risqué for a church statue. Mrs. Weisskopf stated that it was nevertheless done in a tasteful, "artistic" manner. "Over the years, some of the ladies of the church knitted shawls to cover her." She then chuckled and added, "Of course, the shawls never lasted." She hinted that the older boys of the church used to play pranks and try to steal the shawls. She admitted that many of them succeeded.

As the statue sat amid a number of graves, reclaiming the interred was made more arduous by the destruction wrought by the rushing waters, which altered the banks somewhat, making it difficult to find the original plots. Some of the graves were of slaves, and because those were mostly unmarked, and also very close to the banks, they could not be recovered. Mrs. Weisskopf further stated that most of the other graves were reclaimed and are safely reinterred in the old Washington Cemetery, formerly known as Germantown Cemetery.

Mrs. Weisskopf is one of the last survivors of the old church, and a current member of the brand-new Church on the Bayou. She said one of her dying wishes is to see the statue again, even though it is highly unlikely that it can ever be found.

"The statue was a mystery," she said. "She had one hand open and the other closed. When we were kids, we always tried to figure out what she might be holding in her hand." Even if she's found, that part of the mystery will be forever unsolved.

If anyone has any knowledge of the whereabouts of this statue, you can contact this reporter to make arrangements to restore her to Mrs. Weisskopf and the last remaining members of the old church.

Soleil Broussard

Soleil wasn't at all sure whether or not Cade would meet her at the church. She has been living in the mystery of it, a mystery filled with prayers. Lots of prayers, not a few of which were about asking Jesus to forgive her for so clumsily using Him for her own ends.

So when Soleil steps into the hallway of the Church on the Bayou and sees him there, her heart says, *Rejoice!*

But then she sees him look past her, as if she is the only obstacle between him and the door. Plus, he blurts out a word that she is sure has likely never been uttered in this particular spot on the planet. She looks at his face. Escape is written all over it, and she immediately knows that he isn't going to stay. She steps closer to him.

He starts doing that rocking thing. Heel. Toe. Heel. Toe.

"I'm sorry, but I have to go," he says.

She swallows. Hard.

She needs to say something, but before she can, he speaks first. "Look," he says, "I'd stay, but I just remembered that I have something I need to take care of."

His face has an expression of determination, as if the very act of standing there is costing him. Several seconds pass. Where is her voice? She should tell him it's okay, that he should go. But she cannot get her jaws or tongue to engage in this conversation. Maybe, she thinks, this is punishment for misusing Jesus.

Right then she realizes that he has stopped rocking on his heels and toes. He reaches for her right hand, and she watches, as if in slow motion.

There is her hand, resting between both of his, a kind of hand sandwich, which he pulls up to just underneath his chin. She feels the rough skin of his palms against the soft skin of her own. It's as if her hand has found its natural home apart from the rest of her body, and it never, never wants to leave.

They stand there for a full minute, her right hand pressed between both of his, just underneath his chin, where she knows her head would fit. And she prays,

Don't let go. Please don't let go. She chants it over and over and over, just the middle—no *Dear Lord*, no *Amen*.

At last, she takes a chance. "Stay," she says, in her quietest voice. "Please stay." And she realizes that she has never wanted anything ever in the whole history of Soleil Noel Broussard, including her honey bear tattoo, as much as she wants this: for him to stay.

But then he blurts out, "It's just that I forgot . . . I forgot . . . that I have to work on that assignment for Mrs. Franco."

And as soon as he put the invisible period on that sentence, capped off by the invisible quotation mark, the spell is broken. The assignment? Soleil knows exactly which assignment he is talking about, and that assignment isn't due for another week. He is lying to her. Her cheeks blaze.

She pulls her hand away as he rushes past her and out the doors, leaving the air in the hallway all crooked and hot, leaving her there, with the loneliest hand in the Lone Star State.

Zorra

In *A Field Guide to Mammals*, the author said you had *eyeshine golden*. He said, *Skins valuable as trophies; offers sport to the hunter; does little damage because of rareness.*

The metal bowl is cold in the fall night. Empty, it offers no solace. Zorra's ribs protrude underneath her matted coat. She is too weak to clean it with her swollen tongue, swollen from lack of water. It's true she is designed for deserts as well as the jungle, but it's now been several days since the bowl held water, since the rain fell from the clouds.

She is dizzy with grief, trapped in her wooden cage, trapped in the tangled roots of a hickory tree.

Zorra, your motherland wants you back.

Zorra, rare girl, so much damage has been done.

240

Only fifty of your brothers and sisters, your grandmothers and grandfathers, your uncles and aunts remain at Laguna Atascosa, refuge on the border, whispering winds and saw grass. They need you.

Zorra, come home.

Zorra. Eyeshine golden.

Mother River Church of God's Blessings

The dirt in Houston is a rich, dark black, shot through with sand and clay and sediment from the frequent floods. Dig down a foot and the soil is soft, perfect for planting azaleas and camellias. Dig down two feet and a layer of thick red clay will stick to the blades of your hoe or shovel. Dig some more and soon water will seep into the hole, and before you know it, what you have to show for all that digging is a hole filled with muddy black water.

It's why there were never any basements underneath the new citizens' dogtrot houses. Even the wealthiest among them, who built large homes with two stories and wraparound porches, never thought to put in basements. If they did, the water would eventually trickle down the earthen sides and turn the floor to a gumbo of mud and mildew. It wasn't worth it. No one needed a large hole filled with dirty water underneath the house.

No, hardly ever could you find a basement in early Houston.

But Major Bay, he knew how to dig into the hard, packed clay, how to use that clay as a barrier to the water. He knew to come at it from an angle, to make the most of the clay's natural veins. He knew exactly how to cure lime and paste it to the sidewalls and the floor to make a hard, solid crust, knew how to set the bricks in a way that left little room for seepage.

Major Bay built a basement.

The Reverend Phillips blessed it.

Miss Celia stocked it with jars of peaches and honey and pole beans.

And candles. There were candles made of tallow. On a small shelf built into the wall, right next to the wooden steps that Major Bay built, descending from the entrance. And matches for lighting those candles? There, on the shelf beside them.

In the corner, they spread a layer of cotton batting on the brick floor and covered it with flour sacks. And in another corner, there was a small barrel of drinking water, with a wooden ladle for dipping it out.

If James Morgan knew there was a basement underneath Mother River Church of God's Blessings, he'd
likely take a ball-peen hammer and bust through the
floor of the small, lovely chapel. If he did, all he'd find
was dirt.

But the basement was there nonetheless. Its hol-
low space six feet below the altar was what made Miss
Celia's piano ring out like a cathedral's pipe organ.

But you couldn't get to it through the church floor,
or the church door, either. Not the basement that Major
Bay built. Not the basement that wore its blessing like
a gown. Not the basement that Miss Celia filled with
God's gifts from her garden.

It was ready.

It was waiting.

And so was the barge that would arrive in two days'
time. The Reverend Phillips and Major Bay had made
the arrangements a day earlier in Harrisburg. The barge
would drift up close to the banks, its deck laden with
cotton bales, harvested in the hot sun of the Brazos
Valley and tied fast with twine. It would float so close,
it would go so slow, that say there was a person sitting
on the edge of that barge's deck, feet dangling off in the
water—that person could reach right down and grab
the arms of another person, if another person happened

to be waiting right there in the dark, hiding amid the tangle of vines and tree roots that protruded from the banks, and then keep on going until it reached the port in Galveston, where a tall ship waited for all that cotton to take to Mexico.

Two days. They had two days left for the barge to not stop as it drifted past, its cotton bales stacked in neat, solid rows, still smelling like the sun.

The basement. The barge. The tall ship. All waiting. And the Lady too.

Achsah and her girls . . . where were they?

James Morgan

James Morgan could wait. Achsah had a day's lead on him, but he had time on his side. He also had the reward money, and since he had sent his boy to paste the flyers on doorjambs and windows all up and down the rows of shops and houses along the wharves, he knew that soon enough someone would find her and the two girls.

The reward was a handsome sum, one hundred dollars for each of the girls and fifty dollars for Achsah, all in US dollars. The girls and their mother were far more valuable than that, but he could go higher if he needed. He hadn't become successful at what he did by giving up money he didn't have to. He also knew that US dollars were twice as valuable in Texas as they were in the US. Three times more valuable, maybe more, especially with the high probability that Texas would join the United States soon. Very soon.

A day ahead. That's all they were.

Morgan knew that as long as it didn't rain, her scent was still fresh enough for the dogs, the "Negro dogs," as they were called. They'd never failed him. Last time one of his field hands tried to bolt, the dogs had him cornered in less than five hours. Brutus, his big mastiff, took three fingers off as compensation, and would've taken his face if the man hadn't covered it with his hands. Can't get much work out of a man with no face.

He had told his handler not to let that happen to the little girls, to keep the dogs on leashes, even though he realized that would slow them down. It was a chance he could take. He knew that his quarry—a woman and two small girls—couldn't go that fast, even with their day's advantage.

"Don't let the dogs harm them," he had told his handler. "Or I'll set them right back on you. Understand?" The man tipped his hat and spat a huge wad of tobacco onto the wooden plank of the hotel porch. Morgan hadn't looked down. That was two days ago.

Now James Morgan sat on the porch of the Hotel de Chene and stared at the busy wharves on the other side of the street. Ever since the Allen brothers had staked out this new city and named it after the president of the Republic, Sam Houston, it had exploded in growth. Thousands of new residents had arrived, primarily from the southern United States. And since the Texans had defeated Santa Anna, a significant number of those new residents were black slaves. And that suited James Morgan.

He relied upon slave labor to work in his sugar and cotton fields, not to mention his stables and his house.

The Captain had promised him those two girls. Mary Ann and Juba. *Until the age of twenty-one, when they shall be given the status of Freewoman.* He had read the will. He knew the girls were only five and three. They weren't too young to pick cotton, they weren't too young to scrub floors. They weren't too young. . . .

And besides, well before they turned twenty-one, their bellies would be filled with their own babies. He'd see to that. And then who would ever remember the will of a long-dead sea captain? Why, he doubted that he himself would remember it. And it wouldn't take very much to buy off the court, now would it?

Truth be told, he could probably convince the court to give him custody of Achsah herself. Who, after all, would vouch for her? And besides, it wasn't good policy, was it, to set a Negro free just because she was the mother of your children. Thinking about it, he nearly started laughing. That would be rich, wouldn't it? Three for the price of two.

He swirled the liquor in his glass, lifted it to his nose and breathed it in.

He wiped his forehead with a clean white handkerchief and took a deep sip of whiskey, imported from Tennessee where he was born, and waited while it burned its way down his gullet. It was a far way from that rocky terrain to this flat, swampy plain. If his wife, with her sour face, had her way, they'd go back there. Every day he half expected her to pack up her belongings and leave.

And every day, he wished she would. But she had remained loyal to him, and that meant something to James Morgan. On the rare occasions when she smiled, he confessed that she was a handsome woman. She also set a fine table, which impressed the other gentry, along with the officers of the fledgling government. His status required an acceptable marriage. Mrs. Morgan gave him that.

He realized that he needed her. But that didn't mean that he liked her, nor did he like her company. And even though, technically, the Captain had given Achsah's girls to *her*, not him, he also knew that she wouldn't care who they served.

He wiped his face with the handkerchief again and raised his glass to the "Negro dogs," especially Brutus. "Don't eat their fingers, you stupid cur!" Then he threw the whiskey back in a single gulp and waited for its slow burn to shave off the last edges of his heart.

Achsah

1845

The predawn air was still, the bayou like glass. Achsah clung to her burning-up girl, her Mary Ann, held her tight against her chest. Beside her, Juba gripped her skirt. Soon the sun would uncover them. They had been on the go since just after midnight by Achsah's reckoning. There was a sliver of moon that urged them on, step after step, until at last, the river haints cried, *Stop!* So she did, and that's when she saw her: the Lady. Glowing in the early grayness of dawn, just at the top of the banks. And there, right in front of them, embedded in the bank, the wooden steps that would take them right to her.

Achsah resisted the urge to cry out. Even in the pale light, the Lady was so beautiful. Was she an angel?

Achsah didn't have much truck with angels, but if she had, the statue in front of her might be one. She blinked hard to make sure she wasn't dreaming.

Achsah pushed Juba ahead of her up the steps, and once on the top, gripped the back of Mary Ann's head and gently lowered her to the ground, still under the cover of the shrubbery and vines that lined the edge of the churchyard. Every muscle in her body screamed from carrying her daughter over the last couple of miles, miles that had felt interminable, miles that took them through the soft mud of the bayou's banks, mud that sucked at her feet, pulled on her legs, soaked the bottom of her skirt and made it feel as heavy as the girl in her arms. The relief of setting her down was enormous, and for a second, she felt as light as the morning air.

She patted Mary Ann's swollen face, wiped the sweat off it with the hem of her sodden skirt. Juba crumpled on the ground beside her. Exhaustion crawled up Achsah's spine and down her arms. But she could not let it overcome her.

Looking at the statue, Achsah knew she had found her destination at last, knew that this was the right place. Now all she had to do was to figure out how the Lady was supposed to help her. She looked at her through the curtain of vines. Only a few yards to the left of the statue was the small chapel. Achsah didn't think that the chapel was where she should go. The trackers would expect that, would expect her to seek refuge in a church. It would be the first place they'd look.

So she scanned the churchyard, noticed the large pecan trees, the stately pines, noticed the open grounds that surrounded the statue. It seemed like the whole area was uncovered, unsheltered. She couldn't detect anything that resembled a hiding place. She could also see that the church itself sat so low that she was sure there was no crawl space underneath it.

She sat down hard on the ground next to the girls, pulled up her knees, and rested her head on them. If she weren't so tired, she knew she'd break into tears.

But she also knew that there was no time for crying. They had come too long and too hard, and she had to find help for Mary Ann soon, very soon.

She raised her head and stared hard at the Lady. The statue glowed in the gathering light. It had taken them three long days and nights, with little food and sleep, to make their circuitous way to this spot. They had avoided the gators and the snakes, they had been fodder for a thousand biting mosquitoes. Every inch of her body hurt. Her skin was raw from the insects that had chewed on her. Her mouth was bone-dry from breathing so hard while she carried Mary Ann. She could not have come this far, only to fail because she couldn't see what she was supposed to see. She had memorized the instructions passed to her, slave to slave, from Major Bay, but they only got her to the statue. They didn't tell her what to do once she found it.

Achsah!

She cocked her ears. The river haints, the ones that had slid beside them through the water all along the way, rose into the air.

Achsah, they sang. *Hurry!*

She wanted to hurry, knew that as soon as the sun cracked the sky, the hounds would resume their howling trail. Time was slipping away, but where? Where was she supposed to go? She knew she could not just fall at the feet of the statue, not out in the wide open like that.

At once, anger rose up her neck, a bright heat that surged into her cheeks and forehead and through the top of her skull. One daughter was burning up on the ground beside her. The other was crumpled down in a heap, weary to the bone.

She wanted to run up to the Lady and shove her. She wanted to take something hard, maybe a hammer, and smash her to bits, to watch her slump on the ground like her quiet Juba.

Instead, she pushed the vine aside again and stared at her. Hard. The Lady's body was turned in a particular direction, as if she was squarely facing the front of the church. Was that a bluff? It seemed so. The church didn't offer any solution. So she followed the curve of the Lady's outstretched hand, her palm up. Was she making an offering? It seemed she was facing one way, yet pulled in another.

When Achsah looked down, she saw that the arm that was not outstretched hung by her side in a fist, as if she were holding something. Instinctively Achsah patted her pocket. The tiny figurine was still there. She took a deep breath and stood up, and that was when she saw what she was supposed to see. The Lady's head was tilted so that her face nodded toward a copse of shrubs, just to the side and behind the building. At once, Achsah knew where to go. The Lady could not have been clearer if she had spoken out loud.

Quickly Achsah gathered Mary Ann back up, limp and heavy and hot. She pulled on Juba's arm and whispered, "Run, baby. Run." And like that, she flew to the opposite side of the churchyard, as fast as she could, the vanishing stars tracing their steps. With Mary Ann in her arms and Juba holding on to her skirt, she hurried to the hidden brush arbor, cloaked in wild roses and yaupon bushes and stinging dewberry vines, paused only long enough to see the thin stream of light from the opening, hardly large enough for a woman and two little girls to step through. There, in front of them, barely distinguishable from the ground itself, a door. Achsah laid Mary Ann down again and pulled on it. As soon as she did, she saw the wooden steps, and right beside them on a shelf, a candle, glowing in the darkness.

Achsah, sang the river haints. *Achsah!*

But she paid them no mind. For in that moment, she and her little girls were safe. Safe in Major Bay's basement, blessings all around.

Buffalo Bayou

HOUSTON

She has always been a nursery for sun perch and bull-frogs and river rats and dragonflies and mosquitoes. But her favorite? Alligators.

At her most toxic, during the years when she served as a sewer for the city, when she was filled with runoff from the sawmills and breweries and cotton gins, when boats emptied their bilges into her silty bed, even then, she has raised alligators.

She admires their clever ability to hover on the bottom, to lurk beside the banks, to lunge at unsuspecting prey. She respects their sturdy jaws and their ruthless grit. Alligators have always been her special pets.

Major Bay knew this. He waited for Miss Celia to give Achsah and her girls a fresh change of clothing.

Then he took the old garments, shredded them, coated them with blood from a slaughtered rabbit, and dragged them upstream along her banks. When he reached a hidden cove, he set the clothes and the rabbit right at the water's edge.

Bait.

For her alligators.

By the time the dogs got there, the handler tugging on their long leashes, whistling to them with his shrill call, all they found were bits and pieces of bloodied clothing, alligators resting on the banks. Alligators love hounds, so it was good that the handler called them off. He stood as close as he dared, pulled his hat from his head, and held it across his chest.

"God have mercy," he said, and lowered his face and wept.

Zorra

The famous artist Salvador Dali kept an ocelot. He called her Babou, and he took her everywhere. To restaurants, to the theater, on the train. She was a beautiful creature, and he knew it.

But Babou did not belong in sidewalk cafés and movie houses and glamorous hotels. She belonged in the rain forests of Brazil and Uruguay. She needed to be in the ravines and canyons of Mexico and Baja California. Not in Paris or Rome or New York City.

She was a wild thing.

Zorra too is wild. She does not belong in a wooden cage with an empty metal bowl for company. She needs to return to her Laguna Atascosa with her cousins. She needs food. She needs water. She needs for someone to open the door of her cage before it's too late for her.

Oh Zorra, gato bonita.

Where is the angel of ocelots?

Does he even know you're here?

Cade Curtis

Cade wakes up wishing he could redo the night before. Of all the excuses to give to Soleil, he used his assignment in Mrs. Franco's class in order to leave the church and skip out on the party. *Aarrghh!*

He is fairly certain she could see that he was lying. She isn't stupid.

And he can't stop thinking about her. Her soft hand and the disappointed look on her face when he lied to her.

But ringing in his ears like a chant, he is also thinking about what Paul said: *If only we could find one of those, it would be the last one we'd ever have to steal.*

A knot forms in his gut as he recalls the article from the night before.

It was dated 1945. That means that for a good part of a century, more than eighty years, the statue has been missing. It also means that in that same time span, someone else might have already found her. Maybe she was in somebody's attic or garden or garage, maybe she was wrapped in a tarp and tucked out of sight. It was possible.

She might even be in a museum somewhere. Again, possible.

It could also be that she is like the mystery of the Twin Sisters—a pair of famous cannons that a group of Confederate soldiers buried only a few yards from the edge of the bayou in a copse of pine and oak trees, just as the Civil War came to an end. The soldiers did it in order to keep the cannons from being sent to a foundry and melted down. They—the cannons—had been important weapons in the victory at the Battle of San Jacinto, the decisive battle that ended Mexico's hold on Texas.

Years later, during the Civil War, they were used again in the Battle of Sabine Pass. The soldiers loved them too much to let them be turned into church bells or plowshares. So, in 1865, they stole them from the arsenal where they were stowed, burned the wooden carriers that held them, and buried the guns in shallow graves. As they covered the ground with leaves, they marked the trees nearby, to signify where they were. But years later, when one of the veterans returned to uncover them, he saw that the trees had grown, the banks had shifted. Despite repeated efforts to find them, the Twin Sisters are still, to this day, missing.

How does Cade even know about them? He remembers reading about them in his seventh-grade Texas history class, a class every single seventh grader in Texas has to take. Who doesn't know about the Twin Sisters?

It's also possible that, like the cannons, the statue is still hidden along the banks of the Buffalo Bayou. At least once every six months or so, someone comes by Walker's Art and Antiques with an object that they've found in or around the bayou, things the bayou has kept for years and years, and then, for whatever reason—usually a flood—has given them up and tossed them onto her banks.

More often than not, the objects are coins. Cade has seen coins from every era and from dozens of different countries, all discovered along the bayou. There is a small display of them in the front jewelry case, along with a cache of old guns—derringers, Colts, a tiny pocket flintlock with gold finish.

Clients have also dropped off other odd objects—hand-blown glass bottles, rusted tools, pottery, even a carved wheel from a horse-drawn wagon. Aside from a few rare coins, however, none of the bayou's gifts have been particularly valuable. Most of them fall into the same category as the Dutch windmill salt and pepper shakers. Sentimental, but not worth much.

Cade also knows that it's highly probable that the statue is at the very bottom of the bayou, covered with several feet of silt. By now, it might even have made it to the Gulf of Mexico.

Nevertheless . . . what if? *What if?*

The article said that the churchyard was in the Sixth Ward, which meant that if the water had been able to push the statue off her pedestal, it should be downstream from there, which would put her . . . where?

The Buffalo Bayou is long and winding. There are big stretches of it that are wide open. Then again, there are stretches that are completely grown over by the thick underbrush and vegetation that tropical Houston nurtures. It is tame and wild and tame and wild. Take a canoe and float down it. You will see vines as thick as your arm, and grass as neat as a lawn. You will float right through the middle of downtown, next to the glittering arts district, and then past the old industrial alleys of railroads and warehouses. You will hear birdsong and traffic and wind and peepers and sirens and machines and automobiles.

Where on the Buffalo Bayou should Cade start?

Paul is still snoring. Cade knows his dad was puzzled last night when he called to come pick him up so soon after dropping him off, but when Paul asked what the deal was, Cade used the same excuse he told Soleil: "I forgot, I have this assignment due."

Paul just shrugged and said, "Okay, Li'l Dude," which Cade realizes he is pretty tired of hearing. What is he, three?

And just as he asks that question, his gaze falls upon the old baby stroller folded up in the corner. Paul never stashed it, never moved it out of their bachelor pad. According to Paul, for almost half a year, Cade slept in that stroller, until at last he outgrew it.

Cade stands up and walks to the window, careful not to wake his father. He should tell Paul about the article, about the possibility of finding a Luc Bel James statue, one that might be worth half a million dollars.

He should.

And maybe he will, but not now. Now, he wants to do this on his own. After all, he's sixteen, almost seventeen, the same age his dad was when their shared history began. Now it is Cade's turn, and he knows exactly where to start. He looks through the slats of the blinds. It's a clear fall day, a perfect day to hunt for an angel.

He should tell his dad. But he doesn't.

Zorra

Zorra dreams of the jacaranda tree, its branches loaded with purple flowers. She dreams of cool water from a tiny branch that flows to the pond. There is a dream of wet sand beneath her feet, between her toes, and a blazing hot sun that warms her thick spotted coat.

Zorra dreams of marsh hares and the hidden eggs of the bobwhite's nest. She dreams of thunder and the sweet howl of her coyote.

Dream, Zorra, the river haints sing.

Dream through the night.

Dream through the day.

And Zorra, her coat stiff from the bayou's mud and silt, her eyes half-closed, her body limp from hunger and thirst, dreams a thousand dreams. What else can she do?

Soleil Broussard

What is the truth?
  Cade told her a lie.
What, *what* is the truth?
  Cade held her hand between his. Her hand. His
    hands.
What else is the truth?
  Their hands.
Seriously the truth?
  Foolish. She feels foolish.
What is the truth, anyways?
    He held her hand.
    He told her a lie.
And both of those things are true.

Achsah

Achsah, she held tight to Juba's small hand. In the bitter darkness, the only sound they could hear was the *dip-pull, dip-pull* of the oar punching into the quiet bayou as the barge approached their spot on the bank.

Major Bay stood next to them. Achsah thought that if Major Bay wasn't right there, she'd run back to the hidden basement and grab Mary Ann up in her arms. She'd carry her all the way to Mexico.

As if he could hear her thoughts, Major Bay whispered into her ear. "You got to go. The boat won't wait, and she's too sick now."

But that wasn't what Achsah wanted to hear. All night, all day, in the tiny basement, lit only by candles, her Mary Ann had slept, her body burning like the sun while the yellow jack coursed through her tiny self.

Reverend Phillips had prayed. Miss Celia had prayed. Major Bay had prayed. And all Achsah could do was wash her baby's face with the cool water from the small barrel.

"You got to go," whispered Major Bay. "Another boat won't come for weeks now." Plans had been made. The boat was coming—it was only yards away. Achsah and Juba would climb aboard the cotton barge and duck between the bales. Then, in Galveston, they'd board a tall ship, which would take them to Costa Chica, to Mexico, to freedom.

The boat drew close, so close. Achsah tightened her grip on Juba's hand. She should turn around. She should hurry back to Mary Ann. She should . . . But the river haints were having none of it. While the trio stood there, the fog rose up and made a blanket around them, cover for their escape.

Achsah, they sang.

Achsah heard them. But she didn't want to. All she wanted was to hold her baby girl. What would happen to her? Would Mrs. Morgan find her and take her away? Then she gulped. What if she never saw her again? Like her own mama, Happiness, torn away from her? Achsah had never stopped missing Happiness.

Now, here she was, leaving her own baby. How could she even breathe without her girl? She took a step backward.

Major Bay gripped her arm, just above her elbow. "You got to leave now. Got to catch this boat." Achsah nodded, then nodded again. She grasped Juba's hand even tighter. Stepped onto the edge of the bank, felt the water come up over their shoes, felt the fog haints swirl all around them, felt her hot tears stream down her face. Even the water said her name: *Mary Ann. Mary Ann. Mary Ann.*

Achsah, cried the haints. *Achsah.*

She heard their song, she listened, she reached into her pocket, felt the tiny figurine. She pulled it out and handed it to Major Bay. She knew he would give it to Mary Ann, just as the tall boy had given it to her. But as soon as she dropped it into his broad hand, she felt a piercing stab in the middle of her own palm, as if the figurine had been ripped from its skin. She gasped, but resisted taking it back. Instead, she watched as Major Bay tucked the tiny carving into his own pocket. Safe.

"I'll give it to her," he whispered.

And then the boat bumped against the bank. One bump. Two. And just like that, back it sailed into the very middle of the bayou, Achsah and Juba curled up into a tight cocoon between the bales of cotton.

Achsah, the bayou will never forget you.

And she never has.

Juba and Mary Ann

"Mexico means freedom," her mama told her. But to Juba, freedom didn't sound right without Mary Ann. As she held Achsah's hand, there on the edge of the bayou, she looked back over her shoulder. In the darkness, she could barely make out the outline of the Lady, the marble statue. She saw the black shadows of the brush arbor with its drapery of wild roses and yaupon bushes. Underneath, in a small, dark basement, her sister burned with fever.

Mary Ann! she wanted to cry out. All her life she, Juba, had been so quiet, as quiet as a stone. But now, she wanted to make a giant noise, to let the water and the trees and the ink-black sky know that she was calling for her sister.

Instead, she held herself as still as the Lady herself, not making a sound. But the haints, they heard her, the humming she made just underneath her breath, her sister's song, so low, so sweet.

In her deep, burning fever, the refrain played in Mary Ann's head, over and over, "*. . . and who shall wear de starry crown, Good Lord, show me the way.*"

Cade Curtis

Cade leaves the house before his dad wakes up. That isn't unusual. Paul loves to sleep in, and since Mrs. Walker is usually the person who opens up the shop, there is no hurry for him to get there. Unless she has something special for him to do, Paul normally wanders in around ten or so. Cade learned years ago to get to school without Paul's assistance.

Because he knows that Martin might wonder where he is, he sends him a quick text.

Hey, back in bed. Stomach flu.

That's all he needs to say. Sure enough, in less than a minute:

Stay home see u L8r.

After toasting and eating a pair of cherry Pop-Tarts

and gulping down a glass of orange juice, Cade grabs his backpack. In it he puts a bottle of water, a hand trowel for digging, a small pick, and on an impulse, he throws in a box of Raisinets. *Don't go anywhere without them,* Paul always quips. *You never know when you're going to need them.*

In his wallet, Cade has seven dollars and some change, enough for a burger and a Coke if he gets too hungry. He's realistic enough to know that even if he finds the statue, he'll have to come get his dad to help move her. For a split second, he thinks about taking the stroller to put her in, but of course he realizes it is not built to carry four hundred pounds.

He checks his phone: 7:19. He has all day. Even if he doesn't make it back before four thirty or five that afternoon, no one will realize that he is gone. Besides, he isn't actually going that far. Less than a mile, to be exact.

He steps out onto the landing of the garage apartment and hurries down the steps. The cool air of the morning feels good against the bare skin of his arms. He shivers. Maybe he should grab a hoodie?

He looks up at the rising morning sun.

Nah. It will warm up soon. This is Houston. He steps forward, walks past the antiques store, and bounds down the street—in the opposite direction of Henrik Brenner High School. He stuffs his hands in his pockets to keep them warm, and when he does, he thinks about Soleil's soft hand between his.

The memory of it settles on his fingertips, circles his palms. He wants to hold that hand again. Thinking about it makes him pick up his pace.

If he can just find the Lady, there will be nothing to hide. He and Paul and Mrs. Walker could get out of the angel relocation business. A half million dollars would be more than enough.

They could say adios to the Cowboy.

All he needs is a statue carved by a onetime slave named Luc Bel James, a statue last seen more than eighty years ago, in 1935.

He picks up his pace again until he is practically jogging. As he nears the intersection to the trail that will lead him to the bayou, he slows down. The bayou is beautiful this time of day, with the early sun gleaming on her silver surface.

The bayou. She is like an artery, pumping through the very heart of Houston. Cade pauses for a moment, catches his breath. He has seen her change a million times. But right now, she poses no threat. Even though the water is a bit higher due to the recent rains, it is nothing like she was after the hurricane. He'd never seen her run that high, broiling mad, hissing past the bridges, tearing limbs from trees and hauling cars and even eighteen-wheelers down to the river and all the way to the ship channel. Cade rubs his arms and speeds up. When he gets to the bridge, he takes his bearings.

From where he stands, if he looks directly across the bayou and to the right, he should be gazing at the southernmost boundary of the Sixth Ward. So if he crosses over and makes a U-turn in that same direction, by his reckoning, if the statue was pushed downstream, she very well could be in the area just beyond the bridge.

There is a wide swath of grassy parkland, but Cade figures that the park area has been shoveled and leveled so many times that it is highly unlikely that she would be there. But there is also a thick stand of old trees and brush that grows along the banks. It will be difficult mucking around in there, but it seems to him like it's a good place for something to hide, a good place to start.

He pulls his pack up tighter on his back and heads across the bridge. As he crosses, he stays inside the narrow bike lane while dozens of commuters rush by. As

Cade walks over it, he knows that thousands of bats, Mexican free-tails, are roosting under his footsteps right now, a thought that makes him smile.

Once on the other side, he makes the U-turn that takes him into the underbrush. It isn't that far from the water, but it's steep. Instead of going directly down, he veers south toward the wooded area. He pauses. Can he even get in there? He takes a deep breath, and with both hands, he pushes aside a web of vines and steps forward.

The darkness surprises him, and he blinks to adjust to it. Had the light not been so fractured by the trees' leaves. Had it not been so thick. Had he not been so intent on what he was doing, he might have paid more attention to the slick ground underfoot, to the way that the black clay of the bayou's banks was greased from the recent rains.

But he didn't, and before he knows it, his feet fly out from underneath him. He reaches out to grab something, anything, but the slippery clay is unforgiving. It teams up with gravity and jerks him sideways.

All he can see is a dizzy whirl of green. Deep, vibrant, muddy green. All he can smell is the oily dirt, grinding into his face, his hair, his fingernails. All he can hear is the rush of his own blood, pumping into his ears. All he feels is the blinding blow to the back of his head as he pitches backward into the solid gray piling of the bridge. At last, all he remembers is the flash of stars in his eyes before they fade into black.

That is all.

And the haints in the bayou spin in their watery bed.

Cade, they sing. *Cade.*

But he can't hear them.

Soleil Broussard

Soleil does not believe that she can go to school today. She starts to tell her mother that she is sick, but then realizes that that would be yet another lie, so instead, she simply announces: "I'm taking the day off." She will stay home and clean her room. She will scrub the kitchen. Wash windows. Walk the dog if they had one.

But her mom is not having it. "Perfect," she says. "I can use your help today." It seems that the chief administrator of the Church on the Bayou always needs an extra hand, and today, the minister has planned a luncheon for their senior members, and there is plenty to do to get ready.

"Your choice," says her mom. "School or church."

And for a moment, Soleil almost regrets the thing about being sick. At least Cade will not be at church, she's sure of that, and right now, he is the last person in the entire universe she wants to see.

Church it is.

Soleil puts tablecloths on the long tables in the community room and sets up the tea and water station. Then she sets a stack of napkins beside the cookies, along with some paper plates. There is another table with sandwiches and chips. She can smell the egg salad and tuna. Why, she wonders, is it always egg salad and tuna? Can't there ever, just once, be pimento cheese? She stares at the sandwiches, as if staring would magically change them from egg salad and tuna to pimento cheese.

"Soleil!" says her mom. "Why so cranky?" How can her mom always tell? "Take a walk," says Mama.

Fine. She spins on her toes, and all of a sudden, without even realizing it, she finds herself in the front hallway.

The scene of the lie.

Her eyes begin to burn, and her immediate impulse is to turn around. Go back to the egg salad and tuna sandwiches, go any place but here. But instead, she slows down. The faces in the photographs seem to be looking at her, as if they are letting her know that there is something here she needs to see. She stops. These photos are familiar to her. She's seen them a million times. But right now, they all look brand-new.

There are dozens of them: portraits of men with long, bushy beards and bowler hats; group shots of women in white dresses with striped belts and white shoes; children in their various Sunday school groups. Soleil even finds a photo of herself with her first-grade class. She's in the first row, right between Channing and Grapes.

It seems to her that the photos are random. Some are old and some are recent. Some are in black and white. Some are in color. Some are posed and some are just snapshots.

There doesn't appear to be any particular chronology, either. They are basically jumbled up, as if the times and places of the members of this old church were all mixed together, as if the ancestors and the new babies all lived at once.

She pauses in front of the painting of the country church, the one painted in oil by someone named Magnolia Phillips, and dated 1862. More than 150 years ago.

She steps closer and squints. In the corner opposite the signature are the letters *MRCGB*. She wonders who Mr. CGB was.

She stands back and looks at it again, this time without the squint. Why does it seem so familiar? From out of the blue, Mama walks up to her. "It's sweet, isn't it?"

Soleil nods. It is sweet.

"It's the original church."

"It is?" But of course. How could Soleil not know that?

"It was built in 1840 or thereabouts," says Mama. "Can you see something familiar about it?"

So there is something. Soleil looks harder. And that's when she sees them. "The doors!" The ones in the painting are the same ones that lead into this building. The ones with the prayer carved into them.

Soleil has recited it thousands of times. It's the mission of their church, written by the original pastor.

> *Oh Lord, let this beautiful place be a*
> *refuge for all who need it.*
> *Let us be worthy. Let us be brave. Let us*
> *be kind.*
> *Amen*

"The doors were the only things left of the old church after the flood of 1935," says Mama. Then she points to the news article about the Lost Lady. Soleil reads it. And as she does, she realizes that she is standing in the exact spot in the hallway as she stood last night, holding Cade's hand.

"Did anybody ever find her?" asks Soleil.

Mama just shakes her head. "I don't know, baby. I never read anything else about her." She pauses. "But isn't it wonderful that the old doors were recovered? Just think, they're almost two hundred years old, the same age as the church."

Just then a group of folks drop by for lunch, and Mama has to lead them to the community room.

Soleil stands in the empty hallway. Where is the Lady now? And what does she have to do with Cade?

Buffalo Bayou

HOUSTON

On a clear blue day, she takes her time, moseys from her underground springs in the prairie reservoir. She and the White Oak play crisscross and together they twist and turn, bump into each other, sidle past the minnows and the turtles, sunning themselves on fallen logs.

On a clear blue day, she glistens underneath the Texas sun.

But give her some rain, days and days of rain, which she gobbles up like a drunk with an open tab. Give her water and more water, water from the pouring sky, water from the spilling-over reservoirs and lakes, and she will fill your cup and then some.

She takes out cars and houses and massive century-old trees. She grabs hold of railroad ties and semitrucks and grain silos. She even sucks up old graves, carries their bones to the sea. It doesn't matter to her what the color of their skin might have been. Bones are bones.

She fills up underpasses and low-lying pastures and underground walkways. And once, she even discovered a basement built of brick, built by a former slave. Who knows how many people stayed there, waiting for a ride to Mexico? Dozens at least. Maybe a hundred? There aren't any records.

But the bayou? She remembers. She remembers Major Bay. She remembers Miss Celia's piano. She remembers the statue made of Georgia marble, pink with a vein of red shot through, carved by a tall, thin boy who once knew a girl named Achsah.

If you can find the basement, all caved in and filled with mud, you might find the Lady. But I will tell you, it's unlikely. Once the bayou hides something she's particularly fond of, something she admires, she's reluctant to give it up.

Cade Curtis

Cade blinks his eyes. Everything looks blurry. He tries to focus, so he blinks again. For a second, he has no memory of where he is. He rolls onto his back, and when he does, his head pounds. "Ow!" he moans. A flock of tiny, thumb-size kinglets scatter through the brush, startling him. His whole body starts to shake, so he rolls onto his side and pulls his knees into his chest.

What hit him? What time is it? He pats his front shirt pocket. At least he still has his phone, but when he tries to turn it on, he sees that it has run out of juice. Dead.

He pushes himself up to a sitting position and tries to focus again, shaking his head. The blurriness clears, a little. Next to him, he sees his backpack. He unzips it.

When he finds the bottle of water, he feels like he might cry. The water is cool and welcome and it seems to tamp down the pounding in his brain.

How stupid could he be?

He starts shaking again, and he can feel the water start to boil in his gut. He swallows hard to keep from throwing up. He clamps his arms around his chest to try to stop the shaking.

What made him think that he could find an old statue that had been washed away decades ago? Chances are good that it is several feet underneath the bed of the bayou, lost for eternity. Even if he had a backhoe, his chances of ever finding it are minuscule.

Stupid. Stupid. Stupid. That's how he feels. He came out here completely alone, in an attempt to find a statue that could be *anywhere*, all without telling a single solitary soul where he went.

He takes another long slug of water and lies back on the ground. The pounding in his head eases a bit more. His stomach calms a little. He looks up at the patches of sky that peep through the leaves. He has no idea what time it is, but he can tell by the deep color of blue that it must be leaning toward evening. By now, Paul is surely starting to wonder where he is.

Cade needs to gather himself up and go.

He sits back up, slowly, and looks around again. Despite his throbbing head, he suddenly feels seriously lucky. It could have been so much worse. And if he had died here, in this thick stand of trees, it might be weeks or months or maybe never before his body was found. He swallows the rest of the water and tucks the plastic bottle into his pack. He needs to get out of here.

He stands up, but he does so too quickly, because as soon as he gets his feet underneath him, he hears a whistling noise in his ears, and like a deflated balloon, down he goes.

He slides a few more feet before he stops. This time at least he doesn't pass out, but his vision is all blurry again. He reaches out to his side and feels the sturdy trunk of an old hickory tree. He blinks his eyes some more until he can focus a little better, and when he does, he realizes that he is only a few feet from the edge of the water.

"Thank you, tree," he says, patting it as if the tree can understand him. It doesn't matter. He is grateful to the tree whether it understands him or not. He decides to hold on to it as he tries again to stand up. This time, he takes it slow.

He rubs his eyes. *Focus*, he thinks. He looks down at the water, just a couple of feet below him. Then he looks over at the thick roots of his now-favorite tree.

And that is when he sees it, the wooden cage, caught on the bayou's bank in the tangled roots that held it like a nest.

It wasn't what he was looking for.

But it was what he found.

And Cade Curtis, thief of angels and teller of lies, does a very big Something Good.

Zorra

Zorra. The bayou didn't forget you.

Zorra. Bonita gatita.

Zorra. Wild girl.

The bayou sent you your very own boy, a boy who didn't wait, who carried you home, as fast as he could go.

Cade Curtis

There is no hissing, no clawing, no growling. Her eyes are half closed, fur covered in dried muck, so when Cade first pulls her out of the trap, he thinks she is just a large cat. It's not until he gets her home that he realizes that she's not. It is Mrs. Walker who says, "It's definitely not from these parts." It's Paul who says she might be an ocelot.

Whatever she is, she needs help. So the three of them bundle her in a warm towel, and Paul drives the old Oldsmobile like crazy down the freeways to the opposite side of Houston, to a place called Houston Wildlife Center.

Cade knows that time is not on the ocelot's side. As he holds her, he can only barely feel her heartbeat under the palm of his hand.

"Hurry," he tells his dad.

When they finally arrive, the vet—Dr. Jo Farrish—puts the cat on an IV to rehydrate her. While the ocelot is so limp and quiet, Dr. Farrish asks her assistant to try to clean her up. Then she asks Cade if he'd like to help, and he wants to, he really does, but just now he feels a little queasy.

Dr. Farrish insists upon taking a look at the bump on the back of his head. She shines a pin light into his eyes, checks his reflexes, even takes his temperature. Then she tells Paul, "Make sure he doesn't go to sleep for another few hours."

That is easy, because Cade can't leave the cat just yet anyways.

So the three of them sit in the waiting room, drinking coffee that seems to have been brewed two weeks ago. So far, no one has actually asked him what in the world he was doing underneath a bridge by himself when he should have been at school, but he can tell by Paul's expression that that conversation is in the near future.

"For now, we're just grateful that you're all right," Paul says. And for once, his dad does not call him "Li'l Dude."

At that moment, Dr. Farrish walks back in. With

his vision becoming a bit clearer, Cade can see how kind she is by the way she rests her hand on Mrs. Walker's shoulder. Then she says, "You must be so proud of this grandson of yours." Cade sees Mrs. Walker's face. She's beaming.

"Your boy got her to us just in time," Dr. Farrish tells Paul. Then she explained about the poachers who dealt in exotic animals, and the enormous amounts of money they made at the animals' expense. "These guys are almost impossible to catch, and it usually doesn't end well for the animals."

Cade starts to say, *Asshats!* But he keeps his mouth shut. Still, asshats! He doesn't think he's ever seen a sadder animal than the one he bundled into his arms, pressed against his chest. Only a supreme asshat could let that happen.

In the middle of his thoughts, Dr. Farrish turns to him. She looks directly into his eyes. "You did such a brave thing, Cade Curtis." And he can tell that she means it. But then, she chides him a bit. "You also have no idea how lucky you are." Cade looks down because he knows what is coming next. Sure enough, she says, "Never—and I mean it—never try handling a wild animal, especially one who is sick, again." She goes on. "So many things could go wrong."

Cade nods. Then Dr. Farrish tells him that while the cat is still unconscious, he can touch her. So he reaches into the cage and puts his hand on her soft clean fur. Once again, he can feel her faint heartbeat just beneath her protruding ribs.

Beside him stands his father, whose strong hands cradled him when he didn't have to. And Mrs. Walker, with her soft hands, hugging him up in the way that grandmothers do. And then there was Soleil's hand, resting right between his. It was a chain reaction, Cade realized, and at each point, someone ultimately took a chance on love. *Ultimate Love.* He rubs the ocelot between her silken ears. And because they are the best words he knows, he whispers to her, "I'm here for you."

And Zorra, small wild beautiful girl . . . she gets the message.

Soleil Broussard

What would Soleil carry? When she sat down to write her essay for Mrs. Franco, she couldn't help but think about the Byrds. They finally made it to California in their PT Cruiser. There's a photo of them on the wall of the church, with the Hollywood sign in the background. Soleil remembers how they arrived during the hurricane with a single grocery bag that held a few diapers and a bag of puppy chow. How Tyler cried and cried and wouldn't stop. How the puppy that matched the puppy chow was finally found, miles away from her ruined home, and only days before the Byrds left town. Kisser. Her name was Kisser.

And the honey bear jar. Soleil knew that no matter

where Tyler went, he would carry his honey bear jar, his trophy.

Soleil is quite sure that her father would carry his accordion. Even if he had to walk through a flood, he would carry it over his head to keep it dry. It's a fine accordion, though it's not always in tune. "It's all the mule's fault," says her dad.

She tugs on the tiny gold cross that hangs from her neck. She would miss that if she lost it. And of course, she would definitely carry her Bible. It was a gift from her parents when she was baptized. In fact, it's her Bible that she writes about in her essay. She had plenty to say about why it mattered to her.

But the truth is, there is something else that she loves. A marble. It's a cat's eye, golden, with flecks of dark brown. If she holds it in the sunlight, it seems to glow. When Cade gave it to her, he pressed it into the palm of her hand, warm and smooth.

She holds it there, feeling the weight of it, then she slips it into the pocket of her skirt, safe. Tonight, she thinks, she will need to ask the truth about the Lady and why Cade lied to her.

But right now, it is almost sunset. Cade takes her to the bridge where he found the ocelot. He reaches for her hand, just like he did in the hallway of the Church on the Bayou, holds it between his two hands, and pulls it directly under his chin. She is buzzing from head to toe.

She starts to speak, but just as she does, a thousand bats pour out from under the bridge and fly directly over their heads, taking all her words with them.

Cade Curtis

It's early morning, and the air is crisp and cold. There's a low-lying fog resting on the ground, the kind that swirls around Cade's feet as he makes his way to the trail beside the bayou. Once he reaches the water, he pauses. The fog shifts and twists above the currents.

Cade feels his own strong currents coursing through his body.

The little ocelot—which Dr. Farrish and the staff call Buffalo Girl—is getting stronger by the day. Soon they'll release her back into her natural habitat. Dr. Farrish told him there's a refuge in south Texas right along the border where there is a small population of ocelots.

"She should be good there," the vet said. When

the time comes, Cade will ride along with them, even though it will be hard to watch the cat go.

Now, as he stands on the banks of the bayou, Cade shivers.

He pulls his jacket tighter and watches the fog hover just above the water's surface. The sky is turning as pink as roses.

He needs to tell Soleil what is true, something about angels, including an angel with a crack that ran from the corner of her eye to the collar of her robe. And when he tells her this, he will also have to tell her about the lost Lady and why she mattered so much.

Soleil? She could walk away, and he wouldn't blame her if she did.

For now, he puts his right hand over his chest and feels the beating of his very own heart. Below him, the bayou slides toward the sea. The ancient haints rise from the water's silver surface, linger for a moment, then disappear into the morning air.

Gabrio

The boy tied his shoelaces, then tied them again in a double knot. He could not risk stumbling over his laces, couldn't risk losing a shoe. These shoes had to carry him a long ways, over unfriendly ground.

He climbed into the back of the truck, an old army truck with canvas sides. There were other people already in there, sitting on benches in tight rows, side by side. In the boy's left pocket he carried every bit of money he had, plus some that his tía and tío had scraped together. He knew they had given him every last peso they could find.

They were all counting on him. Every single person in his family needed for him to make it to Texas. He could do it. He had his St. Christopher medal, the one his abuela had placed around his neck. The cash in his left pocket should get him there, plus some for when he arrived.

And in his other pocket? A small figurine of a woman, carved out of marble, her eyes closed, her mouth an open O, as if she is taking in a deep breath, and maybe the whole world with it. It was handed down to him from his mamacita. It was given to her by her mama and hers before that.

All the edges of it were smooth from being rubbed and rubbed some more. Whenever he held it, it warmed up in the middle of his palm. He patted his pocket to make sure it was there, looked around the truck at his fellow travelers, and prayed.

"Señor Dios," he said. "Enviar ángeles, por favor."

Buffalo Bayou

HOUSTON

The bayou, she remembers all her names, she remembers the names of those she's met, and some she hasn't, she remembers their deepest dreams, their keenest prayers. She knows all about love, how it's lost, how it's found. How it can save the world.

Listen. There are angels.

Amen, they whisper. *Amen.*

104. **THE GOOD OLD WAY.**

As I went down in de valley to pray, Studying about dat good old way, When you shall wear de starry crown, Good Lord, show me de way. O mourner,*let's go down, let's go down, let's go down, O mourner, let's go down, Down in de valley to pray.

* Sister, etc.

Bibliography

For further information about the times and places that occur in this story, I recommend the following resources:

BOOKS:

Aulbach, Louis F. *Buffalo Bayou: An Echo of Houston's Wilderness Beginnings*. Houston, TX: Louis F. Aulbach Publisher, 2012.

Baker, T. Lindsay, and Julie P. Baker, eds. *Till Freedom Cried Out: Memories of Texas Slave Life*. College Station, TX: Texas A&M Press, 1997.

Blanchett, Sara Louise. 2013. *The "Other Side": Public Memory and the Life of Sylvia Routh in Houston 1837–1859*. Thesis, Department of History, University of

North Carolina at Charlotte, Charlotte, NC: University of North Carolina at Charlotte.

Burt, William Henry, and Grossenheider, Richard Philip. *A Field Guide to the Mammals: Field Marks of all North American Species Found North of Mexico.* Boston, MA: Houghton Mifflin, 1952.

Dunbar-Ortiz, Roxanne. *An Indigenous Peoples' History of the United States.* Boston, MA: Beacon Press, 2014.

Francis, Lee. *Native Time: A Historical Time Line of Native America.* New York, NY: St. Martin's Griffin, 1996.

Glancy, Diane. *Pushing the Bear: A Novel of the Trail of Tears.* New York, NY: Harcourt Brace, 1996.

———. *Pushing the Bear: After the Trail of Tears.* Norman, OK: University of Oklahoma Press, 2009.

Hoxie, Frederick E., ed. *Encyclopedia of North American Indians: Native American History, Culture, and Life from Paleo-Indians to the Present.* Houghton Mifflin Company. Boston, MA, 1996.

Keith, Bill, and Baker, Bill John. *They Call Me Eddie Morrison: Cherokee National Treasure.* Gretna, LA: Pelican Publishing Company, 2016.

Neeld PhD, Elizabeth Harper. *A Sacred Primer: The Essential Guide to Quiet Time and Prayer.* Austin, TX: Centerpoint Press, 2011.

O'Brien, Tim. *The Things They Carried.* 20th Anniversary

edition. Boston, MA: Houghton Mifflin Harcourt, 2010.

Shelton, Gilbert. *Fabulous Furry Freak Brothers*. Issues 1–14,.San Francisco, CA: Rip Off Press, 1971–1997.

Sipes, James L., and Zeve, Matthew K. *The Bayous of Houston*. Charleston, SC: Arcadia Publishing, 2012.

Steptoe, Tyina L., *Houston Bound: Culture and Color in a Jim Crow City*. Oakland, CA: University of California Press, 2016.

Torget, Andrew J. *Seeds of Empire: Cotton, Slavery, and the Transformation of the Texas Borderlands, 1800–1850*. Chapel Hill, NC: The University of North Carolina Press, 2015.

Tucker, Phillip Thomas. *Emily D. West and the "Yellow Rose of Texas" Myth*. Jefferson, NC: McFarland & Company, Inc., 2014.

WEBSITES AND PAGES:

The Baby Moses Project: babymosesproject.org

"The Black People 'Erased From History'": bbc.com/news/magazine-35981727

"Born in Slavery: Slave Narratives from the Federal Writers' Project, 1936 to 1938": loc.gov/collections/slave-narratives-from-the-federal -writers-project-1936-to-1938/about-this-collection

Buffalo Bayou Partnership: buffalobayou.org

"Constitution of the Republic of Texas":
tshaonline.org/handbook/online/articles/mhc01

"Georgia Marble":
aboutnorthgeorgia.com/ang/Georgia_Marble

"New Orleans Grave Theft: Nothing's Sacred":
nytimes.com/1999/02/16/us/new-orleans-grave
-theft-nothing-s-sacred.html

Operation Jungle Book: bigcatrescue.org/operation
-jungle-book

Texas Slavery Project: texasslaveryproject.org

Texas State Historical Association: tshaonline.org/home

"The Underground Railroad: A Study of the
Routes from Texas to Mexico": uh.edu/honors/
Programs-Minors/honors-and-the-schools/
houston-teachers-institute/curriculum-units/
pdfs/2003/african-american-slavery/
redonet-03-slavery.pdf

"Their Stories to Tell": chron.com/news/article/Their
-stories-to-tell-2007485.php

PLAYLIST*

*With the exception of "Thinking Out Loud," these are songs commonly found in the public domain and sung through the years by a wide variety of performers. These are simply my favorite versions and don't actually reflect the way they might have been sung in the context of this story.

"Down to the River to Pray," sung by Alison Krauss:
    youtube.com/watch?v=zSif77IVQdY
"Jolie Blon," sung by Clifton Chenier and The Red Hot
    Louisiana Band: youtube.com/watch?v=yteXz_J1Nlk
"Lead, Kindly Light," sung by David Beck:
    youtube.com/watch?v=MVX3G_stfwg
"Thinking Out Loud," Ed Sheeran:
    youtube.com/watch?v=lp-EO5I60KA
"This Little Light of Mine," sung by Sam Cooke:
    youtube.com/watch?v=OdsIjwwfhjk

VIDEOS

"Houston Flood Defense Traces to Flooded
    Past, Rachel Maddow, MSNBC":
    youtube.com/watch?v=sACC2jBzjis
"Ocelot Attack!":
    youtube.com/watch?v=2oSh_zOaVFk
"A Tale of Two Rivers: Mississippi
    River Flood of 1927, excerpt, Part I":
    youtube.com/watch?v=UGy4DgeaZNo
"When the Roads Turned to Rivers: Texas in the
    Aftermath of Hurricane Harvey:
    youtube.com/watch?v=l6V8Kxyvivw

Author's Note

I grew up on the south end of Houston, on the corner of Mayo Avenue and El Buey Way. I can count my Houston ancestors from at least seven generations back. So I've wanted to write a story that was set in my hometown for many years. And I've always known that if I ever did, it would take place along the Buffalo Bayou. The bayou of my story is far more fictional than real, and while I've hewn to historic maps of the wards and streets and bridges, as well as the various paths of the ever-changing bayou itself, I've definitely taken some liberties with their actual geography. Considering how often the bayou herself has shifted in her banks, I let her be the guide location-wise.

A few years ago I happened across a small article

by Louis Aulbach about a woman named Sylvia Routh, who was brought to Texas as a slave in the early 1830s. She was owned by a ship's captain, James Routh. When he died, he set her free, leaving her a substantial amount of property. He also set their two older sons free, and he left his ship in their care. However, he did not do the same for their two young daughters. Instead, he put them in the custody of a friend until they reached the age of twenty-one. So my character Achsah is loosely inspired by Sylvia's story.

Reading about Sylvia led me to some further research about pre–Civil War Texas and the very startling discovery (to me) that one of the reasons that the Texans fought for independence from Mexico was that Mexico had made slavery illegal. The Texans who had come to settle there rejected that law. Because they wanted to entice settlers from the southern slave states to locate in Texas, it was important to them to maintain the legality of slavery, especially in light of the two major cash crops—sugar and cotton—which were labor intensive.

If you read the constitution of the Republic of Texas, you'll find the inclusion of the infamous Section 9, the section that embeds slavery into the fabric of Texas's history and that mimicked the Constitution of the United States.

One of the underreported facts of American history is that in the years before the Civil War, there was a southern Underground Railroad, but instead of it leading to the northern states or Canada, it led to Mexico. It wasn't as organized as its more famous northern route, but it nevertheless existed. Among the narratives of enslaved people that the Works Progress Administration (WPA) writers of the 1930s wrote down, there is at least one that talks about walking to Mexico and crossing the Rio Grande into freedom. The city of Costa Chica, along the eastern coast of Mexico, was partly settled by enslaved people who escaped.

There have been so many dark moments in our history as a country, and one of the most bleak and horrifying was the forced removal of thousands of Cherokee, Seminole, Choctaw, Chickasaw, Muscogee (Creek), and other indigenous people from their homes and land in the southeastern United States to Indian Territory west of the Mississippi. Genocide is the only way to correctly describe it, as thousands died along the trail.

One of the many things that were stripped from the Native Americans when they were forced out were the marble fields of Georgia. The marble there is uniquely beautiful and arises in a variety of shades and colors.

Many of our public buildings, as well as private homes, were built using Georgian marble, including the United States Capitol Building and the Lincoln Memorial. It's also used for the vast majority of US military headstones.

About the cemetery angels . . . Several years ago I accompanied my grandmother to the funeral of her younger brother. He, along with many of my ancestors, is buried in the old Washington Cemetery, one of Houston's oldest graveyards. My grandmother's family—the Brenners and Brinkmans—all arrived here beginning in the 1830s. So there we were, my grandmother and I on a rainy fall day, and as we drove out of the cemetery, I noticed that many of the angels—not just a few—were headless.

Those angels haunted me. And that's when I began to learn about the black market in stolen cemetery statuary. So yes, it's a thing.

Sadly there is also a thriving black market in exotic pets and their fur, which is where sweet Zorra comes in. The wild animals that make their homes in Laguna Atascosa and other refuges in the Rio Grande Valley are all at risk. If a border wall is actually constructed, migratory animals will be terribly disrupted. But even nonmigratory animals, like ocelots, require large swaths of land for their survival. If those lands are cut in half, many of them will suffer, and some species may be seriously diminished, especially if the wall obstructs them from accessible water and habitat.

I'll never be the sweet believer that is Soleil, but I do believe in love as the key to restoring the darkness that can be so pervasive. I do believe in gathering in circles, sharing our stories, and learning to see one another for who we truly are—messy, conflicted, angry, smart, joyful, driven, funny creatures, who have the capacity for being lamps in the world. I also believe that if the world is to be saved, it'll be because young people join together and get the rest of us to stop being asshats.

Acknowledgments

I believe in angels, largely because a host of them set aside their own work to become my saving graces. Cynthia Leitich Smith, Rita Williams-Garcia, Kevin Noble Maillard, Jennifer Zeigler, Elizabeth Harper Neeld PhD, Anne Bustard Fusilier, Susan K. Fletcher, Liz Garton Scanlon, Lindsey Lane, Professor Andrew Torget, and Marion Dane Bauer. I'm indebted.

When I needed expertise, two people, who shall remain nameless, not only did close reading, they read between the lines. This book is so much better for their care and attention.

Diane Linn, you always ask exactly the right questions at exactly the right time. And Erika Barosh Ervin, thank you for deep breaths and encouragement.

Thank you to Marco Wagner for the gorgeous jacket, and to Debra Sfetsios-Conover for the design. To Jeannie Ng and her steadfast crew of copy editors, you are the ever-loving best. I appreciate you more than you know.

In so many ways, the entire team at Simon & Schuster feels like family to me. I feel so fortunate to work with each and every one of you.

I'm beyond grateful to Holly McGhee, agent and muse, and to Caitlyn Dlouhy, editor and guide.

And what about Ken? He just keeps taking a chance on love, and that is all that matters.

Angel Thieves

ABOUT THE BOOK

Each person makes an impact, touching the lives around them whether or not they know it. The objects we encounter have histories, and impact lives they come in contact with. Large or small, the items that we see, feel, and use throughout our days affect the experiences we have. *Angel Thieves* gives insight into these sentiments with a collection of histories that intertwine and influence in ways that none of the characters imagine. Soleil Broussard feels adrift without the previously displaced Byrd family in her life, and she is overwhelmed, too, by her attraction to the boy who sits behind her in American literature class. Cade Curtis steals marble angels from old churchyards to help support his makeshift family, but knows that he can be so much more. Achsah, a freed slave, is willing to give up everything she has in this world, including her life, to save her daughters. Zorra, an ocelot trapped in a cage by a terrible man, faces her own mortality as the waters rise. And the bayou itself, swirling around all these lives, gives up secrets and drowns others for an eternity. Each one has a story, and it is the connection between these stories that will stick in your heart.

DISCUSSION QUESTIONS

1. Kathi Appelt begins the book with an anthropomorphized depiction of the Buffalo Bayou, a technique that she continues throughout the book with various objects. Why do you think she gives human traits and thoughts to things that are not typically thought to possess them? What does this add to the story? How do the characters react to these objects?

2. Why do Paul and Cade steal the marble angels? What is it about this act that bothers Cade so much? Given his misgivings, why do you think he continues to participate in the thefts? What would you have done if you were Cade?

3. What is Soleil's connection to Tyler Byrd? Why does the family's move to Los Angeles affect her so strongly?

What is the significance of the honey bear tattoo on her wrist?

4. Is Achsah's freedom a gift? Did the captain intend it as a gift or a trick? What makes Achsah so determined to save her daughters from James Morgan? How might this kind of determination change someone's motivation or behavior?

5. Why is Juba so good at being quiet? Where did she learn this skill? How is this a helpful trait both before and after her escape? Why do you think Mary Ann is not quiet?

6. Why do you think Appelt chooses to dedicate a chapter to the marble fields? Why is marble so important to the story? Does the process by which marble is formed make you think of anything or anyone else in the story? What makes the angels carved from marble more valuable to collectors?

7. What was Paul's promise to Evie? Why does he break this promise? What repercussions do his actions have for Evie? For Cade? Does Paul make any other promises?

8. At one point Soleil thinks of prayer as "the one thing that she knows how to do for sure." How did prayer come to play a role in her life? How would you characterize her communications with God? Do you think

prayer brings her closer to others in her life? Do you think prayer provides her with answers?

9. Achsah believes that she lost her son at birth, not because he "wasn't good for this world," but because "the world wasn't good for him." What do you think she means by this? Do you think she feels her world is good enough for Juba and Mary Ann, or even herself?

10. Do you see any similarities between white treatment of Native Americans and white treatment of slaves? What are the differences between the two groups' situations? Why does Achsah feel such a connection to the thin boy she's chained to?

11. Why does Celia Phillips declare her husband's prayer at the consecration of the new church "perfect"? What meaning does it have for the people present that day? Do you think it continues to have meaning in the present?

12. Why won't Luc give his real name to Etienne? Why doesn't he tell Achsah his name either? How does his namelessness compare to the bayou, which we learn has had many names over the years? What does a name mean to each of these characters?

13. Is Mrs. Walker a member of Cade's family? Why does she grow so close to the Curtis men? What role does she fill for Cade? What does she think about stealing the angels? What is her reasoning for that belief?

14. What is the Moses law, and why is it important to Cade? What are the similarities and differences between Cade's story and that of Moses?

15. Why do you think Reverend Phillips allows his church to be segregated while he is also helping escaped slaves? How can he reconcile or justify these two very different actions? Do you think his abolitionist stance comes from his religion or his personal beliefs? What might happen to the reverend if his activities are discovered?

16. What does Zorra want? How is this different from what she needs? Are there other characters who want the same things as Zorra? How does Cade feel about finding Zorra instead of the statue?

17. When Cade sees Zorra's cage and rescues her, he is described as a "thief of angels and teller of lies," who "does a very big Something Good." Is this how you would describe Cade? How does this viewpoint compare to his other acts in the book? How many past deeds does he need to make up for?

18. Why does Achsah leave Mary Ann behind? Do you think she had other choices? How do we know what happens to Mary Ann after her mother and sister leave? How would you have reacted if you were Mary Ann? What would you have done if you were Achsah?

19. How does Major Bay communicate with the runaway slaves, or even with those slaves thinking about running? Why do you think that Major Bay stays with Reverend Phillips?

This guide has been provided by Simon & Schuster for classroom, library, and reading group use. It may be reproduced in its entirety or excerpted for these purposes.

The store with one hundred Chinese blessings.

The bridge on Fourth Street.

His friend Playa's house.

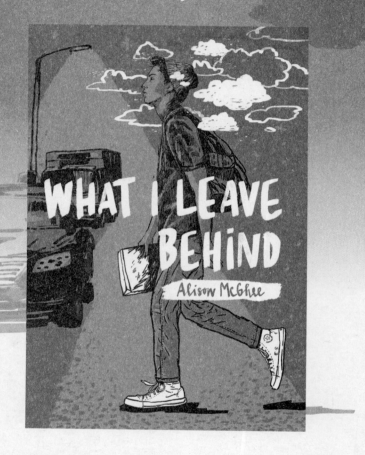

These are the places Will can't—won't—go.
But what happens when the things you're walking away from
turn out to be exactly what you should be walking toward?

From atheneum   A Caitlyn Dlouhy Book   simonandschuster.com/teen